D0869876

A SPECIAL BREED OF MAN

ED EDELL

A RANGER BOOK

Published by

Ranger Associates, Inc.
600 Washington Court
Guilderland, New York 12084

ISBN: 0-934588-08-2

1st Printing - August, 1984
2nd Printing - July, 1985

With profound respect
I dedicate this book to

General Edward C. Meyer, Chief of Staff of the Army

William A. Connelly, The Sergeant Major of the Army

Also to Lieutenant General James J. Lindsay

and to members of his

XVIII Airborne Corps

The Association of the U.S. Army

and

All Vietnam Veterans

who have finally come home

ACKNOWLEDGEMENTS

As destiny willed it in the Spring of 1979, I rescued two vacationing Special Forces master sergeants, who were stationed at Fort Bragg, North Carolina. Both were desperately clinging to a Sombraro Key Channel buoy, approximately five miles northeast of Marathan, Florida. Their tiny sailboat had capsized and had sunk with most of their personal belongings. During their week long stay in my home at Key Colony Beach, I became fully aware of their Vietnam experience. In appreciation for my hospitality, they gave me a copy of Robin Moore's best selling novel, *Green Berets*.

"This is the naked truth!" the senior non-commissioned officer told me with a wry grin, over a cup of coffee. "We lived it!"

Several months later, I was the guest of the renowned General Mark W. Clark at his home in Charleston, South Carolina. At the time he was President of the Citadel. When I told him about rescuing the two sergeants and about Robin Moore's blockbuster, the Grand ol' Soldier's lanky-lean posture became habitually erect.

In a lengthy dissertation he praised the Special Forces under his command, which spearheaded the Fifth Army in Italy during 1944. In retrospect, the four star general who accepted General Von Vietinghoff's formal surrender at the Brenner Pass and who in July 1953 signed the armistice agreement between the UN Command, the North Korean Army and the Chinese at Munsan-ni, recalled how his Special Forces distinguished themselves at the inpregnable Monte La Di Fensa Fortress, where they were dubbed the *Devil's Brigade* by the retreating Nazis.

At General Clark's implication, I contacted the Commanding General of the XVIII Airborne Corps at Fort Bragg and requested permission to start my research there.

I am particularly indebted to Lieutenant Colonel Patrick F. Cannan of Public Affairs, who supervised fulfillment of my needs. His guidance, information, patience and red pen were invaluable to me. At times, when words and ideas failed to materialize, I would sit in his office and drink coffee, or chat with his deputy, Mike Shutak. I also spent time at the enormous Womack Army Hospital, at the Advanced Airborne School under the command of Major Kotulas, with Captain Kevin D. Chaffin, his executive officer, and with his leading non-commissioned officer, Master Sergeant Jim Cole.

I am most grateful to Lieutenant Colonel "Ike" Isaacson of the John F. Kennedy School of Special Warfare and his deputy Mrs. Beverly Lindsey. SFC Ron Freeman helped me tremendously with Special Forces history, standard operating procedures, films, action pictures and eventful field trips to Camp Mackall, where men were trained with cold steel.

I profited greatly from Colonel Charles Beckwith's generosity and spirit of strength. Colonel Beckwith led SF personnel in Korea and again in Vietnam, as well as on that ill-fated Iranian hostage recovery mission, which President Jimmy Carter terminated. My appreciation also goes to Colonel George Maracek and Sergeant Major David Brock for their support. A distinct "Thank You" is extended to MSG Fred L. Foster of the JFK Museum for shepherding me as I gathered information there and at the "Hall of Heroes."

At Fort Jackson, in Columbia, South Carolina, Major General Lucien E. "Blackie" Bolduc, Jr., LTC William A.

Cauthen, Jr. and MSG Willis Johnson were invaluable when, among other things, they insisted I should witness first hand how today's young soldiers are developed.

LTC Charles G. Belan invited me to Fort Benning to learn and understand what is really meant by the "Challenge of the Airborne," then furnished me with the historic Fort's literature "In Peace and War."

At the Army's Recruiting Command Headquarters, I feel indebted to Public Information Officers Jack Muhlenbeck, Major Patrick Hirsch, LTC William A. Knapp, and the local recruiter, SFC "Mike" Dollarhite, for assisting me with special information on recruiting.

In Hawaii, Major General A. M. Weyand was most receptive, furnishing me with heretofore unpublished pictures of the Jap-strike-force's butchery of Hickham Field and Schofield Barracks.

I absolutely owe a special debt to William A. Connelly, the Sergeant Major of the Army and members of his staff, MSG Dale D. Ward, SFC Fred LeBlank and their lovely secretary Miss Ely Shepheard. Bill Connelly's profound encouragement, discussions, recommendations and years of wisdom about Army matters in general in the Pentagon and the field were necessary and priceless.

Since I personally served 20 years as a medic specialist and am a survivor of hand-to-hand combat which meant either kill or get killed, I was happy to get valuable information from Womack Hospital Adjutant, Captain Joe Pigford, regarding Vietnam casualties at the time.

I also treasure Mrs. Glenna Taylor's friendship and enthusiasm during the writing of this book, giving me a mother's feeling on the Vietnam experience, since her only son Ted served there with other countless thousands of - as she said - "Unsung Heroes of the United States."

With profound personal appreciation, I laud the straightforward moral support of Major General Robert F. Cocklin, Command Sergeant Major Al Kaczmarek and numerous active and retired officers and NCO's from the Association of the United States Army, of which I am a life member.

A sentimental thank you goes to Captain W.I. Lewis with the 6th Fleet, Attorney Carroll Gardner, Timothy O. Reilly, SFC Dennis Carter and PFC Kim Godon of the Green Beret Parachute Club, at Fort Bragg. Likewise, to Thelma M. Pitts, General Clark's Secretary; to Catherine B. North of the Daniel Library at the Citadel, and also to Ronald L. Lane, for his confidence and his friendship.

Thanks are due also to Dean Bray, Paul H. Scott, Gail Spane, Thomas Woltz and Pamela and Bill Crouse. At times they overwhelmed me with their encouragement, enthusiasm and their friendship.

With sagacious admiration and delight I especially wish to thank SFC Bryan J. Parker for granting me permission to use his photograph on the cover of this book. His image has for a number of years characterized the special breed of men who compose the United States of America's armed forces.

With profound respect and dignity, I acknowledge that Reverends Frank B. Cook and Julian M. Aldridge, Jr. guided my principles, spiritually of right and wrong, ethical and ideal, moral and virtuous throughout.

Everlasting appreciation to Mary Lee Epperson, her family and Mike Hayes of the First National Bank of Stuart in Ararat, Virginia. Without their financial support, this book might never have been completed and published.

Conclusively and indeed with self-esteem, I recall that after I presented the final draft of this work to Major General Lyle F. Barker, Jr. and to Colonel Michael A. Vargosko at the Army's Public Affairs Office in the Pentagon, they, like General William Westmoreland, reflected that the people of the United States have never really had a clear cut picture of what actually happened in Vietnam in the coverage they had seen. They applauded my effort to present our outstanding soldiers in an accurate portrayal and considered my work a highly worthwhile project.

Ed Edell

GENERAL MARK CLARK

FOREWORD

"The lessons of World War I, Pearl Harbor, and the ensuing devastation of World War II, Korea, and Vietnam have been put away like museum pieces in the hearts and minds of the American people.

"We need somehow to resurrect the lessons of those conflagrations and the spirit of heroism that inspired so many to sacrifice so much in defense of freedom. Those lessons must be imparted to young people today if we are to avoid leaving them a legacy of future battlefield horror.

"We can accomplish this by teaching the young that we can survive as the free people only if our nation remains strong. That is the lesson not only of the wars mentioned but of the total American experience."

Mark W. Clark
General, US Army, Retired

Chapter I

JOURNEY INTO HELL

Early in August 1966, 6 foot 3 inch, 210 pound, 20 year old, sundrenched and crew-cut Sergeant Raymond Heller from Key West, Florida, finally received his long awaited orders for the Military Replacement Center, Military Assistance Command in Saigon, South Vietnam.

The night before Sergeant Heller departed from Pope Air Force Base at Fort Bragg, North Carolina, his adopted mentor, Sergeant Major Jim Cartwright, had arranged a farewell bachelor banquet at the main enlisted men's club. The party was a total surprise to Heller.

When Sergeant Major Cartwright and his non-commissioned officer instructors from Camp Mackall, the John F. Kennedy School of Special Warfare and other commands entered the club's semi-public dining hall, with Sergeant Heller in their midst, the bartender shouted, "ATTENTION!"

At once, all personnel in their starched Army fatigues arose and froze until Cartwright and his entourage were seated. At that moment, the bartender roared, "CARRY ON!"

After an elaborate roastbeef feast with all the trimmings, many Special Forces NCO's showered Sergeant Heller with lofty-style speeches which echoed through the large hall, crowded with NCO's from other commands and units of the XVIII Airborne Corps.

Finally, the sergeant major hammered his powerful fist upon the table for attention. "Comrades!" he said solemnly. "Let's all stand and drink a toast to our guest of honor, Sergeant Heller. Eighteen months ago, he was a member of my staff in France, where I had the pleasure of observing him, as he sacrificed his passes and his leave to learn the French language and, of course, the Army way of life. Since his ambition was to get to Bragg, one way or another, I kinda helped him get there. All of you know he has just graduated with honor from the Special Forces class. Tonight, he is finally headed for Vietnam, where he will systematically help to eliminate the Viet Cong."

After a brief pause, the sergeant major explicated further, "Certainly, those who know Sergeant Heller will not doubt that he'll give a good account of himself wherever he may be. His attitude is that of a true Special Forces professional. . . Comrades, we share his concerns and interests in a common bond of esprit de corps. So, let us all drink a toast to Sergeant Heller and hope that he will honor us with a few words of his own. In conclusion, I say again that I consider it a personal pleasure to have helped with his mold. Gentlemen! Let us drink a toast to Sergeant Heller's good health and success oversea's. . ."

Heller literally jumped out of his chair. He was so overwhelmed with Cartwright's tribute, he embraced him with sincere admiration and indeed with the approval of the entire room of soldiers.

As he stood before his peers, his face had turned hard. The set of his jaw revealed toughness, self-assurance, and confidence. Finally, he cleared his throat and began to express his thoughts and feelings. "I adore this giant among us," he remarked looking at Cartwright. "This soldier with prowess and lordly strut, who loves and breathes the Army, joined almost 29 years ago. . . this tough and wise old warrior who taught me Shakespeare's enduring 'THIS ABOVE ALL, TO THINE OWN SELF BE TRUE, AND IT MUST FOLLOW

AS THE NIGHT THE DAY: THOU CANST NOT THEN BE FALSE TO ANY MAN.'"Comrades," he went on, "let us now drink a toast to our Sergeant Major Cartwright and wish him well and indeed a long life."

After Heller's short eulogy of Cartwright, the soldiers rose to the occasion. Their expression was tumultuous. The barroom vibrated from the applause, and as the spiked punch took its toll, some of the younger NCO's rocked back and forth like the pendulum of a grandfather clock. Indeed, it was an evening to remember. A night to write home about.

Shortly before the festivity came to an end, Heller produced a piece of paper from his green beret. "Comrades! Comrades!" he shouted. "I have a worthy poem, which I would like to read to you on this special occasion. . . if you don't mind."

"Read it! Read it!" Cartwright said loud and clear, as the Special Forces troopers settled back to listen.

"It goes like this," Heller declared:

"One day, a Special Forces instructor knocked at the
    Pearly Gates,
    His face was scarred and bold;
    He stood before the man of fate
    For entry to the fold.

"Well sir! What have you accomplished,"
    Saint Peter asked, "to gain an entry here?"
"I've been a Special Forces soldier, sir," he told him,
"For many a trying year."
    Suddenly, the Pearly Gates swung open,
    When Saint Peter touched the bell.
"Come in" he told him, "and choose your harp,
    You've had your time in hell!"

At 3 o'clock in the morning, when Cartwright drove Heller to Pope Passenger Terminal, he handed him a large brown manila envelope.

"After you're airborne, take a good look," he told him. "When I was in Nam, I would have given my eyeteeth for what's in that envelope."

"Can I have a look over coffee in the terminal?"

"No! Do it after you're airborne," his mentor repeated positively before he augmented, "Unequivocally and definitely the information was compiled by Special Forces veterans who lived through hell and high water, including my own experiences."

"Thank you, Sergeant Major. May I ask why you waited 'til now to let me have this information?"

"You didn't need it before."

Until fifteen minutes before the giant DC-130 departed, the two men were engrossed with questions and answers, such as, "Does this manuscript mention animal life in Nam?" Heller wanted to know.

"I'll give you a few facts now," Cartwright remarked, toying with a cigarette lighter in his hand. "There are a number of pythons and poisonous snakes, like the cobras in the south. . ."

"Hold it! Hold it!" Heller interrupted. "What about those poisonous cobras, sergeant major?"

"Well! I've seen a few of them around six feet long. They are easily recognized by that loose skin just behind the head, kinda' like a hood. Like our rattlers, they have long, hollow fangs through which they inject their venom in whatever they hit."

"Have we suffered casualties from snakes?" Heller asked anxiously. "Anybody die from a snakebite?"

"Let me tell you this, Heller. . . The snakes aren't out there looking for people to bite. It's those damn VC gorillas who capture them, put a collar or a band around their necks and attach a leash to control them. The VC's know cobras will cause confusion and horror. So, they plant them as they retreat. At times, they'll use them for watch-dogs at the entrance to their own fortification. These damn snakes are almost as bad as the hidden bamboo stakes, with razor-sharp and poisoned points, piercing and penetrating through our jungle boots as if they were wet cardboard."

"Dear God in heaven!" Heller exclaimed. "No wonder we're not doing too well over there. . . Please go on. . ."

"The giant Mekong Delta is loaded with crocodiles and sharks, which reminds me of an experience I'll never forget."

"I'm all ears, sergeant major. . ."

"Toward the end of my second tour, I was in charge of delivering 15 hard core VC guerillas to Phu Quoc Island, in the Gulf of Siam, somewhat south of Ha Tien. Enroute, when our prison cruiser ran with the waves close to shore along the Delta, five of my prisoners jumped ship. Make no bones about it, these characters were tough, and obviously thought they were pretty good swimmers. Before our boat's pilot could find deeper water to turn and chase after them, they had reached a good sized shallow sandbar. The VC's knew we couldn't follow them with our boat. So, they cheered and called us stupid, softhearted American fools. . ."

"How about that? Why didn't you wing a few with your. . . whatever you were carrying?"

Sergeant Major Cartwright ignored the question. "Yep, they really thought they put one over on us, when all of a sudden the tall weeds on the sandbar parted and a school of sharks attacked them. Heller, my boy, you talk about hysterical screaming? Well, since I was responsible, I fired my pistol near the point of attack, but to no avail. By the time we got close, the only sign of the VC's was their blood, while many other prowling sharks roamed about in a frenzy, their sinister backfins menacing and visible, waiting for another meal. I'll tell you one thing, Raymond," Cartwright recalled, "after that, the rest were model prisoners."

At 0550 an Air Force NCO stormed into the passenger lounge and glancing at his watch, impetuously barked, "You two have five minutes to get aboard! The tower has cleared this C-130 for 0600!"

The sergeant major apologized to the frowning NCO who disapproved. Explicitly, he reminded the Special Forces soldiers that indeed the Air Force is well aware of the war in Vietnam. Sergeant Major Cartwright was surprised at the NCO's outburst. Both men grabbed Heller's luggage and hurried from the lounge toward the roaring aircraft, warming up for take-off.

"One last word, Raymond," Cartwright shouted into

5

Heller's ear after they had reached the aircraft. "Surely you know this is your journey into hell! You can see there's nobody to cheer you on! There's no flag waving! No rituals! No sanctification by an Army or Air Force Chaplain! No affirmation! There are no brass bands! No women! No embracing, or kissing from relatives or sweethearts. The only parades in the country are from the anti-war protesters, and many times led by misinformed and misguided clergymen, who are encouraged by an avalanche of uncensored media reports and are spreading and preaching with their artificial eloquence, that our soldiers are murderers and baby killers. . . I've been praying that perhaps someday, when our soldiers return from that stinking Vietnam war, the silent indifference, the abuse, the insults, and the accumulated horrors of what most of them have to endure there, will turn into a hero's welcome. . ."

Heller noticed a strange muscular twitching in the sergeant major's throat.

"Although it's historical that most, if not all, societies the world over honor their departing soldiers with respect, and reward them for their sacrifices, most of our men depart almost in secrecy and without recognition from the politicians, who created this Vietnam monster. God bless you and protect you, Raymond," Cartwright remarked in conclusion, as they embraced like father and son.

At that instant, Heller was so choked up he could hardly breath. He swallowed the saliva in his mouth, trying to suppress his feelings. Without uttering another word, he turned on his heels and quickly entered through the partially opened hatch which swung shut a moment later.

When Heller entered the cargo compartment, the crew chief instructed him to take the only available seat up front. "And fasten your seatbelt! In three hours and ten minutes, we'll arrive at Travis. I don't think I need to give you further instructions. I can see your silver wings. . ."

"Thanks!" Heller told him with a wry grin, adjusted his seatbelt and relaxed.

Alone now with his thoughts and memories of his father, of Cartwright, and among other things his tour of duty in

France, he was positive about his sense of purpose, his mission, his duty. His biggest concern was about Army leadership and structure in combat. But to him, his entire life came under the heading of DUTY, HONOR, COUNTRY. The extraordinary statement of President John F. Kennedy: ASK NOT WHAT YOUR COUNTRY CAN DO FOR YOU. ASK WHAT YOU CAN DO FOR YOUR COUNTRY, was foremost on his mind all the way across the American continent.

At Travis Air Force Base, 40 miles north of San Francisco, Heller boarded a chartered aircraft which headed directly for Tan Son Nhut Air Base in Saigon.

During the long flight, he read Sergeant Major Cartwright's mimeographed manuscript four times. He knew that every word was factual with no surprises. According to the manuscript, Heller reasoned, one needs to understand the war between the factions in Vietnam. As the sergeant major revealed so positively, "It should be remembered that the Vietnamese people have been struggling for nearly 2000 years for independence. After centuries of Chinese domination, the people took a stand against the warlords who had invaded the Red River Delta. The Chinese were finally repelled at the battle of "Bach Dang." Thereafter, an independent Vietnam became a reality and thusly remained for 900 years.

The very first reign of the Ly Dynasty, which was established in the year 1009, ushered in a period of cultural development, territorial expansion and prosperity. After an interval of confusion, the Ly rulers gave the country the form of government it retained until the French conquerors defeated and subdued those who resisted them. Nevertheless, the role of the Vietnamese emperor was dominant. He was the father of the nation, the absolute spiritual monarch, the leader and intermediary between his rule and heaven. The mandarinate, a group of high officials, performed the governing functions of the country until mid-13th Century, when Kublai Khan and his Mongol tribes invaded Vietnam. This time, however, the people were determined to fight for their freedom, and repelled the invaders time and time again.

In the 16th Century, European influence affected Vietnam

when a Portugese sea rover arrived in Da Nang harbor. The Portugese dominated the nation, including all commerce, but failed to impose their will upon the people, as indeed they had done in the West Indies.

Numerous Catholic missionaries entered Vietnam during that century, but Confusian oriented officials discouraged the people from learning about another religion. The Vietnamese suspected it as the forerunner of conquest and feared its effect upon the traditional religious order, which had been the foundation of the state for centuries. Nevertheless, Christianity spread over the years.

In the middle of the 19th Century, France, like England and many other nations of Europe, applied pressure to Vietnam in a power squeeze and a desire to protect their missionaries, who they claimed were being persecuted. The French seized the city of Da Nang and shortly thereafter Saigon. In 1867, the western section of the southern delta, then known as Cochin China, was completely under French control. For the next thirty years, the French expanded their control over all of Indochina, or, what today is North and South Vietnam, Laos and Democratic Kampuchea, formerly Cambodia. During that time, most basic decisions were made by the French, whose rule demoralized the emperor and the mandarinate in the country.

French occupancy also had a profound economic effect on the region. Absentee ownership grew as large scale agricultural and rubber plantations appeared. The most prosperous Vietnamese moved into the cities, and more and more of the land was tilled by peasants who did not own it.

In the fertile Mekong Delta, the French encouraged the building of large scale canals to exploit the rice production. Early in the 20th Century, the French managed to produce a considerable rice surplus for European markets. European ideas and culture permeated the country, especially among the upper class Vietnamese. The European influence stimulated the movement for Vietnamese nationalism which began to develop, initially among urban intellectuals.

During that time, many anti-French societies developed. Most were improperly organized and lacked positive political objectives. The clandestine nationalist leadership movement in Vietnam was eventually taken over by the Indo-Chinese Communist Party, which was formed in Hong Kong in 1930. The leader of the party was Ho Chi Minh.

When France fell to Germany in 1940, the Vichy government ceded all of French Indo-China to the Japanese. However, the French administration was permitted to remain intact with many lucrative agreements being made between wealthy French interests in Vietnam and its occupation forces. Meanwhile, Ho Chi Minh's party adopted a policy of collaboration with all non-Communist nationalists to broaden the social and political base of its activites, calling itself the Vietnam Independency League, or the Viet Minh. Shortly thereafter, the League formed guerrilla bands, which operated against the Japanese and French nationalists in Vietnamese territory. Although Ho Chi Minh was jailed in 1941, the League remained active, effective, and strong. Under the guise of "Nationalism," Ho Chi Minh overcame much of the opposition to him by establishing countless communist cells throughout the country. The next five years left the country in further turmoil and confusion, since the French had left for a time, but then returned again late in 1945. By December 1946, the Viet Minh, under Ho Chi Minh, decided that the only way to achieve independency would be through a "War of Liberation."

For the next nine years, the French fought the Viet Minh. The French army was conclusively defeated at Dien Bien Phu, which in fact ended French rule in its entirety on May 7, 1954. Then the so-called "Big Four Geneva Conference" turned its attention to the French Indo-China War. The outcome, as with all disputes of that kind, ended in a sham, where the big four powers fixed a provisional demarcation line along the 17th parallel, and provided for a complete French military evacuation and the removal of Ho Chi Minh's forces from the South. Although the powers set up an International Control Commission to supervise the truce agreement and the French handed over their control, with general elections scheduled to be held in 1958, the well organized Viet Minh underground continued to press for the realization of Ho Chi Minh's dream of unifying Vietnam under a Communist regime.

Although the United States was not an active participant in bringing about the end of the Indochina War, our government worked quietly behind the scenes. At the same time, groundwork for the South East Asia Treaty Organization, known as SEATO, was being activated. The treaty was signed in the city of Manila. South Vietnam was included in the treaty as a protocol state, with the signatories accepting the obligation, if asked by the government of any SEATO member nation, to take action in response to armed attacks against any other member and to consult on appropriate measures if it were subjected to subversive activities.

In late 1954, President Eisenhower instituted economic aid for the new country of South Vietnam. To understand the events which followed, we must examine the development of North Vietnam, the rise of the Viet Cong who received assistance from the North, and the tremendous economic and military aid to the South furnished by the United States.

Ho Chi Minh began feverishly to consolidate his forces. Ninety thousand of his cohorts moved north of the 17th parallel, while many thousands of his loyal party members were ordered to remain behind, hide their weapons and wait to be called.

Actually, the Hanoi government and Ho Chi Minh presumed that the South would fall by subversion and that force would not be necessary. When the South became more prosperous in spite of Communist penetration into government agencies and attempts at agitation and propaganda, the Communists of the North were in a state of shock. Agitators and agents were exposed by the people of the South, which caused Communist morale to hit an all time low and caused many defections.

One of many problems of the North was food production, which dropped by ten percent, while the South's improved by twenty percent. Despite the immense industrial complex in North Vietnam, the South's per capita income was 50% higher, causing a major revision in overall Northern strategy. Ho Chi Minh and the Communist party in general agreed that military force would have to be employed to take over South Vietnam. The Communists accelerated terrorism and recruiting. Their propaganda exploited every avenue and propounded confusion and fear. All activity was directed from the North.

In 1960, the National Liberation Front boldly announced that the disguised colonial regime of the United States Imperialists and the dictatorial President Ngo Dinh Diem of the South must be overthrown. The propaganda hierarchy of the North tried to establish that acts of terror, fear and political executions and violence to intimidate, was in reality the work of discontented groups who were against the Diem regime. They also insisted that the Viet Cong obtained their weapons by capturing them from American and French stockpiles. When such propaganda failed to influence the world, an estimated 40,000 trained soldiers of the North infiltrated South Vietnam through Laos between 1958 and 1964. The other infiltration route was by sea with simple looking fishing boats departing from North of the 17th parallel. Hanoi and Ho Chi Minh were determined to conquer the South one way or another. They activated Mao Tse-tung's three part plan: 1 - harass the enemy and weaken them with guerrilla attacks. 2 - engage in battalion size combat mobile operations of strike, disappear, and fight another day, and 3 - if need be, deploy total warfare by regular Army forces for an ultimate victory.

During phase one, from 1954 to 1960, the United States under President Eisenhower, believed that *"The loss of South Vietnam would set in motion a crumbling process that could, as it progressed, have consequences for us and for freedom."* President "Ike", with Congressional approval, assisted the South Vietnamese with economic aid and shortly thereafter added military advisors. By 1961, the guerrillas from the North had reached a point of open warfare, being reinforced by the entire 325th North Vietnamese Regular Army Division. The Viet Cong finally standardized their supply line with the North.

In 1961, the United States had approximately 600 advisors in South Vietnam to help stem the "Red Tide" from the North. President John F. Kennedy declared in 1961: *"The United States is determined to help South Vietnam preserve its independence, protect its people against communist assassins and build a better life through economic growth."*

President Kennedy decided to increase United States commitments and increased the number of advisors, which were called *SPECIAL FORCES*, and which he praised for their dedication, their courage, bravery and fearlessness, especially in battle. He granted them permission to wear the *GREEN BERETS*.

Although the United States involvement in Vietnam was officially recognized in July, 1965, the establishment of a Military Assistance Advisory Group, Indochina, goes back to the 1950's. After committing itself to the defense of Southeast Asia under the Geneva Agreements and the Southeast Asia Defense Treaty, the United States provided economic, military and technical assistance until late in 1961, when South Vietnam declared a state of national emergency and asked the United States for combat troops.

The first combat units of United States Special Forces arrived in December, 1965, together with the 9th Logistical Support Team, stationed on Okinawa, forming the nucleus which evolved into USARV (United States ARmy, Vietnam.)

While the Army units increased in "Nam", the U.S. Army, Ryukyu Support Group, Provisional, took over logistics control of U.S. Forces in South Vietnam.

Numerous combat missions spurred the creation of two subordinated field commands: I Field Force, Vietnam, was located at Nha Trang to command U.S. Army Units in II Corps Tactical Warzone, and II Field Force, Vietnam, located in III Corps to Command Army Units there. General Bruce Palmer, Jr. paid tribute when he said:

". . . USARV is a fighting command of dedicated soldiers, young and not so young, career men and citizen-soldiers, but All-American, in the truest sense."

In 1965, President Lyndon B. Johnson appraised the war 9,000 miles from the American continent. Said the President: *"The central issue of the conflict. . .is the aggression by North Vietnam. . . .if that aggression is stopped, the people and the government of South Vietnam will be free to settle their own future and get on with the great task of national development."*

United States involvement in South Vietnam increased sharply. Australia, New Zealand and South Korea committed ground combat troops, in answer to the Communist challenge of the North. At the same time, the war developed from guerrilla activities and terrorism to a large unit action on the part of the Viet Cong, reinforced by regular army units from the North. The South Vietnamese Army and the communists were now committed against each other in battalion and regimental action. But, guerrillas and Viet Cong terror action continued.

On February 7, 1966, the VC's finally attacked a U.S. compound at Pleiku and Camp Holloway close by. Later that same day, U.S. aircraft struck a North Vietnam army barracks, just north of the 17th parallel. From that time on, President Johnson authorized bombing of the North, and he initiated the immediate evacuation of all U.S. dependents from Vietnam. The President's concern was warranted. Several days later the Viet Cong blew up a hotel in Qui Nhon, which housed U.S. Army enlisted men. In the attack, 23 Americans died and 35 were seriously injured. Also, in February, 1966, a North Vietamese supply ship, loaded with 80 tons of arms and ammunition at Vung Ro Bay, was sunk by U.S. aircraft. By mid March, Navy and Air Force war planes were delivering staggering blows, striking Communist targets both in North and South Vietnam.

According to verified statistics, the South Vietnam "Pacification" was working. Individuals and families managed to slip out of Viet Cong controlled villages, joining other resettlement communities for safety, protection and a new way of life. Those in the resettlement villages received a small plot of land, providing them an opportunity to build again what they lost. As early as 1965 and 1966, at least forty nations responded to the needs of South Vietnam for equipment and advisors, in nonmilitary assistance, which fell into five categories: (1) medical aid, (2) educational and vocational aid, (3) technical assistance, (4) agricultural and (5) resettlement programs.

One of the most serious problems was the shortage of medical personnel, which was rectified somewhat by participation of 13 Free World governmental and private organizations, medical teams from New Zealand, Australia, Korea, the United

Kingdom, the Philippines, the Republic of China on Formosa Island, Germany, Japan, Spain and, of course, the United States. There was the German hospital ship *Helgoland*, docking at numerous ports along the coast to provide unique medical service. Canada provided almost a million vials of anti-polio vaccine and conducted a massive immunization program with the Vietnamese Department of Health. The Brazilian government sent three tons of medical supplies. The team from Taiwan sent medical personnel to work at the Phan Thiet Hospital. Many doctors from Canada and Cuban refugee medical personnel, were on the staffs of the Quang Ngai Clinic and the hospital by the same name.

Doctors and their staffs from the Philippines worked in several provinces, including Tay Ninh. New Zealand had a surgical team at Qui Nhon. A Korean mobile unit worked in the coastal city of Vung Tau. A Spanish medical team was operating in a provincial hospital in Go Cong. Last, but not least, over 150 private physicians from the United States, on leave from their practices, had volunteered and served in South Vietnam under a program sponsored by the American Medical Association. Other countries provided several million textbooks for school children of all ages. Still others contributed technical training aids, and others gave machines to schools to give the young opportunities to carry on where they left off before the Viet Cong attacked them. The U.S. gave the Vietnamese 48 railroad locomotives and over 225 freight cars for their system.

***

At the very minute Sergeant Heller stepped from the aircraft in Saigon, a Special Forces sergeant first class in a military jeep whisked him from the airport to the Military Replacement Center, Military Assistance Command, Vietnam (MACV), for processing. Shortly thereafter, he sat impatiently in front of the personnel officer's desk, as if he had received a summons to defend himself in some kind of kangaroo court, with the attendant disregard for ethics and procedures.

Abruptly, a youthful lieutenant appeared, who half-heartedly returned Heller's salute and handed him a large manila envelope.

"Sergeant Heller! Since your record is exemplary, we decided to assign you to the Army, Republic of Vietnam (ARVN) Ranger Battalion at Loc Ninh," he told him deliberately. "It's about 45 minute flight by chopper."

Heller simply said, "Yes, sir!"

"The sergeant who brought you here will take you to the helicopter pad. You'll join three other SF instructors with the Rangers at Loc Ninh. . ."

"Question, sir!" Heller temporized, glaring at the inimical, rather hostile officer.

"Well?" he frowned.

"Why the hassle?" Heller asked pointedly, examining his orders. "I see no change on my original orders, sir. . ."

The officer swallowed before he clarified what seemed questionable to Heller.

"We were thinking of assigning you to an A Team earlier this morning. When you got here late, we had to assign another sergeant from our office. . ."

Heller's heart pounded. "What do you mean, when I arrived late? Lieutenant! I'm not due in til tomorrow. . ."

Later while flying toward Loc Ninh, deep down inside he bitterly resented the manner in which he was received. "That little man musta never heard of ethics, integrity and/or morals," he mumbled to himself. "It takes all kinds."

From 1500 feet up, human beings were barely visible. The landscape with countless little straw huts and houses appeared tranquil and orderly. There were marshy and swampy rice fields, in perfect harmony with the orderly dikes to keep the precious water from running free. Although signs of war were noticeable, farmers were working the fields in their traditional manner, with their oxlike water buffalos pulling the rough farm implements, turning and breaking the soil for their mainstay food, rice.

Heller had read such books as *The Smaller Dragon, The Struggle of Indochina, The Story of Vietnam* by Hal Dareff, *the Two Viet-Nams,* Ho Chi Minh's book, *From Colonialism to Communism,* whatever he could get his hands on, which gave him an overall view of the national resources of a small country in Indo-china known as Vietnam. At first, it was the French who really began the large scale cultivation of rice for export. They grew coffee, and tea, and mined coal, tin, tungsten and zinc. "No wonder North Vietnam wants the riches of the South," Heller remarked to the pilot of the helicopter now approaching Loc Ninh.

After the giant blades of the chopper were resting above the fuselage, Heller was met by Captain William Armstrong, who was the senior American advisor to Captain Ho Tieu of the ARVN Rangers. Later, Heller was impressed with their friendliness and expression of respect toward each other as the two officers gave him the grand tour at base camp. For defensive reasons, a moat with bamboo stakes and barbed wire fences surrounded the entire camp. Vietnamese soldiers were everywhere, working, lubricating and polishing their rifles, or doing their laundry. Amidst mortar and machine gun fortifications were Strike Force Billets. Helicopters were delivering supplies near the teamhouse. Mortar pits and flood dikes, guy wires to support antenna poles were in the center of the ambitious camp. An SF medic was passing out pills and bandaids to children near the camp dispensary.

After Heller had checked in at the team house command office, he met the three other SF sergeants from Fort Bragg and their Vietnamese counterparts. Finally, the first sergeant took him to the strike force hut. Heller was surprised that Armstrong and Tieu both rose politely from the orange crates they had been sitting upon and once more extented their hands to make him welcome. After all, he was an enlisted man and they were officers with the rank of captain. Heller was even more surprised to get an apology from Captain Armstrong regarding his humble BOQ (Bachelor Officer's Quarters).

"Please grab yourself one of those crates and sit, Heller," the captain told him. "It's the best we can do."

Heller thanked the captain, who was most anxious to continue an indoctrination chat with his new advisor.

"By the way, Heller, you'll have Doc Blanchard for your hutmate. He's cross trained in demolition and went through Fort Sam Houston for his medical training."

"I know him from Bragg, sir. I recognized him as he was passing out bandaids, when I arrived earlier."

"You'll get along. He's been around Loc Ninh for some time," the captain advised Heller. "He'd give you the shirt off his back."

"I look forward to seeing him again." Heller replied good naturedly, then asked if there was anything else he ought to know.

The captain asked, "Do you understand the CIDG program which is beginning to mature in the country?"

"Yes, sir!" Heller replied. "CIDG, which stands for Civilian Irregular Defense Group, is essentially a defensive effort characterized by the overriding goal of securing control over the native minorities, and winning their allegiance, so that they won't fall victims to communist domination. Actually, sir, the mission of the CIDG is to control the Viet Cong, either through area development, or border surveillance. The word from Bragg is that the CIDG and our people are actually hunting the VC now, since our commitment of conventional forces has distinctly accepted an offensive role. As a matter of fact," Heller continued with his synopsis, "I studied a department directive which defines the counterinsurgency program as a military civil effort, designed to accomplish the destruction of the Viet Cong and create a free environment, establish firm governmental contol over the population and enlist the people's willing support and participation in the program. Border control operations against VC infiltration routes and hitting them and their bases in the south and in the north, should bring that old whiskered Ho Chi Minh and his communist cohorts to their knees. I believe, gentlemen, if the strike force people are recruited from the area which is exploited by VC, we can get the information to wipe them out quickly and decisively."

Heller stopped talking for a moment. He turned toward Captain Armstrong. "Sir! Shall I continue?" he asked, while his eyes were fixed on a bracelet on the officer's wrist.

"Not now, thank you, Heller," the captain grinned, shaking his head in disbelief. "I'm amazed what they teach at Bragg these days. . ."

"Sir! The instructors at Bragg are all experienced soldiers, professionals, like yourself. If the politicians will let the generals fight the war, we'll win it and be home by Christmas."

"Not so loud on the political aspects, " the captain stressed. "Are there any questions from you, Heller?"

"One sir!"

"Please."

"Sir! That bracelet. I believe I've seen a few like that on Special Forces instructors at Bragg."

The captain smiled. "I got mine at a Montagnard tribal ceremony, which was given in my honor, Heller. Back in the mountain country, getting a bracelet is a token of respect, an act of appreciation for helping that particular hamlet to fight the VC, who were about to take their 14 and 15 year old sons and whatever food they could carry."

"Was it much of a fire fight, Captain?"

"No! Not that time. There were five reckless VC and just two of us. We were expecting them. When they got into our kill zone my Montagnard rifle expert and I fired our M-16's simultaneously. After the short encounter, we looked the dead in the eye. As per plan, I hit them between the eyes, while my loyal mountain-man hit them in the rear. . ."

Suddenly, there was considerable laughter in the hut. Heller thought he heard a giggling female voice. "Am I hearing things?" he wondered out loud. "I thought I heard a woman's voice, Captain."

"You did, Heller," he acknowledged. "Her father, who was also the mayor of the hamlet, insisted I take his pretty daughter along. You know the rest. I didn't want to insult him. So, I accepted the girl, and have become rather fond of her," he said affectionately, suddenly taking a tiny native in oversized Army fatigues in his arms. "Sandy, please take your garrison cap off and show Sergeant Heller your long beautiful black hair," he said with great gentleness.

Like a docile wife, she complied wholeheartedly.

18

After the Special Forces captain had concluded his interview with Heller, he suggested that he meet and get to know his hut-mate, Doc Blanchard. Heller saluted sharply and departed for his strike force billet, fifty yards from the team house. He found it as immaculate as an operating room. The chemical odors were a combination of pine oil and a substance used to kill insects. There were two bunks, with sleeping bags ready for occupancy. The top bunk was occupied. Harsh vibrating sounds whistled through the hot air. Doc Blanchard was sleeping, snoring like a sow. Heller laid his personal gear carefully on his bunk, so he would not disturb his hut-mate. Then he went outside to scrutinize the simple fortification, and the sandbags surrounding the encircled billet.

Suddenly, he realized he was still without a weapon, which should have been his very first priority. He found the ammunition hut, not far from his and chose a M-79 Grenade Launcher, together with 75 rounds of "Buckshot" and 25 standard grenade projectiles, knowing he would be comfortable with it in close combat, should that time come.

"And it will," he thought to himself, in the broadest application and mental acceptance. "But, if and when that time comes, I'll take a bunch of Viet Cong with me."

The next morning, Captain Armstrong requested that the leaders of the CIDG, - the 4 Special Forces soldiers, 4 South Vietnamese Rangers, 3 interpreters and 27 civilians, would meet in the team house for another general briefing. Rumor had it that Captain Armstrong had seen captured enemy documents and information from a recon reserve force, obtained while they were patrolling near the Cambodian border less than 5 miles to the north of the camp.

"Gentlemen!" said the captain slowly. "I assume all of you know what mobile strike forces are? Some time ago, General Westmoreland created them to protect "C" Detachments for reinforcement and reaction. At that time the units came under the 5th Special Forces Group (Airborne), with a strength of about 200. Like anything else in Nam, it took time to recognize their capability. Their recon work was remarkable. Their efforts produced excellent results, and I am delighted they had few casualties. Last, but not least, each mobile strike force has an A team with it.''

The captain stopped talking for a brief moment. His sharp eyes traversed hastily over the men in front of him.

''If you have any questions, please raise your hand,'' he said with strong emphasis.

When no one raised a hand, the captain continued. ''Although our own patrols and our night ambush troops have failed to bring in live VC, we know they are out there. We know they are probing our outer defenses. We've combed every crack and crevasse, every barn, pit and shack, with negative results.''

Sergeant Heller raised his hand. The captain was immediately responsive. ''Yes, Sergeant Heller?''

''I have several questions, sir.''

''Please ask them, sergeant?''

''Sir! What about this mobile strike force?''

''Army intelligence gave us the word that a mobile strike force ran into a rather large VC unit at Bo-Duc, 10 miles northwest of here. After the VC took heavy casualties, which they left on the field, they crossed into Cambodia, and are now regrouping for another assault. The commander of the strike force was a friend of mine from Bragg, who was wounded during action, but he came by to tell me he believed we would be next on the VC's list.''

''Are we ready for them, sir?'' Heller asked impatiently, biting his lower lip.

''Saigon is well informed, but of course there's always inept and inaccurate intelligence information, especially in the numbers of Viet Cong who come down each day from the north.''

''I realize that, Captain. I'm more interested in the kind of cooperation we can get from the so called unified command system, when and if air strikes are necessary, sir.''

''You amaze me, Heller,'' the Captain remarked thoughtfully. ''Specifically. . .?''

''The word at Bragg has it that unit field commanders have problems with bureaucratic red tape. For example, when battle field commanders have urgent need for close support air strikes from the Air Force, it takes an eternity before they get it, if at all. We were told there's still considerable inter-service rivalry, which stifles and smothers missions. Since I'm still working on theory and have little actual field experience, sir, I would feel much better, if you can clear my questions."

"Heller! At this time, General West. oreland is supreme commander. Let no one question that he's in charge. Also, let me assure you, all of you here, Captain Tieu and I know what numbers to call to get immediate results," the captain emphasized. "Any other questions from anybody?"

"As I asked before, sir, are *we* ready for the VC?"

This time the captain chose not to answer Heller's question. Instead, he asked him what his other question pertained to.

"Sir! I'd like to know if your patrols have searched for VC hardware under buffalo stalls, native outhouses, perhaps even under the fire pits in their shacks or in their burial grounds? Every other grave might contain VC weapons."

The officers and NCO's who were present looked mummified. Captain Armstrong's face seemed to shrivel up. When he regained his composure he slapped at a flying insect on his brow and promptly remarked "Sergeant Heller! I'll give you a qualified no!"

Captain Tieu shrugged his shoulders. Some senior enlisted men clearly expressed indifference, doubt and reluctance to accept Heller's suggested digging in graveyards.

Heller finally realized he had struck out. "Captain! I request permission to take a patrol of volunteers into the field to prove my point."

"Sergeant Heller! Let me see if I understand you correctly? You believe the VC excavate and hollow out tunnels, even under the dead?"

"Yes, sir!"

The captain glanced at his counterpart, then back at Heller. "You have your patrol! But for the time being please keep out of the graveyards."

"Sir! After you dismiss us, I would like to see all available maps. Then, sir, I'd like to discuss the actual terrain and the general habits of the VC with your other three SF NCO's. I assume they know the lay of the bush, paths and trails. For my intended search and seizure patrol, I'd like to have Doc Blanchard and an interpreter, with weapons of their choice. I'd like seventeen volunteers who will carry their regular equipment and four hand grenades each. I wanna be sure that we'll have six M-15's and six M-16 rifles. Since I carry an M-79, I'd like to have one more. Each of the riflemen must have 15 magazines with tracer and ball ammunition. Two grenadiers will carry a dozen high explosives and their sidearms. We'll need flares and canister rounds. As I've said, if I can get Doc Blanchard, I'd like him to carry at least 2 claymore mines, since he's an explosive expert."

The captain leaned forward and nodded his head. "That's very good, Sergeant Heller. You sound like a soldier with experience?"

"Thank you, sir!" he replied honestly. "So far it's all academic theory and intuition. Of course, the instructors at Bragg directed their lectures toward this type of mission."

"Anything else, Sergeant Heller?" the officer inquired with a serious face.

"Yes, sir! I'll need a strobe light, a couple of flashlights, a half dozen picks and shovels, and finally, the most important item beside our weapons..."

"Which is?" the captain interrupted, wondering what it could be.

"A starlight scope, sir!"

"You got it! Anything else, Sergeant Heller?"

"Oh! I almost forgot, sir," Heller answered. "We'll have to have one of your crackling two way radios to keep in touch with you, sir."

"I assume you'll wanna inspect your volunteers and have them test fire their weapons?" the captain asked.

"I was coming to that, sir," Heller told him grimly, adding, "if it pleases you, sir, I'd like to do that at 1600 hours. If you have no objections, sir, each soldier test fires his weapon at his convenience."

The captain nodded affirmatively. A moment later he asked his counterpart, Captain Tieu, if Heller's patrol was acceptable to him.

22

"Yes, it is, Captain Armstrong. I believe this untried, young SF sergeant has a real concept about his operation. All I can say is that he impressed me with his positive intent. I almost wished I could go along."

Heller thanked the officers for their cooperation, saluted sharply and returned to his hut to discuss things with Blanchard.

Doc Blanchard was waiting for him. "Congratulations, buddy!" he said sprightly, as Heller bent to enter the hooch. "If your reconnaissance sweep brings in the bacon, you'll get a medal for sure. . ."

"A medal? The hell with medals, Doc! We got a job to do," Heller reminded Blanchard harshly. "I simply wanna prove to my superiors, my equals and those below me that traditional ideas don't work at times."

"True!" Blanchard acknowledged. "How about an example?"

"Well, I understand that none of the patrols have come in with either the goodies or information pertaining to buried or concealed stores of ammo. True or false, Doc?"

"True!" he answered quickly, adding, "Heller! You've gone way out on a limb and you haven't got much of a leg to stand on. But, for some reason I kinda believe you. As a matter of fact, I'll shadow you just to see for myself what kind of trooper you really are."

"Thanks, Doc. I can use all the help I can get."

There was a moment of silence. Finally, Blanchard asked, "Heller, got an opinion of Ho Tieu?"

Without a moment of hesitation Heller said, "Ho appears to be a dedicated freedom fighter. He's been trained by our advisors. He was a POW up north and escaped."

"Somebody told you that?" Blanchard asked intensely.

"I could tell at a glance he had been in irons."

"How?"

"I saw the ring marks of the shackles on his wrists and his eyes told me he has been broken, humiliated, starved and tortured. Tell you what, Blanchard. Let's stop this twenty question game. We're wasting valuable time. How about a short resume, without interruption or conversation? I don't wish to look like an idiot the next time I come in contact with Captain Ho Tieu."

In a concise summary Blanchard succinctly narrated how Captain Ho Tieu of the ARVN Rangers had been trained by 5th Special Forces personnel in counterinsurgency, guerrilla and unconventional warfare, psychological warfare, assassination, kidnapping, ambushing and how to infiltrate into North Vietnam. The captain was also jump qualified and was totally familiar with Hanoi and Haiphong, as well as the North Vietnam major rail links going to China. After President Johnson authorized retaliatory air strikes in the middle of February, 1965, the highly trained captain was sent on a mission to North Vietnam. He found the first part of his mission simple. As bombing the North gradually was accelerated, the air drop was uneventful. However, when Captain Tieu entered the house of one of his cousins on the outskirts of Hanoi, his relatives had left it for the South. As it was, the vacant house had become a VC officers quarters. Thus, in a matter of moments he was beaten into unconsciousness and taken to Hoa Lo Prison, which was an old French hotel, eventually named "The Hanoi Hilton", primarily used for downed American airmen. Since Captain Ho Tieu knew that North Vietnam had been a signatory nation to the principals of the Geneva Convention, in 1949, at first, he showed considerable respect for his captors, his guards and most certainly for his interrogators. But, when it became obvious that they wanted to use him for international propaganda and ordered him to confess that the "American Imperialists" had ordered him to spy and sabotage the major rails in and around Hanoi, he refused to give them more than his name, rank and serial number. After they classified him as a common criminal, his preferential treatment stopped. After a final quiz, his interrogators struck, whipped, and tortured him into a helpless heap. After more of those gruesome, horrifying and grisly sessions, they put him in irons, tortured him until his bowels and urine emptied involuntarily. When he still would not cooperate, they stopped feeding him, broke his ribs and consequently threw him into a cell and left him there to die. In one of the most incredible schemes ever contrived by Vietnam POW's, an American pilot in leg-locks, declared to the guards that Tieu had died and that he would be only too glad to carry his stinking carcass outside, to save them the trouble. "Somehow, Tieu survived," Blanchard told Heller. "And, with superhuman strength managed to reach South Vietnam. End of story."

That particular night, Sergeant Heller did not sleep. Intermittently, he closed one eyelid and then the other. He tossed and turned. Although he realized he had no positive information of how Viet Cong guerrillas managed to get their hands on heavy military hardware, he recalled his father telling a group of Florida fishermen stories that many years before the horrifying surprise attack on Pearl Harbor and other military activities, Japanese soldiers, disguised as fishermen, buried large quantities of guns and ammunition on strategic Pacific Islands, which they activated at their convenience and much to the surprise of our forces.

Heller thought about the many dirty tactics of our Asian enemy. "Traditionally, our enemies think of us as fools, gentlemen and sportsmen," Heller argued with himself. He thought about initiating more positive methods of search and seizure control by hard muscled veterans, with determination, aggressiveness and versatility. He also recalled how his father shed some light on the dangerous Nazi Fifth Columns, which undermined local establishments in Europe, or, going back to the classic Trojan legend, about a huge, hollow wooden horse, filled with Greek soldiers and left at the gates of Troy. According to legend, the soldiers of Troy believed that the Greek conquerors had abandoned the war, and had departed for home. The Trojans jubilantly brought the horse into the city. But their happiness was short lived. That night, the soldiers in the horse opened the gates to the city for their compatriots who completely destroyed it.

At 0300 hours, Heller bailed out of his bunk. He grabbed one of two canteens filled with water and quickly splashed some on his face. He gulped down four or five big swallows, then literally flew into his jungle fatigues and his boots. Still filled with self doubt, he adjusted his belt and the M-79 bandoleer

25

across his chest. As he concentrated on his forthcoming mission, he also gave some thought to Captain Ho Tieu and wondered what he might do under similar conditions. Heller hoped that the captain would eventually discuss with him how he succeeded and finally got back to South Vietnamese forces. He also wondered just how many American POW's were in the Hanoi Hilton, Alcatras, Briarpatch, Dogpatch, The Riveria, The Vegas and Son Tay. Heller swore on his mother's grave, "Come what may, no enemy would take him alive and imprison him in the Hanoi torture system." After he checked his grenades, the projectiles for his grenade launcher, he whipped his Jim Bowie knife from its sheath and felt the sharp edge of the steel. All of a sudden he realized that his hut mate was still sleeping soundly under the mosquito net.

"Hey! Sleeping beauty!" Heller mocked gently. "If you're going with me, how about getting your butt out of the sack?"

Before Heller had uttered the last word, Blanchard had landed on his feet, completely dressed in his fatigues, jungle-boots, harness and everything else required for action, with the exception of his explosives and ammo for his weapon.

"You were saying, ol' buddy?" he boasted. Heller smiled, as he observed the medic grab his pouch, his bandoleer, his M-16 rifle, and his claymore mines. They left for the team house without another word.

When the two leading NCO's arrived at the team house, the seventeen volunteers and interpreter were there drinking strong, hot coffee.

"When all of you get back early in the morning," the cook told them, "I'll have a hearty meal waiting for you. Meanwhile, good luck!"

Captains Armstrong and Tieu were pleased. They knew Sergeant Heller was motivated, capable and determined, as the detail of the twenty troopers marched over the rolling hill in front of the CIDG compound.

The patrol passed the barbed wire fences, spaced at various internals, zigzaging with its barbs in alternate directions, and at various heights. They walked by the massive concertina implacements winding and twisting in ringlets and coils. They came to the ricepaddies close by which gave the camp's defenders a clear line of fire for approximately three hundred yards.

As per planned diagram and arrangement, the overnight security patrol was spotted by Heller's pointman two thousand yards from the edge of the wooded area. Without incident Heller's force moved cautiously through the night patrol. There was an exchange and words of caution between Heller and a young Special Forces officer that a small unit of VC were operating in the area and that they might have followed the early withdrawal of his troops in order for them to probe the outer defenses for an eventual attack.

According to plan, the point man was fifty yards to the straight front, followed by three security front soldiers. On the left flank were four soldiers, as well as on the right flank. Heller was in the middle of the main body, with a cross-trained communication expert, carrying his radio on his back. Three CIDG volunteers protected the rear. At a hand signal from Heller, they moved forward.

Although the moon was almost full, there were moments of complete darkness, as it played hide-and-seek with the clouds.

At the onset of dawn, the small force of South Vietnamese CIDG personnel led by Special Forces Sergeant Heller, slithered through the jungle. Suddenly the pointman gave a hand signal for a halt. A quick moment thereafter another signal indicated he wanted Heller for a conference. Heller moved forward like a panther, in a crouching position, ready to pounce on whatever confronted his pointman.

When Heller got there, the pointman told him that he had spotted 5 VC carrying rifles, with his starlight scope. Heller looked in the direction of where the soldier had said he had seen the enemy and could not confirm it.

"In another moment, the moon will come out from behind the clouds, and. . ." the Vietnamese soldier emphasized.

"I see them! Five, like you said."

Heller pulled the map from his harness to have a look at the area. "I see swamp and dangerous marshland to their left. If they wanna probe toward our camp, they'll have to pass on this narrow path. What do you think?"

"Right!"

At that moment, Heller raised his arms over his head, brought his hands together and intertwined the fingers of both hands, as if he were giving praise to the Almighty to glorify Him. It was in fact a pre-arranged signal for an immediate ambush.

There was instant response from the force with some light rustling of grass being trampled. There was the rubbing of branches and other sounds. Here and there early birds started chattering indistinctly, but incessantly. Daylight was almost at hand.

In a matter of sixty seconds, Heller's entire force was lying in wait to attack. The ambush was set. The Rangers and their American advisors were in position, waiting for the VC to come into the kill zone.

"If only that enemy detail will not deviate from the path," Heller hoped, thinking about what he must do if they did.

When Heller saw the five man VC detail again, walking boldly at early light, he told his pointman, "This will be like shooting fish with a double barrel shotgun in a rain barrel."

Doc Blanchard, who had come up to be near Heller, remarked in a whisper, "I've never seen them that stupidly reckless. They are committing suicide!"

"It might be a trap," Heller whispered back.

"It's my Rubicon," he remarked a moment later.

"That's a word I'm not familiar with," Blanchard whispered. "Is that something new?"

"Hell no! It means, when you take an irrevocable step, there's no turning back."

"Oh! Something Napoleon said?"

"No! It was Caesar crossing a river in Italy."

Heller pondered over the problem in contemplation of using twenty professionals to kill five well armed VC guerrillas. "Might as well," he thought silently. "If they are decoys for a larger force, the firepower from my patrol will probably sound like a full company fire fight, and they might take off in the other direction. We can't lose this opportunity."

At that moment the five VC's entered the kill zone. Their

frontman moved cautiously forward, with his automatic rifle at the ready position, as if he were stalking deer.

Suddenly Heller dropped his arm and all hell broke loose. The VC's never knew what hit them. Before their bodies hit the ground, each had been literally torn to pieces by instantaneous, massive saturation, annihilation fire.

Heller was first to stand up. He kept his finger on the trigger and kept pointing his weapon at the dead. "Look at them when we move out," he instructed. "Take their weapons and let them lay where they are. If they're still here by the time we get back, we might take them with us for show. Meanwhile," he told Doc Blanchard, "search these characters for documents, papers, etc. Then get with our radio operator to inform the skipper that we sighted five VC and killed same. No casualties. Patrol now enroute to objective."

"Yes sir! I consider that an order," Blanchard said, grinning with satisfaction, knowing that Heller was truly a well trained and now experienced Special Forces non-commissioned officer, who would as time goes on earn the love and respect of all those who came in contact with him.

Several long minutes later, Heller's small force took the narrow pathway toward the nearby hamlet. After they arrived, Heller, Blanchard and the interpreter were directed to the mayor's thatched roof house, while eight Special Forces CIDG soldiers acted as security men. When the interpreter told the mayor of Heller's mission, which was to find and destroy Viet Cong hardware, the old man shook his head and said the only word he knew, which was "No! No! No!"

"Tell the mayor, unless he will tell us where the VC hid their weapons, we will take building by building apart, starting with his house," Heller said with determination.

The old man repeated, "No! No! No!". When two men with picks started digging in the mayor's sleeping quarters, he summoned Heller to inform him, via the interpreter, that it was possible that the VC had buried weapons under the buffalo manure pit.

"Thank the gentleman," Heller instructed the interpreter, who passed the word to the old, white whiskered native.

Among other things, Heller had read books about early civilizations, about the science of archaeology and excavation, which made him appreciate mother earth's secrets even more. "It is written," he said with humor in his voice to the men standing with their picks and shovels ready to dig, "modern archaeology began when the ancient city of Pompeii was discovered under massive volcanic ashes and rocks, after Mount Vesuvius erupted 2000 years ago and buried it."

The men looked at each other. They wondered what manner of man the twenty-one year old sergeant really was, eventhough he revealed his uncommon leadership at the ambush of the five Viet Cong earlier. Sergeant Heller knew what they were thinking.

"Let me take a sounding," he said, poking, probing and prodding with one of five type 66 AK47 Chinese-communist, 7.62 mm assault rifles, they took along. After poking again and again, he thought he heard a hollow sound. "Start digging, right here!" he ordered positively. "There's some kind of a tunnel down here."

The men started digging. Buffalo and human manure started to fly in every direction. Doc Blanchard got a shovel full down his back-side, when he turned to chat with Heller, who had just told him to move the cattle to another place. "By the time you get back, we might have found gold," Heller told him.

"You got to be joking!" Blanchard laughed, trying to get the crap off. "Let's face reality. Nobody, but nobody, in his right mind would wanna hide weapons under this pile of crap!"

"Not so loud! You're discouraging the diggers," Heller said distinctly. "Please get the animals out of here before the whole stall collapses."

Suddenly one of the diggers hit something solid. "I think I got something," he told Heller directly above him.

"Keep digging 'til we can make it out. It looks like some kind of grave stone."

"Yeah, sergeant. I think you're right."

Heller jumped into the hole. He put his strength on the rock and started to twist it. "Help me with it," he asked the man who found the big stone. Finally both men managed to move the barrier rock, which had covered the entrance to a three by three foot tunnel, just big enough for Heller to crawl into.

"We hit gold!" Heller shouted with joy, as he passed the weapons from the tunnel. Each rifle was in a polyethelene sack. There were 15 SKS carbines, the Russian AK47 assault rifle which can be fired at a rate of 150 rounds a minute. There were 15 Russian RPG7 rocket launchers and B41 rocket AT grenade launchers, Chinese-communist type 56. Finally, Heller said, "Praise the Lord! Here comes a baby carriage with wheels!"

Everbody looked. "It's one of those Chinese communist type 53, 7.62 mm machine guns."

"And look at all that ammo...mostly 7.62 mm stuff," Blanchard remarked to Heller, who repeated what he had previously stated, "We've found gold right here!"

"All right, my friend, now that we have the VC equipment what are we gonna do with it?"

"Get on the radio and ask number one for instructions. Throw him a hint that all of us are kinda tired and hungry."

Without asking for help, Heller took one of the shovels and started filling in the big hole. When the rest of the CIDG soldiers saw their laboring leader on the other end of the implement, they almost fought each other for a shovel.

Meanwhile, Blanchard got in touch with Captain Armstrong, who was elated. He regretted choppers were simply not available for a pick-up. "Bring in what you can. Destroy, wreck or burn the rest!" he ordered.

When Blanchard informed him what the captain had said, Heller's jaw bone hit the upper frame of his mouth, as if he were trying to squeeze blood out of his teeth. He spit on the buffalo manure, scratched his face with his dirty hands and finally said, "I'd appreciate if all of you will help me get that ammo about a hundred yards out of this hamlet, where we'll blow it sky-high. Then each of us will carry two or three VC rifles. Blanchard and I will bring the baby carriage."

After the destruction of the ammunition, Heller lead the troops back to camp via a different path.

At 1000 hours, twenty hungry, thirsty, tired, sweaty physically and mentally exhausted soldiers laid thirty enemy rifles and one machine gun in front of the team house. Heller was certain that Captain Armstrong would be waiting to greet his patrol. When no one, not even the first sergeant appeared, Heller's face turned red. He was embarrassed. "Where in hell are the officers and where in damnation are their combined values, responsibility, integrity and military ethics?" he wondered. "Surely Captains Armstrong and Tieu will show their appreciation for our extraordinary accomplishment."

Although Heller's mouth was parched and dry and the salty moisture was still pouring in droplets from his body, he had the men stand at attention, waiting for the senior officer, who did not show.

"Gentlemen!" Heller spoke loud and clear. "Why don't all of you find some water and get cleaned up first? Next, get the special breakfast the cook promised us before we left this morning, then hit the sack. And thanks for putting up with me," he added before he shouted, "Dismissed!"

Heller was perplexed. Once inside the team house, he confronted the first sergeant. "Where's everybody, Top?"

"After Captains Armstrong and Tieu heard how well you did, they took off to Saigon for a CIDG directors' conference," he told him, adding, "In case you've forgotten, today is Sunday. So, if you and that special detail wanna eat your late breakfast, first, I'm ready to issue all of you a 36-hour pass."

"I forgot all about Sunday."

"Confidentially, Heller," the first sergeant injected, "I can assure you Captain Armstrong will brag about your find under that big pile of bullshit," he laughed.

"Right now, Top, my men and I just want a good meal under our belly. After that it's sack time for the next 24 hours, that is if the Viet Cong will let us."

"Heller! You don't think the VC might hit us this weekend? Tonight?"

"It may not be today or tomorrow," Heller told him. "But I'll assure you it's coming soon."

The following morning, Heller and Blanchard appeared at the personnel office to get a two day pass to Saigon. A supply truck took them to a heliport in Phoc Vinh, where the two noncoms caught a hop on a Huey helicopter to the big city of over a million people. After arriving in Saigon, the two Special Forces sergeants, wearing their green berets and their jungle fatigues, walked through the main gate leading to Plantation Road. When they saw the 3rd Army Field Hospital across the street, Blanchard mentioned that he had been there recently, drawing medical supplies and some small equipment.

At the main gate the two sergeants showed their special passes to the MP's. Once outside, they were literally mobbed by peddlers, pimps and pushers, who were ready to sell their wares from trinkets by nameless vendors to vicious narcotic merchants, actually displaying heroin, morphine, cocaine, marijuana, LSD, hashish, MDA and methaqualone.

"You name it and they'll have it!" Blanchard remarked between his teeth. "What really bothers me is that the Saigon police close their eyes to drug problems, and, we, according to facts, can't touch them with a ten foot pole."

By the time the two soldiers got to the corner, a nine or ten year old native youngster made his proposal with a big grin and determination, which brought some laughter to Heller and Blanchard. Said he, "G.I.. .you want good time with my sister? Long time? Short time? She much pretty, like me," he told them. "Do anything you want. . .only 400 piasters."

While Blanchard and Heller had a good laugh, the little boy would not be denied. "G.I. . . .you say yes?"

Blanchard said, "Maybe. Where are your sisters?"

Heller simply said, "No!"

"For you, G.I., I have a special deal, today. . .only 300 piasters with my smaller sister."

"What do you think?" Blanchard asked Heller. "I really just wanna see a good looking woman again. I honestly don't particularly care to take one to bed. I'm engaged to my childhood sweetheart, and if and when I get back to Bragg, we'll get married. How about you, Heller ol' boy?"

By the time they got into a Vietnamese 3 wheel taxi, (lombret) which took them to MACV Headquarters, Heller had informed his companion of how his childhood sweetheart, Susan, had taken off with another, three weeks before graduation, how another girl rolled him in a West Palm Beach motel, and how he eventually met the girl of his dreams in the Palace of Versailles. "I've just had my 21st birthday. I believe I'll wait 'til I get married, someday. Right now I could eat a Kodiak brown bear."

While at the headquarters building in Saigon, they were told how to find the snack bar. Shortly thereafter, they entered. When the two non-commissioned officers saw nothing but silver and gold leafs and even stars on uniforms, they wondered if they were in the right place. "This must be for officers," Blanchard thought.

"Brass or no brass, I got to eat," Heller remarked, pushing Blanchard toward a pretty native waitress with fair skin, long black hair and a beautiful smile, who asked if she might take their order.

"Yes, please. We need four cheeseburgers, two large french fries, four sodas and," Heller said glancing about the snack bar, "a place to eat it."

"While you buy it," Blanchard said softly, "I'll whisper into one of those bird colonel officer's ears, we'll need one of their tables."

In less than three minutes, the waitress had the order on a tray. Heller handed the lovely Eurasian girl a ten spot. "Keep the change. Buy yourself a pink ribbon for your beautiful hair."

The waitress seemed speechless for a moment. After she recovered, she said, "That's the very first time anyone has ever given me a tip," she said with a straight face. "If I may, the next time you come, I'll promise to sit with you and watch you eat it."

"I'll look forward to that," he told her, searching for Blanchard, who was sitting at a table with a green beret Major.

When Heller got to the table, Blanchard stood up, and told him that the gentleman had obviously noticed their predicament and motioned for them to join him.

"Sergeant Heller, this is Major Beckwith," Blanchard told him with a feeling of happy satisfaction.

Openly and enthusiastically, with a high degree of pleasure, Heller recognized the name. There could be no other. He knew it was Major Charles Beckwith, well known at the John F. Kennedy Special Warfare School, one of the truly remarkable officers who embraced special training for missions, tactics and strategy for Special Forces combat A, B, and C teams.

Heller placed the tray of food on the table. He snapped to attention and saluted sharply. The officer returned the salute and told Heller, "Do sit down, won't you? It seems the three of us work for the same organization. How did you manage to get off on a Monday?"

Heller shook his head and grinned. "Major, would you believe my commander insisted we take a trip to the big city and relax?"

The major's serious ruddy face turned from a frown to a light hearted grin. "May I know how you earned that kind of praise?"

"Yes, sir!" Heller said with pride, and proceeded to tell the green beret officer of volunteering for a patrol, which not only encountered five heavily armed VC, but discovered an arms cache and destroyed approximately 1000 lb of ammunition.

"Let me congratulate you, sergeant," Major Beckwith said sincerely. After a moment of hesitation, he added, "Heller, if you had done for me what you did for Captain Armstrong, I'd get you the Army Commendation Medal with a bronze V, a pass, plus a promotion. 'Course there's no money in medals, except for the Medal of Honor."

"Major, I really don't think I deserve a medal. I did what Special Forces prepared me for," Heller said seriously, with an absence of assertiveness. "Another stripe really would look good for pay purposes, and of course my ol' dad would have something to brag about in Key West."

During their hectic and unexpected encounter at the snack bar, the three Special Forces soldiers exchanged action packed stories of uncommon accomplishments and about the missions and purpose of the United States in Vietnam.

Major Charles Beckwith's extraordinary critique was told with such soldierly and intellectual depth that Blanchard and Heller were stimulated and impelled to greater achievements. The satisfaction that they had been consorting with one of the very great professionals, who had distinguished himself earlier in Korea and now in Vietnam, would be something they would treasure and remember.

After Major Beckwith left them, Heller and Blanchard remained to relish the air conditioned splendor of the snack bar, an anomaly to the oppressive heat they had experienced just one day ago.

At the table directly behind them, three distinguished Army colonels with silver eagles on their collars and one lieutenant colonel in fatigues were rehashing what they obviously considered improper management of the war in Vietnam.

"Jack," commented the colonel sitting opposite the junior officer. "Since you're one of the interpreters in the intelligence community, will you tell us ol' battlefield commanders what we're doing wrong? Are we really bungling things? After all, we have massive air and ground firepower. We have highly sophisticated equipment, damn good reconnaisance, and I'm told we have well over 200,000 troops, not to mention what our allies have..."

"Gentlemen!" the light colonel acknowledged at once, sympathetically, trying to spare them further pain. "First and foremost, although we have at least 25,000 paid interpreters, we are not getting hard facts. Frankly, gentlemen, we are linguistically poor. With few exceptions most Vietnamese interpreters are unreliable. I'm sure you have all heard that the Viet Cong have infiltrated everywhere. Most of our so called interpreters are uneducated. They simply can't translate, deduce the meaning of, or even give a firm opinion of what they see."

"I've been present at a prisoner interrogation," one of the other colonels mentioned. "The result was negative, nothing. I've been told our friends torture VC's to get info.."

"What really makes me angry," the light colonel went on, "is there's too much double talk from uninformed but optimistic visiting firemen from back home. Then, when we do clobber the VC's decisively, the media ignores our gains and successes. By the time the news gets to the States, things are distorted."

"As is right now," said one of the other colonels, "regardless of what we do under General Westmoreland, Ambassador Bunker, President Cao Ky and our allies, the Viet Cong, using their sanctuaries in Laos and Cambodia, have the military initiative, which in itself is an absurdity."

The colonels discussed many other aspects and subjects related to the war, such as the massive desertions from various South Vietnam army units and CIDG's, search and destroy missions, science of methods used to gain military matters and strategy, large scale operations, even how the atom bomb could be used, if nothing else would stop the Communists.

Abruptly the colonels stood up, adjusted their hats and stormed out of the building.

Later in the day the two Special Forces troopers took another 3 wheel taxi into the city, hoping to eventually get to the Army PX on the other side to purchase routine necessities, like tooth brushes, tooth paste, razor blades, shaving lotion, chocolate bars and soap.

Wherever the two soldiers looked, they saw signs of VC sabotage, distruction of bridges, uprooted rails and bombed out hotels. Assassinations had been rampant and unchecked. Violence and signs of death were everywhere. The city of Saigon looked as if it were under siege and out of control. Refugees were crowding the streets and the sidewalks. The massive influx of the stranded had aggravated the already overcrowded housing conditions, which posed extreme burdens on the overtaxed public utilities. Many thousands had been uprooted by Viet Cong terrorism. They had managed to get to the big city where conditions were even worse than they had been in their hamlets.

While the wealthy people of Saigon lived in spacious villas, built of brick and stone and fully equipped with electricity, running water and sanitary facilities, the middle and low class families were living in multiunit one story structures, occasionally with a small inside toilet and perhaps a small shower. Most tenants had to use Kerosene and gasoline lamps. Water had to be hauled from the nearby canals, all polluted and defiled with human excrement. During this turbulent period, traffic was uncontrolled. Smuggling, blackmarketing, gambling, vice and prostitution were running wild.

Blanchard shook his head in disbelief. "What do you think, Heller ol' boy? Can we save this country, or is it too late?"

Heller shrugged, but he wanted to give a more positive answer. "Once more, if and when Johnson turns the fighting over to our generals, we'll run the commies and their ilk back to where they came from in less than sixty days. Otherwise, it'll be a terrible waste of time, money and our youth," Heller emphasized.

As the taxi rolled slowly down the main section of the city, it appeared to be a soldier's mecca. There were topless clubs, stage shows showing raw burlesque, and there were the ever present massage parlors.

Suddenly, the sidewalk became alive with swinging and swaying ladies of all ages. They displayed lovely clothes and lovelier full breasted and delightful profiles of femininity. With some exception, all had long black hair.

"With their inviting smiles and high heels, they sure look like Hollywood models out for a stroll," Blanchard remarked, as both men stepped from the vehicle. "This is a sex supermarket! Wild! Devastatingly tempting! What do you think, Heller?"

"I see it, ol buddy," Heller replied. "I've seen it in Paris and in New York. I wasn't interested then and I'm not now."

When the girls came closer, the smell of perfume and incense pervaded the air. At one moment, they were completely surrounded by teenage girls, who made no bones that they were most anxious to earn a few American dollars for what they called "long time."

It was sheer torture for Blanchard. The opportunity for a moment of earthly bliss was his for the taking. Impulsively, he flung his arms around a Eurasian beauty, yelling at Heller to grab one of her girlfriends and as he shouted "Let's fly."

Heller shook his head. "Sorry, ol' friend. Nothin' doin'!"

"Very well. In that case, I'm sure you don't mind if I take off," Blanchard reasoned, not waiting for an answer, while the girl pulled and pushed him in the direction of the hotel.

"Damn it, Blanchard! Have you forgotten the buddy system? If somebody doesn't kill you, you'll probably catch VD."

"I'm gonna live a little, Heller," he remarked over his shoulder, with his arm around the girl. "I'll see you in a jiffy!"

Heller watched his buddy disappear in the crowd. He took several steps toward the nearest corner and waited, when a French speaking pimp came too close for comfort. Heller simply asked him to please move back and told him that he wasn't interested, in French. When the man further crowded Heller and even stepped on his jungle boots, Heller pushed him away. When the man was still not satisfied, Heller tapped him slightly with his fist on the chest.

"Sorry, pal, I'm just not interested," he told him in simple French language. "It's against my religion."

Suddenly the pimp pulled a switchblade from his pants pocket and started to circle Heller, who made an automatic defensive move. For a split second, the words of his Camp Mackall instructor rang in his mind, regarding defensive procedures, disarming and inactivating an enemy barehanded.

"This is no ordinary South Vietnamese pimp," Heller thought to himself, as he scrutinized the man. "I'll better take him seriously. He might even be a Viet Cong."

Quickly Heller tore his fatigue top from his body and wrapped it around his left hand. He kept his hands high and apart to deflect a possible slash and to keep the attacker off balance. By this time, many people had gathered to see the struggle of an unarmed soldier and a well built VC pimp, who would undoubtedly butcher the American, who was alone.

Heller was in control of his moves. He was barely breathing. When the pimp literally hurled himself prematurely at him, he sidestepped like a matador in a bullring. There were countless thrusts, slashes, stabs and swipes from the determined adversary.

"Don't defend yourself against that gorilla!" some older woman cried with desperation in her voice. "Run!"

Heller tried a bit of psychology. "Hey! Hold it, buddy! I've never seen you before!" Heller cried at him, backing away. "Why are you trying to hurt me? What do you say? Let's forget it."

"I'm not trying to hurt you, you American pig! I'm gonna kill you!" the punk shouted in English, wielding his knife skillfully, confident and sure of himself.

The decisive turning point came as Heller maneuvered a tactical retreat and deliberately leaned against a wooden door, which led to a side entrance to the hotel where Blanchard had entered with the girl. Heller threw up his hands and now begged the punk to stop. At that moment the punk leaped at what he believed was a young helpless soldier. But Heller moved like a panther. It was close, but the blade plunged into the door behind him. During that split second, Heller delivered a sledge hammer blow behind the punk's neck with his fists, which put his lights out. Heller was instantly on his back, riding his face and head into the cement sidewalk with his knee in the small of his back.

Sergeant Heller's foot was on the punk's right hand preventing the Vietnamese from further flailing. Heller grabbed the would-be assassin's chin and viciously jerked it toward himself. cracking the pimp's spinal column. The punk squealed like a sow in the slaughterhouse, after the butcher has plunged his knife through its heart, then all was quiet. For all intended purposes the fight was over. The punk, whoever he was, closed his shifty eyes and stopped struggling. As Heller stood and dusted himself off, the pimp came suddenly to a sitting position and drew a second concealed knife and threw it at the unsuspecting Heller's back. Miraculously, the knife missed Heller by fractions, probably because of the punk's dazed condition.

Without mercy, Heller grabbed the punk by his long hair. He dragged him like a sack of stinking fertilizer to a nearby open sewer trench, submerged his head, neck and shoulders by putting his jungle boots and the full force of two hundred twenty pounds of muscle on him. Heller's wrath to punish or kill was now very real. He wanted no playing possum for a second time.

"No, Heller, no!" suddenly came the voice belonging to Blanchard. "Get off the bastard, you're killing him!"

"Well!" Heller muttered. "I hope you've had your pleasure, while I fought for my life. Go back to her and stay there!"

At this time the MP's had arrived. They verified that the unknown assailant was dead and began to take statements from witnesses. They arrested Heller and took him and the dead man to military headquarters for positive identification. When they finally removed the punk's clothes, they found a loaded Russian automatic pistol and three distinct sets of numbers tatooed under his right arm.

The MP officer in charge scrutinized the body in front of him, as did numerous others.

"Yes, sir!" remarked the officer, glancing at Sergeant Heller. "You did us one hell of a favor. We've been trying to pick him up for the last three months..."

"Is that so sir?" Blanchard chimed in, looking in the direction of the body. "That VC punk couldn't have been too clever..."

"Why would you say that?" the officer wanted to know.

"Because he picked on the wrong soldier, sir."

"True! True! That pimp had it coming to him," the officer smiled. "According to our information this parasite has a stable of infected whores, who had orders to waylay as many of our soldiers as humanly possible, as long as they would make certain that our American playboys would end up with syphilis, or some other form of VD."

"I guess soldiers who get caught that way are as much a casualty as if they had been brought down by a bullet?" Heller thought aloud, now facing the officer. "Sir! Will I have to appear before a military tribunal? I've made my report. As you know I killed that VC with my bare hands in self-defense..."

"Personally, Sergeant Heller, I'd like to recommend you for a medal and keep you in my command. But," he went on, "you may return to your command, and, while I think of it, I would like to ask you if you've ever heard of the buddy system? You know, going and returning from town with one of your own, shepherding each other?"

Heller glared steadily at Blanchard, before he muttered in a very low but distinct tone of voice, "Yes, sir! I'm aware of the buddy system."

"Good!"

"Sir?"

"Yes?"

"I'm hoping we'll all forget about this thing, sir. I did what I had to do to stay alive?"

"That's noble of you, sergeant," the officer affirmed as he rose to shake hands. "Good luck, sergeant. Next time 'round, stop by, won't you?"

After a warm handshake, Blanchard and Heller saluted and left through the long passageway leading to the exit of the Military Police complex.

"Heller, ol' boy," Blanchard confessed sheepishly, "I've wanted to tell you something, regarding that small skirmish you had with that punk..."

Heller's face dropped. "Well, spit it out!"

"By the time we got to that Asian doll's room, I had second thoughts," he told him. "I had almost undressed when I heard the commotion on the street below. I opened the window, just in time to see you take your jacket off..."

"Then what? You decided to..."

Blanchard cut him off. "Damn it! With my pants in one hand, I flew down the stairs and rushed into your corner, just in case you weren't as sharp as you were against that new colonel at Mackall..."

Heller was appalled. "Are you telling me you watched me waltzing in the street with that Viet Cong pimp?"

"Yeah! I was right behind you, just in case you couldn't handle him by yourself."

"Some pal you are!" Heller remarked with disbelief.

"They call it the buddy system...remember?"

Chapter II

THE BATTLE OF LOC NINH

Sergeant Heller and "Doc" Blanchard stayed the night at the Tan Son Nhut Air Base in Saigon, as the guests of the Military Police Commander there. After a restful night and a hearty breakfast, a CH-47 Chinook helicopter dropped them at Loc Ninh. From there a jeep delivered them to the entrance of the teamhouse, where they checked in.

The first sergeant greeted them with a friendly grin, before he told them that Captain Armstrong wanted to see them on the double. The two sergeants were announced to their commander. After routine protocol and other niceties, Captain Armstrong told Sergeant Heller that he had a surprise for him.

"A surprise for me, sir? Good or bad, sir?"

"You be the judge, Staff Sergeant Heller..."

Heller's ears and posture perked up. "Captain! May I call your attention that I reported to you as Sergeant Heller, only recently, sir?"

The officer smiled at his advisor. "True! You did and you were. But, as it was, I discussed your remarkable leadership achievements with my group commander in Saigon. He asked me if I, as your superior officer, intended to recommend you for the Army Commendation Medal, for meritorious achievement, with the Bronze V device, denoting bravery, courage and fearlessness?''

Unpretentious, Heller wondered if indeed he was recom-mended for the medal.

"As a matter worth mentioning, I knew that each Group Commander was allocated a certain number of stripes, so, I held out for Staff at the same time..."

With unassuming humbleness, Heller was grateful. "But," he mumbled.

"But what, Staff Sergeant Heller?"

"Well, sir! The patrol had hoped that you would receive us after we got back with those five kills and 30 odd rifles and Chi com machine gun."

The captain apologized. "The first sergeant should have told you that I had to go to Saigon. I'm truly sorry, Heller and Blanchard."

"We hoped you wouldn't mind our bringing up the subject, sir."

"Not at all. Not at all," the officer repeated and offered them a cup of coffee. "But" he went on, "I wanted to ask both of you if you have ever heard of the buddy system?"

"Of course, sir," Heller answered. Blanchard did likewise.

"Sir! May I summarize our trip to Saigon?" Heller volunteered, looking at Captain Tieu, who had just entered.

"You may and you should," Tieu said thoughtfully, as he flashed a sheepish grin at Armstrong.

"Gentlemen!" Heller admitted awkwardly and in a low tone of voice. "We've been in Saigon. We've seen Saigon. And, we don't want to never, ever go there again!"

"Why is that? Never, ever, is a very long time..." Armstrong said pensively.

"It's really quite simple, gentlemen," Heller told them regretfully. "Both of us have been under the delusion that the function of our multi-million dollar post exchanges, including the commissaries for that matter, are here to provide us soldiers with necessary supplies the Army doesn't give us for free..."

"Like what, Heller?" Armstrong interjected, glancing at Tieu momentarily. "Like what?"

"Sir! We had hoped to get us some sweets, shaving cream, toothpaste, and things like that..."

"Don't forget the ivory soap," Blanchard harmonized further. "Well, the PX was completely sold out!"

"I should have cautioned you," Armstrong acknowledged apologetically. "The black market thieves, native employees and the politicians probably took their share, as they usually do."

"True!" Tieu added. "Of course, if you had known where to go, you could have gotten the items you wanted in the black market alley in Cholon, no more than fifty feet from the PX..."

"What about the Vietnamese police? Don't tell me they're corrupt?" Heller inquired with youthful innocence.

"The naked truth is," Armstrong explained, "the police don't bother anybody, even if the items are clearly marked or labelled with US-PX markings..."

"I assume you had plenty of MPC (Military Payment Currency) and piasters?" Tieu pondered.

"We still have most of it," Heller admitted. "Later, I discussed the PX plight with an MP officer, who took my complaint but told me that we of the United States have no rights whatsoever in such matters. He also told us that he would file a report with JUSPAO, (Joint United States Public Affairs Office) although he was sure it wouldn't make a tinker's damn."

"That's hard to accept," Blanchard remarked. "I thought we were in Nam to help and that the people would welcome us with open arms. Instead, I'm frustrated to learn that the Saigon bureaucracy, the police malpractices and the black market operations are king. If that isn't a screwed up mess. Surely, General Westmoreland must know it!"

"I can assure you," Tieu intervened, "he is aware of everything. But, the same old song prevails, *All Americans are guests of the South Vietnamese people and have no rights whatsoever!*"

"In other words," Armstrong summarized. "We're up the creek. Even when we win, we lose. Which reminds me, I guess everybody in Saigon envies me having both of you in my outfit, including Major Charles Beckwith, who called me earlier."

"Isn't it a small world, sir?" Heller grinned.

"Yes and what about the MP officer? The one who questioned you at headquarters regarding your defensive action with that pimp?"

"Oh! Sir! I kinda forgot," Heller apologized. "I never knew the MP's name, sir...To tell you the truth, I was hoping he wouldn't remember mine."

"As I said, Sergeant Heller, you're one helluva young soldier. Let me warn you," he went on, "I expect great things from you, now that you're a household word in Saigon."

"I promise I'll do my very best, sir. If and when we go into the field, I'll lead by example and at the head of the troops..."

"Hold it, Sergeant Heller!" the captain said heavily. "When I mentioned that I expected great things from you, I didn't mean getting you up front. All of us know how you can handle yourself. You're confident, mentally and physically courageous, fearless. I think you're unique, loaded with the kind of Army enthusiasm that is rare even at the Point and at Bragg."

"Well, sir!" Heller interrupted grinning. "How may I serve you, Captain Armstrong?"

"Sergeant Heller! I want you to teach leadership and hand-to-hand combat. In fact, I want you to become training officer for our entire CIDG program. We have a lot of greenhorns, as you know."

"Including several young officers on my staff," added Captain Tieu. "Mine need pushing to the limit and I expect we'll probably be committed for a large scale ground assault in our district in the near future."

Heller looked at Captain Armstrong for additional information. The gentleman simply nodded his head and said "True! True!"

"Sir! May I know how intelligence views the situation?" Heller asked apprehensively.

The SF officer left his improvised desk and quickly stepped in front of the four by eight foot plywood board, which was resting on the ground. It contained a map of the entire geographic area of what was called "The Iron Triangle," which included Saigon, Tay Ninh, Loc Ninh, Bo Duc and Bu Prang, close to the Cambodian border and across to Cam Ranh Bay on the South China Sea.

The officer removed a thin flexible stick which was hanging on the side of the board, and abruptly lashed the map with one stroke.

He pointed at the projecting land mass which protruded into Cambodia and firmly shouted. "Damn it! Here's where they are massing! And we can't touch them! Intelligence tells us that the VC will try to overrun us, Bo Duc, Song Be and everything in between..."

"That will take more than a couple of NVA regiments with heavy artillery, sir," Heller said forcefully.

Captain Tieu took the pointer. "Here's where the VC units will strike first!" he stressed. "Right here!"

In a prolonged dissertation both officers, Armstrong and Tieu, took turns and presented what was axiomatic according to intelligence gathering and an analysis thereto from the Vietnam Rangers, Special and other Free World Military Forces, that the VC were positively making preparations for an assault on the Loc Ninh District. Other allied observers thought that the attack would undoubtedly occur late in November. Mobile Strike Force officers, as well as Allied fighting units, had seen VC reinforcements coming into the district. Although Captains Armstrong and Tieu had these reports, they realized it was up to them to verify the accuracy.

"There is a persistent report that the 273rd hard corps VC Regiment has also moved South, as early as last month and is making light excursions into our territory from the Cambodian border. Most recently it crossed the Song Be River and took position northeast of us, becoming our camp's chief adversary."

Tieu spoke, "Also, it is established that at least two or three battalions of the 165th VC Regiment are ready to strike with the 272nd. And, as is," Tieu explained further, "captured documents reveal that elements from the 141st VC Regiment have been identified, together with the 9th VC Division Headquarters, which moved from War Zone D to Loc Ninh. Are there any questions thus far, gentlemen?"

"I have a comment, Captain Tieu."

"Please speak right up, Sergeant Heller."

"I am sure that no one will question that the VC will hit us first," he said with emotion. "I believe if those VC Regiments succeed in running over us, they'll hit Saigon next!"

"If only General Westmoreland had his way, instead of politicians who choose the weapons," Tieu remarked, gnashing his teeth. "He knows how many Viet Cong there are and where they are massing. I can not comprehend how we can honor those sanctuaries on the Cambodian border, when we know full well they'll attack us with everything they have."

"The media watchdogs would have a field day, condemning our own forces if they dared to rout our declared executioners. War is dirty," Captain Armstrong declared. "We are here to do a job, performing effective action, not to win this war, but to deter the North from a complete takeover of the South."

At this moment the first sergeant came into the room, waving two large brownish-yellow envelopes. He handed one to Captain Armstrong and the other to Captain Tieu. Both officers seemed aware of the contents and literally tore into them with intense eagerness.

"Heller! Captain Tieu and I are overwhelmed with personal happiness," Captain Armstrong said convincingly.

"Congratulations, gentlemen!" Heller said joyfully. "How much did each of your babies weigh?"

"Ah! This time you are not correct, Sergeant Heller!"

"Please, sir...the suspense is killing me."

"Captain Tieu will you kindly tell our able sergeant the good tidings?" Captain Armstrong urged his counterpart.

"Happy to, my friend," the South Vietnamese CIDG officer said. "Sergeant Heller! Both of us have been promoted to the rank of major, as of tomorrow!"

"Blanchard! You wouldn't have a tiny bit of some straight disinfecting medicine for our sore throats, would you now?" Heller wondered, waiting for an answer.

"I have some in my hooch!" he told them with a serious face, reaching for a tongue depressor in his pouch to see if indeed some of his special sore throat medicine was an urgent requirement.

"Damn it, Blanchard! Will you stop trying to be so genuinely innocent? It's a celebration," Heller told him impatiently.

Blanchard responded, "Oh! Come to think of it, I have some snake medicine that's even better for special occasions. Would that do, you think?"

"Blanchard! Will you get the snake medicine, or do I have to carry you to the hooch?" Heller wanted to know.

"Just kidding. I'm heading that way right now, Blanchard said loudly over his shoulder, as he finally flew from the room.

After several toasts, the business turned back to the intelligence reports, which were still the number one priority.

On October 28, at 2000 Sergeant Heller volunteered to lead another search and seizure patrol toward the Cambodian border. When he scanned a jungle clearing with his straight scope, he focused in on a large concentration of what appeared to be irregular Viet Cong guerrillas. Heller ordered his men to stay put, while he moved forward like a crawling crocodile, fearless, but cautious, scrutinizing every foot of ground under his stomach. After he thought he was almost upon them, he stopped and lifted his head to evaluate the reckless jibber-jabbering enemy soldiers, as they were setting up 82 mm and 120 mm mortars of Russian design, 122mm rocket launchers, recoilless rifles and heavy machine guns.

Heller was not certain, but he felt that these soldiers were not Viet Cong guerrillas.

"Good God!" he thought to himself, "They must be from that 273 Viet Cong Regiment, or," he concluded, "they may well be from that North Vietnamese Army Artillery Regiment, Majors Armstrong and Tieu had mentioned earlier in the chart room of the team house."

Heller was able to return to his patrol without being detected.

"Where's the radio operator?" Heller whispered to Doc Blanchard.

"Right here," Blanchard said softly. "Wanna tell me what you saw?"

"There's no time for that!" he whispered. "Get me Major Armstrong, or Tieu, and make it quick!"

In less than ten seconds he was in radio contact with the commander. "Sir! We spotted and observed what looks like VC regular Army units, setting up heavy equipment. What are your orders?"

"Wildcat! Wolf here!" came the voice. "Avoid contact. Withdraw cautiously and silently. Your ETA (estimated time of arrival this camp) is approximately 2400 hours. Copy?"

"Wildcat! Wilco! Out!"

When Heller returned with his entire patrol, Majors Armstrong and Tieu, plus all CIDG officers and NCO's were waiting in the teamhouse.

Heller informed all of what he had seen, then offered a suggestion. "I believe the time has come to place Loc Ninh and other smaller camps in the area on Full Alert. As is, after what I've seen approximately 8000 yards from here, we may well have an artillery attack at any moment!"

"Thank you, Sergeant Heller," Major Armstrong acknowledged. "I'm most grateful." Major Tieu assumed leadership of the group and spoke in his native tongue. "All right. You've heard Sergeant Heller's report. Now I want you to get your men and set up defensive positions. Move out!"

Within minutes, light fire teams were at their stations. Mortar crews were in their pits and bunkers. Soldiers checked their weapons and rushed to the ammunition bunker to draw additional supplies. Squad leaders ordered mortar projectile increments pulled for short range action. The command and communication bunkers were manned. The CIDG's patrolling the outer defense perimeter received orders to withdraw and man the defenses assigned to them. Soldiers with starlight scopes strained their eyes for any movements in the moonlit night. All standard operating procedures were carried out without questions. There was no dispute in anybody's mind that, come what may, Major Armstrong and his Special Forces NCO's would lead by example. All were experienced and responsible men.

There were no amateurs in the camp, including the 27 civilians. All of them had suffered from Viet Cong terror. Their families and relatives had witnessed political executions. The "Reign of Terror" was much like the French Revolution in the 12th century. Cruelty and inhumanity, outright butchery, torture and pain to force confessions or information, were known, if not experienced, by all of them. Unwavering, determined and resolute, they stood with the soldiers, come what may.

Suddenly, there was a violent explosion, followed by another, then another. Those who were not in the bunkers, hit the ground. Vicious enemy artillery fire laid down a curtain of destruction. It looked like heaven was on fire, from enemy flares and explosive flashes. VC rockets kept bursting and bullets kicked up the dirt everywhere.

When an enemy mortar shell hit the camp mess hall where native women were preparing breakfast, there were distressing screams for the camp medic. After the bombardment became sporadic at the main camp, Major Armstrong told Heller that the Viet Cong were obviously concentrating their attack on the subsector slightly north first, in order to eventually swarm like cannibal soldier ants toward the main compound.

"At this moment," the major remarked, "they are receiving a hail of 82 mm mortar fire, heavy small arms and automatic weapons fire from the northwest, which certainly doesn't come as a surprise. Heller, take some volunteers up into the subsector to evaluate the situation. If our position is critical and it appears that the sector may be overrun anyway, withdraw and consolidate down here! Good luck, Heller!"

"Thank you, Major Armstrong."

Heller grabbed Blanchard by the arm. "You're a volunteer. Get ten of the same volunteers who were with us on our first patrol. Let's move!" Heller then asked the major to pass the word to the subsector that he was enroute.

When Heller and Blanchard arrived at the subsector they crawled into the first mortar pit, which had been hit by a shell. The three CIDG soldiers who had manned the wrecked mortar were just pieces of bodies now. "What do you think, Heller?" Blanchard asked with compassion.

Heller gazed intently from the pit scrutinizing the devastation to his straight front. "Tell you what, Blanchard..."

"Yeah! Tell me!"

"See if you can get through this small arm's fire to the next gun position, whatever it may be, or whatever is left," Heller said, "and pass the word, to start throwing everything except the sandbags at the VC to expend all live ammunition. We're making our own tiny counter offensive for the sole purpose of gathering our wounded and withdrawing to the main camp."

Blanchard nodded and flew up a narrow trench, stooping low with his arms dragging on either side of the trench. Heller watched Blanchard roll his body over the sandbags into a gun pit. A moment later four or five mortar projectiles chimed in cadence with the lobbing of other high explosives, bursting fragments and shattering explosives, which slaughtered the wave of black uniformed guerrillas as they attempted to overrun the valley of their dead.

When Heller finally reached the subsector command post and found the radio man, dead, with no face at all, he zigzagged in sharp angles and directions, shouting to all he could reach, "SHOOT UP ALL YOUR AMMO...IF YOU CAN'T CARRY YOUR WEAPON WITH YOU, DESTROY IT...THEN TRY TO GET THE WOUNDED BACK TO THE MAIN CAMP!"

In a matter of seconds, the machine guns were spitting bullets. The few remaining mortars erupted like volcanos with a raking, ravaging fire, which not only perplexed the advancing hordes of Viet Cong, it literally threw them back on their heels. Since they obviously thought the concentrated fire came from the subsector directly in front of them, they withdrew momentarily to regroup. This gave Heller and the survivors just enough time to retreat to Loc Ninh's main camp. Heller and Blanchard brought up the rear. Blanchard carried one CIDG trooper with a smashed shoulder. Blood was oozing slowly through his dirty Army uniform. By the time the short Vietnamese soldier was carefully laid down in the medic bunker, he was unconscious.

Sergeant Heller struggled into the compound with one casualty on his back and another in his arms.

"Somebody take these men to the medics," Heller ordered, completely exhausted, with the sweat pouring from his face and arms. "Let's hope we can evacuate the casualties at daylight."

At the precise moment Heller stretched out on the ground, for a much needed rest, a CIDG runner rushed up to tell him that Major Armstrong wanted to see him on the double. Heller opened his eyes and tried to get to his feet. He almost made it, but, his strength failed him. He simply collapsed. When Blanchard saw that Heller had caved in, he rubbed his hands together, as if he were trying to warm them and slapped the seemingly unconscious Heller with the palm of his hand.

Heller opened his eyes just long enough to say, "Myyy fooot...Ssstop..tttt..bbloodddd!!in mmy..ss..shoe..."

Blanchard ripped Heller's jungle knife from its sheath. With one skillful stroke, he split Heller's trousers, while another medic took his jungle boots off, which now revealed a wound just above the ankle of the left foot.

"Somebody hand me a canteen with water!" Blanchard ordered. "We got to see how bad the wound is!"

Blanchard removed a sterile first aid pack from his pouch and told Major Tieu to apply pressure to the wound, until he was ready with the bandage. "Go!" he ordered. "Now, sir!"

Major Tieu was most cooperative, producing the desired results, while an assistant CIDG medical technician assisted Blanchard elevating Heller's lower leg above the level of his heart. Blanchard applied another heavy dressing firmly over the first dressing, which finally stopped the flow of blood.

"Take him to the command bunker!" Blanchard ordered a CIDG stretcher team. "And you, medic, stay here while I try to get some whole blood or glucose for Heller. He's real weak from loss of blood..."

"Don't you think we ought to evacuate him?" somebody asked.

"Hell no! We need him right here!" Blanchard told everybody. "He'll be as good as new in 3 or 4 hours. All he needs is some blood and a few hours rest..."

"But why the command bunker?" the CIDG medic wanted to know. "Why not the heliport and radio for a real doc?"

"Damn it! This is an order!" Blanchard growled. "I'll be responsible! I want him at the command bunker, so that he can tell Major Armstrong what's up front! Is that so hard to understand, you idiot?"

With the subsector in their hip pocket, the 273rd Viet Cong Regiment, supported by a battalion of the 84A North Vietnamese Artillery Regiment, one or two battalions from the 165th North Vietnamese Army Regiment, and the 14th NVA Regiment, and another heavy weapons battalion equipped with anti-aircraft guns and heavy mortars, the North Vietnamese high command, with over 3000 veterans, was applying pressure to the Loc Ninh district.

On October 29, by 0500 hours the area had received 140 rounds of heavy mortar, numerous rockets and a steady tirade of heavy machine gun fire.

"We may have to request tactical air support help from Saigon," Major Armstrong remarked emphatically, directing the defenses with Major Tieu by his side. Sergeant Heller was still in a stretcher at his feet, getting a bottle of glucose from a team of medics Doc Blanchard had summoned.

Majors Armstrong and Tieu were on their second tour of duty in Vietnam. Both had served on General Westmoreland's staff. Before that time, both had been attached to the 5th SF and to Ranger Battalion operations, where they had led their troops from the front. To them, firefights and ambushes had been almost a daily routine. Neither officer would order a PFC to do anything they had not done themselves, or would not do again. Both believed that the officer replacement system with only six months command time did little or nothing for their soldiers.

Rumor had it that Major Armstrong has suggested an eighteen month tour for field commanders when he had been on General Westmoreland's staff. He believed it would improve the morale of soldiers, who many times laid their lives on the line, when in fact, they did not trust their inexperienced officers.

From their experiences, the two officers also knew that their command at Loc Ninh, less than 5 miles from the Viet Cong sanctuaries, was a thorn in the VC side. Indeed, they had known it was only a matter of time until they would finally assemble in full strength from other units already in the area and then strike under the cover of darkness. That time had come. The VC had finally launched their blistering assault against Loc Ninh with nine full battalions of regulars from the North a few minutes after midnight. It was common knowledge that attacks usually ended at early light, with scattered sniping in the early morning hours and then a final heavy mortar bombardment, which allowed them to gather their dead and wounded in an orderly withdrawal. Since it was about that time, Major Armstrong said clearly, ''Any minute now, the VC will break contact. Let's give them a little help!''

Major Tieu nodded his head. ''Let's do that, my friend,'' he agreed wholeheartedly. ''By all means, let's!''

At 0520, Special Forces A-331 detachment and two CIDG companies launched a stinging operation to expel VC snipers. They killed sixteen in short order, wounded a considerable number, then withdrew, as the NVA launched a short counter attack to recover their dead, then also quickly withdrew.

After the attack had ceased at 0530 on the 29th, the Loc Ninh SF camp immediately began to restore and improve its defensive positions, knowing full well that another attack could come at any time.

While Loc Ninh camp remained on full alert, Major Armstrong asked Doc Blanchard if he had decided to evacuate Heller or keep him.

''He stays, Major! He stays! He'd have my head if he found out I consented to his evacuation. If you'll look at him, you can see, sir, by his color that he's comin' around. He's had four hours of rest...''

''Wake him! I got to know how he feels. I need him!'' the Major ordered Blanchard.

Suddenly Heller stirred, attempting to change his position, trying to rouse himself to find out where he was. In another moment he was fully conscious, his eyes searching the bunker for an explanation. When Heller tried to sit, Blanchard tried to help.

"No! I can do it!" he told him, now coming erect in the stretcher, sitting on his haunches with his upper legs drawn up toward his chest.

Frowning with displeasure and disapproval, he asked, "Will somebody tell me what the hell I'm doing on this stretcher? I remember dragging a couple of wounded casualties back to the compound..."

"You did ol' buddy. Then you passed out," Blanchard chimed hurriedly with a rare smile. "Besides that, the major wanted you in here..."

Major Armstrong took several steps toward Heller. "I assume you don't know you had blood in your shoe?"

"Who? Me? Wounded?" Heller queried in uncertainty. "Where?"

"Left ankle," the officer said positively. "The Doc must have found a pint of blood in your boot..."

"Major! I can't feel a thing. May I stand up?"

"Certainly, Sergeant Heller!" Major Tieu responded. "Grab my hand..."

"Thanks anyway, Major," Heller told him gratefully. Without further ado he came to his feet without assistance, first standing on one leg, then on the other.

"Heller! You're one helluva soldier," both officers said simultaneously, smiling now that Heller looked as good as the day he reported for duty.

"As soon as I change your bandage, you'll be ready for duty," Blanchard said without doubt, mingled with curosity.

"All right! But, buddy or no buddy, you owe me a good pair of pants," Heller mentioned briefly with humor in his voice. "What would our friends think of me running around this compound in a one-legged Army fatigue?"

In spite of the seriousness of the past two nights and the unavoidable forthcoming attack by three thousand North Vietnamese Army regulars, the command bunker became alive with laughter. But not from Heller. He simply asked Major Armstrong for permission to run to his hooch to get another pair of pants, and a moment later he was gone.

As anticipated, the VC attacked shortly after midnight. The moment the first salvo of enemy artillery was received from their 82 mm and 120 mm mortars, as well as their RPG 2's, the RPG 87's (rockets) and recoilless rifles of undetermined calibre, the most venerable Air Force C-47, nicknamed "Spooky," started dropping flares to illuminate the countryside below, exposing hordes of advancing VC and, of course their gun positions. Another gun ship, nicknamed "Puff the Magic Dragon" droned above with its miniguns blazing down upon the VC.

One of the pilots reported, "We estimate that two VC battalions are now charging in formation toward the west wall. . ."

Major Tieu and Sergeants Blanchard and Heller hustled from the bunker to the west wall. Although the Loc Ninh defender's withering machine gun fire, in cooperation with well placed air strikes from Army and Air Force sorties, was unrelenting, the suicidal effort from the hardcorps NVA regulars succeeded in breaching the repaired holes in the barbed and concertina wire with their numerous wooden ladders to finally get close to the wall.

When Heller poked his head through a large crack in the wall, he was startled to note that several hostiles were setting demolition charges directly below him. Quickly, he thrust his M-79 barrel through the crack and released a canister, which took the nearest VC's head off and seriously wounded others near him. As the hostiles were swarming to the wall, Heller removed the four hand grenades from his harness. "Now's the time!" he growled, pulling the pins one at a time and lobbing the projectiles over the wall.

After Heller had expended most of his ammunition, he was everywhere, running from man to man and from position to position, offering encouragement and reassurance to the hard-pressed CIDG troops. Heller was calm, confident and unyielding. The vicious attack of the black clothed horde was unending. No matter how many VC's were killed, others kept coming, leaping and vaulting over their dead, as the savage Loc

Ninh defensive dropped and tangled them in the barbed wire coils, which seemed to snatch, snarl, snare, entangle and trap them while well aimed CIDG bullets slammed through their half naked bodies.

When the wall was finally being penetrated by the massive onslaught, a fusillade of small weapons fire from the defenders reeled them from the barrier time and time again. When a CIDG soldier close to Heller shouted that the VC were setting up a Russian rocket launcher fifty meters from the wall, Heller managed to scratch it with a burst from a nearby inactive 30 calibre machine gun.

Doc Blanchard suddenly showed up near Heller's position.

"Where have you been, Doc?" Heller wanted to know without looking at him.

"I didn't think you needed me," Blanchard joked, adding, "It's close to 0500...time for our mortal enemies to run, ain't it?"

"Thanks, Buddy. Thanks," Heller somehow managed a smile. "You are still my buddy, aren't you?"

"Until the end of time," Blanchard shouted and once more snaked his way toward the command bunker, where Major Armstrong was in radio contact with Saigon. He requested a flight of F-100's with napalm at exactly 0535. "I'd be most grateful, colonel," the major told him and suddenly became silent. Finally he spoke.

"Yes, sir! Yes, sir!" Major Armstrong was saying to the officer on the other end of the telephone. After another silence, the Major remarked, "That would be a godsend, sir! Thank you, sir!"

"Major! Do I note a sense of optimism in your voice," Doc Blanchard asked his commander, after he had replaced the receiver.

"Yes! But right now please get the word around to all units not to pursue the VC when they withdraw at first light. Several flights of Air Force F-100's and helicopter gunships are gonna murder them. Also, tell everybody we're getting reinforcements by airlift this morning, right into our camp."

58

"Do the senior NCO's of the CIDG's know that? What about Major Tieu, Heller and all other SF personnel?"

"Not yet! Go! Go! Go!" the commander yelled as Blanchard flew from the undamaged bunker.

When Blanchard got to his position, Heller was firing a 50 calibre machine gun. At once he ordered him to get volunteers to pursue the enemy, but Blanchard shook his head and yelled into his ear, "Not today!"

"What? What did you say?" Heller asked in dismay. "I'm the team sergeant, or have you forgotten?"

"Orders from Major Armstrong!"

"Let's hear them!"

At exactly 0530 the VC began their body recovery offensive operation. Precisely five minutes later, two flights of Air Force F-100's came roaring in to drop napalms upon the fleeing VC. After the F-100's had made their first pass, they looped, climbed, rolled, dipped and suddenly went into a vertical dive which fascinated the VC even in retreat. As if under a spell, many remained motionless as the super jets streaked above them with lightning speed and machine guns blazing. The bullets ripped them apart like so many rag dolls, killing and overwhelming them as they tried to retreat to their sanctuaries near the border.

No sooner had the F-100's made their spectacular passes, than the helicopter gunships arrived, with their heavy machine guns spitting bullets, blasting and raking the fleeing VC, taking a terrible toll.

Later in the day flights of helicopters brought in South Vietnam Army units and the First Brigade of the U.S. First Infantry Division. They also airlifted coffee, milk, hot cakes, eggs and all other food items for the battle scarred fighting personnel in the camp. On return flights, they took with them as many wounded as possible. After the wounded had been evacuated, the returning helicopters evacuated the dead.

Meanwhile, repairing the damage done to the camp and its perimeter, the walls, mortar and machine gun pits and bunkers again became the number one priority. Although reinforcements had arrived, half of the remaining original defenders either ate or worked while the other half stood ready for action, or cleaned their rifles or other equipment in preparation for another day and night of battle.

That day, at 0900 hours, a full bird colonel by the name of Bruce Outlaw, who had been with Special Forces in Korea and was a personal friend of Major Armstrong, arrived at the camp, much to the surprise of Armstrong and Tieu. Upon their arrival, all soldiers not actually on watch were told to assemble near the command bunker for orders and instructions.

Majors Armstrong and Tieu were delighted. Without further ado the two officers introduced their staff and related the events of the past two days.

"Our Special Forces personnel and all our CIDG's fought gallantly and bravely and our periodic practice alerts helped us immensely. Every soldier knew exactly where to go and what to do, without additional orders, kinda like a professional team, each knowing the next play by heart," professed Major Armstrong, with hearty approval from Major Tieu.

"Throughout the attacks our squad and platoon leaders were always on the line with their men, assisting whenever or wherever they were needed. At first, our Special Forces detachment commander and I personally were in the communication bunker, but both of us took position on the perimeter and helped and directed the defense of the camp."

Major Armstrong added, "My counterpart, Major Tieu, served at the point of greatest impact. He assisted most soldiers in resupplying ammunition, even rendered first aid and assisted with the evacuation of the wounded and the dead. Our team medics," he went on further, "not only treated the wounded on the defense perimeter, but also the severe casualties in the medical bunker, which, unfortunately, was partially destroyed by mortar fire. Our weapons men divided their time between the mortar crews and the front. All team members were periodically active and were exceptionally effective in keeping the camp defenses organized. Individual acts of heroism are too numerous to mention. With profound pride, respect and appreciation, I will recommend many men for valor. We want to drive the VC north, or so deep into Cambodia that they decide they've had enough."

Colonel Bruce Outlaw and his staff were extremely impressed. Said he with witticism and jesting: "Major Armstrong and Tieu! We've come because MACV thought you needed help! But" he laughed and added, "we might just as well go back to Saigon."

Somewhat later the officers and NCO's discussed camp defense, alerts, and communication, which was effectively maintained throughout the attacks by underground emergency antennas. Colonel Outlaw was pleased that most, if not all, of the camp's requests from higher echelons were granted without delay, that flare ships (Spookys) were on the scene of battle within minutes after being summoned, then remained as long as they were needed. He was told by Armstrong that air and artillery support were outstanding and logistical support was superb. Supplies and equipment were handled expeditiously. All medical evacuation was swift, either during the battle or after fighting had diminished. All reports were submitted according to standard operating procedures.

"Gentlemen!" Colonel Outlaw said gleefully, "I am amazed with your spirit and the job you've done thus far. It would be nice if General Westmoreland could see to it that your type of battle management would come to the attention of the media, who give our people at home nothing but condemnation and doom. When this is over, gentlemen, I will find the General and make a few recommendations. So! With your permission, Majors Armstrong and Tieu, I hereby relieve you and your men now on battle stations with my entire brigade."

"Might just as well catch some shuteye," Heller suggested to Blanchard. "The VC will be back, probably one minute after midnight."

After Blanchard and Heller had returned to their hooch, they discussed the action of the day. Abruptly, Heller crashed his fist through a nearby orange crate and surprised Blanchard with "It's inconceivable! That's what I believe!"

"What's inconceivable, buddy?" Blanchard asked through his teeth. "This war?"

"Yeah! This war! What's even more ridiculous and far beyond my mental capacity is that we allow the VC's their so-called sanctuaries within shouting distance of the boundary of both Laos and Cambodia..."

"Agreed! Agreed!" Blanchard allowed, slipping under the mosquito net over his bunk. " So, what else is new?"

"They come down the Ho Chi Minh trail just slightly above the demarkation line with little military hardware. I know they organize, retrieve their hidden guns they had buried months and even years earlier, then, when they choose they hit us with the kitchen sink and run to their refuge. Damnation! Damnation!"

"As I mentioned in Saigon, I like your sense of humor. Now, goodnight, ol' buddy!"

"I haven't finished..."

"Is that so?" Blanchard wailed. "Well, finish and let me get some sleep. I'm bushed."

"I'm trying to tell you that this damn war is like the Korean..."

"Not so!" Blanchard interrupted. "You heard that President Johnson finally agreed with General Westy to start bombing North Vietnam targets recently..."

"By the time the AP and UPI, not to mention ABC, CBS and NBC with their 'Selective Personal Judgment' of what's news get through with their psychological and lethal criticism of the bombings, Johnson will stop them just as quickly."

"I say again, as I've said before -- what else is new? Heller! Let me ask you something..."

"Shoot!"

"Ever hear of the Battle of Khe Sanh?"

"Yeah! It was another hopeless disaster...?"

"Like hell it was!"

"That's what I read. Since you put it that way, I guess as usual, it was distorted war news. What really happened?"

"Our Marines killed 12,000 North Vietnam Army regulars."

"What did it cost us?"

"205 Marines, which was in fact one of the greatest victories ever. That sure as hell would have done something for our image and national pride, if it had reached our precious United States. It's most likely the same story with our civic programs.

The so called 'Newsmakers' and editors don't give a good damn about anything, except the horrors of war..."

"By the way, Blanchard, where is Khe Sanh?"

When he failed to answer, Heller brushed under the mosquieto netting and between the blankets. In another moment he entwined his hands in prayer. In humble supplication, he petitioned the Divine creator to help the South Vietnamese people and their friends to bring this ugly war to an end.

Since Heller believed in the need for dreaming, his instinctive mental concentration made the girl he had met in the historic Palace of Versailles in France a reality. He closed his eyes and quickly fell asleep.

Chapter III

THE DEVIL'S BRIGADE

In retrospect, twenty-eight months earlier, Raymond Heller from Key West, Florida, pulled up at a restaurant parking lot in Charleston, South Carolina, for an early breakfast. Before he could turn off the ignition of his car, a South Carolina State Police cruiser stopped abruptly alongside. When the two troopers literally flew from their vehicle and scrutinized his brand new Ford convertible which his father had given him as a high school graduation present, his brazen-faced expression turned to jelly. Raymond had a guilty conscience from the night before, when a girl hitchhiker from Florida invited him to a party in a West Palm Beach Motel, where she drugged, fleeced and left him, before he regained consciousness.

"Hi, gentlemen!" Raymond stammered. "Could you point my nose in the general direction of the Citadel?"

"You're lucky," the sergeant of the two troopers told him. "After a bite, we'll be heading out there ourselves."

"May I follow you...?" Raymond asked, as he locked his car door. "I hate to admit it, gentlemen, this is my first time out of the Florida Keys."

"We've noticed the license plate, Mr..."

"Heller, sir. Raymond Heller," he told them honestly.

"I'm Sergeant Timmerman. This is Jim Norris, my partner."

"Tell me, Mr. Heller," officer Norris asked, "is it really true that the Russians have fished out the entire Gulf Stream? We're told they even bring their can factories in their fleet."

"That's true!" Raymond nodded vigorously. "But I want you to know that my Dad and the Florida Fisherman's Association are applying pressure to State and Federal authorities to get a 200 mile limit established and enforced. Otherwise," Raymond explained, "the Russians will spend their lunch hours right on our beaches and catch the landcrabs, or pick up our sea shells to decorate Lenin's tomb."

Somewhat later, the three men had a lively discussion while eating their breakfast. The sergeant reminded Raymond of his father's ruggedness.

"Would you fellows happen to be ex-Green Berets, or even French Foreign Legionnaires?" Raymond remarked suddenly, to liven the conversation.

The two officers grinned. "You're really not too far from the truth, Raymond," the sergeant told him. "As a matter of fact I've been in Africa, but not as a French soldier. I served with Special Forces in Italy, during World War II. My outfit assembled in Africa. From there we were shipped to Italy, where we spearheaded General Mark Clark's Fifth Army," he declared with obvious pride. "I assume you know I am referring to the same General Clark who effected the successful amphibious invasion at Salerno, drove on to Anzio and Nettuno, then captured Rome on June 4, 1944."

"Sergeant! Are you telling me we had Special Forces way back in 1944?" Raymond wondered.

"Does that surprise you?"

"It does! It does," Raymond repeated. "Several weeks ago I had a lengthy conversation with two Army master sergeants on a routine fishing trip. They told me that they had recently returned from Vietnam, where they had served with Special Forces and were stationed now at Fort Bragg. they had gotten a flight from Pope Air Force Base to Homestead, south of Miami. From there, they rented a car and somehow found me in the Keys.

65

"Did they hook the big one, or did it get away?" officer Norris asked.

"As a matter of fact, each landed a big Sail,"Raymond recalled.

"How big?" Timmerman asked sharply. "Personally, I've given up on Sails. I've tried it for twenty-five years."

"The female was 9 feet 6½ inches and hit 147 pounds. The male was only 8 feet 2 inches, around 129 pounds," Raymond told them truthfully, but with an overweening opinion of himself, since he had been their guide.

"Woweeee!" Norris exclaimed, shaking his head furiously.

"I'll call that beginner's luck," Timmerman said vehemently, still looking for the truth.

"Gentlemen! Yes and no."

"What do you mean, Raymond?" Timmerman persisted, refusing to accept what he believed was just another fish story.

"Of all the people I've ever instructed and guided on basic techique about deep sea fishing, these two Vietnam veterans had the most unorthodox style. Would you believe me, these two guys ran around my boat on their knees?"

"Why in the world would anybody do a thing like that?" Timmerman wanted to know.

"These two soldiers were something else," Raymond laughed. "When I asked them why they were running around the back of the boat on their knees, they told me that they didn't want to spook the fish. I never did ask them why they moved their lips silently and continuously..."

"They were probably praying," Timmerman thought."What do you think, Raymond?"

"They traveled on their knees through the jungle and undoubtedly did a lot of praying, kinda in a whisper, so the Viet Cong couldn't hear them."

As the sergeant and Raymond laughed heartily, Norris had another important question."Raymond, stop stalling. Tell us how those Army pros landed their Sails?"

"Let's see. I cruised on automatic in big circles for about twenty minutes for the first biggie. It probably took a little longer for the second one."

"How did they get those big babies into the boat, or did they tie them to the stern and drag them in?" Norris asked.

"It's one helluva long story, and neither of you would believe me if I told you. Gentlemen, I can't divulge their disgraceful behavior, and I'll ask you to let it rest there."

"I'll be a cockeyed sailor," Timmerman said laughing again. "I'd much rather hear more about the Special Forces in that Italian campaign," Raymond told them seriously. "How about it?"

"It's been a very long time, gentlemen. But, I remember those days as if they happened yesterday," Sergeant Timmerman recalled, lifting his coffee cup at the waitress for a refill. "The First Special Forces consisted of Canadians and Americans. In April 1942 we organized and trained at Fort William Henry Harrison, Montana. Originally, we were trained to fight under ice and snow conditions, to eventually get behind the so-called Nazi supermen in Europe and support a cross channel invasion from England to France."

"Please go on, Sergeant Timmerman, "Raymond urged.

"Well, after fifteen months of concentrated training in winter combat skills, like mountaineering, skiing, parachuting, and close combat with a great variety of weapons, we were committed to clean the Japs out of Kiska Island in the Aleutians. But, after we stormed ashore all psyched up, we were surprised that the Japs had abandoned the island."

"Then what?" Norris urged impatiently.

"On November 19, 1943, we were shipped to Italy, where we formed three battalions, about 800 officers and men in each. Right from the start, General Mark Clark had us up front, under operational control of the 36th Infantry Division in an attempt to break the German winter line. I recall how it rained cats and dogs that November, and that the Third Infantry Division had been taking heavy casualties in their attempt to take two mountain peaks controlling a pass through that winter line. Ol' General Clark pulled his Third Division back, got the mission to take Monte La Difensa, giving the Second Regiment the assault assignment. Late in the afternoon and under cover of one of the heaviest artillery barrages of the entire war in

Italy, our Special Forces troops of the 2nd Regiment moved toward the towering cliffs. I recall that intelligence reconnaisance and our own commanding officer had scouted, appraised and evaluated the almost impregnable German position. While the artillery kept punching, our force slowly but surely moved upward on the barren cliffs, rising sharply, like the walls from the moat of a medieval castle. At the time," Timmerman explained, "some of us offered the first man to reach the top, be he Canadian or U.S., all he could drink and not one, but two women, the next time we got to a town."

"Don't stop now!" Raymond challenged the former Special Forces NCO. "Who managed to get to the top first?"

Trooper Timmerman ignored the question. "Going on, if you'll let me. At dusk the devastating artillery bombardment from our regiment kept punching and hammering, probing frantically, while we were hoping and praying that the Nazis wouldn't find us struggling to get to the top. Yes, sir, we dared to climb where neither beast nor man had ever ascended before. I remember my first sergeant, slightly behind me muttered, 'no tawny-brown cougar, or even a big horn ram from Nebraska, could make the top! How in the hell do they expect us to do it?'

"What made the climb so tough, there wasn't a tree, shrub or any other vegetation to anchor your feet to, and we had to make it while artillery fire from our regiment would support us which was only for three hours." Sergeant Timmerman continued, "You haven't heard anything until you've heard the grumbling from a Canadian. But, the job had to be done. With superhuman effort, some of our very best managed to get near the top. They had orders to wait for others for a precise hand signal, before the Nazi guards were to be silenced with daggers. The Nazis seemed to be loafing and relaxing. They were sure that if there should be an assault, it would have to come from the front. After the guards had been killed, our Special Forces got to the top with their grapnel hooks, anchors with flukes and claws. With unbelieveable speed our men deployed and spread. In a matter of minutes we overpowered the krauts who were unsuspecting in their bunkers and pillboxes, which hadn't even been damaged by our coordinated artillery fire.

We took a lot of prisoners, but if my memory serves me properly, the German General and his staff made a frantic stand and died with their boots on. I'll always remember the General. I changed my boots with him. After all, that General didn't need them anymore."

"Go on, Mr. Timmerman," Raymond pleaded. "Please. . ."

"From the winter of '43 through early summer of '44, our forces fought their way up the Italian peninsula. This gave us the privilege to enter Rome first," Timmerman pointed out. He cleared his windpipe and emotionally continued, "World War II history will show the uncommon valor of our Special Forces, first in Italy and on the 14th of August 1944, when we hit the beaches of Southern France. I remember how we scrambled down the big landing nets to the assault boats. First, we hit the Hyeres Islands. Later, as the right flank of the 1st Airborne Task Force, we finally joined other allied units. For the next three months we fought our way along the French Riviera toward the Italian border. After we had suffered several thousand casualties and over 400 dead or missing in action, the fighting stopped for our outfit. We were finally going home," he said with painful sentiment, all choked up. Mr. Timmerman took a drink of water, glanced at the time, then, once more resumed. "On December 5, 1944, those of us who survived gathered for the last time. At that time our Special Forces colors were cased. There, the Canadians withdrew from our ranks and formed their own battalion. They marched past us, still in rank, with many, many empty spaces to mark the departure of those who fell in combat. Gentlemen," Timmerman said painfully, but with the enormous pride of an unsung hero, "'til all eternity, the Canadian Airborne and the United States Army Special Forces of World War II, can proudly trace their uncommon history of helping to win that grotesque war. General Clark will substantiate what I've told you. It is the naked truth. This is the first time I allowed myself to reminisce and tell that story."

Trooper Norris and young Heller remained seated at the restaurant table in intense silence as Sergeant Timmerman stood up. Overcome with sentiment, the two men watched him enter the men's room.

"You're his partner, Mr. Norris. Tell me honestly. Did you know what Mr. Timmerman told us?" Raymond asked softly.

"Nope! I knew he had been in Italy under the overall command of General Clark. I also knew he is drawing a small disability check for wounds received during combat. But, this was the first time I've heard him open up. If it hadn't been for you, Raymond, I might never have found out. As for myself?" he explained. "I was in that lousy Korean War, just about the time Harry Truman fired General MacArthur, and would you believe it, it was old General Clark who took over MacArthur's command. Come to think of it, on the 27th of July, 1955, General Clark signed the Korean Armistice between the United States command, the military commanders of the North Korean Army and the Chinese People's volunteers at Nunsan-ni. I recall that day because my outfit got its orders to return to Fort Lewis then. I might add that nobody rolled out the red carpet for us after we got back. But," he concluded sadly, "we really didn't care. We were alive and we were home and that was the important thing."

"Needless to say, I'm impressed, Mr. Norris. It's been quite an experience to meet you and Sergeant Timmerman. I've done a lot of reading on my Dad's fishing boats, but, I never have had the pleasure to meet a couple of real pros, except the two sergeants who caught those big sailfish," Raymond acknowledged, just as Sergeant Timmerman returned to claim his seat and once more started relating his experiences.

"While I think of it," Sergeant Timmerman pointed out, "it was General Clark who pulled that eventual coup d'etat on the 400,000 Nazi soldiers and accepted their surrender at the Brenner Pass in the Italian Alps."

"Let me add that we in South Carolina are proud to have General Clark at our West Point, the Citadel. By the time students view the General's 40,000 photos, 60,000 manuscripts, films and countless tapes, newspaper clippings and other artifacts in the Daniel Library, some of his soldierly statesmanship may rub off on them."

Raymond had to say something. "My Dad and some of his cronies rehash battles and wars quite often. Generals Clark, Bradley, Patton and MacArthur are their heroes. I've learned a lot of history listening to them. According to those big old armchair strategists, General Clark had fewer casualties than any other Army commander in World War II, and again in the Korean War."

"I know that first hand in the tough struggle we had with the despicable Red Chinese, who had no value for the lives of their men, while General Clark always thought his soldiers and marines were precious commodities," Mr. Norris added conclusively.

When Raymond reached for the bill, the two distinguished State troopers objected. "Thanks anyway, Raymond. It was a pleasure to sit with you," Timmerman told him, gripping his hand. Trooper Norris also expressed his appreciation.

"Oh! Gentlemen! Don't forget I'm headed for the Citadel. Please don't lose me," Raymond reminded the officers, who looked at each other and shrugged.

"What's your business out there?" Timmerman inquired.

"My cousin is graduating today. I can't wait to see him in his cadet uniform, marching in the parade."

The troopers turned on their heels and came rushing back toward Raymond. "Did you say your cousin is graduating today?" Timmerman inquired.

"Yes, sir!" he answered. "That's why I've come."

"Tell 'em, sergeant," Norris urged his partner.

"Tell me what?" Raymond snapped with uncertainty. "What?"

"Raymond!" Timmerman replied, "the Citadel graduation was yesterday. You're a day late."

Momentarily, Raymond was speechless, "I guess Dad isn't infallible after all," he whispered to himself.

"Anything we can do?" Timmerman asked.

"No, gentlemen," Raymond told them with a smile. "If either of you ever get down my way, ask for me at the King House Marina. Ken, or his beautiful wife Cathy, will tell you where to find me..."

"You're on," both officers said simultaneously. "Good luck!"

Raymond drove to the nearest motel. After a long shower, he placed one of many calls to his father. The line was busy. It was the same ol' story with all other calls he made. At noon he made his way to the motel restaurant. When the counter waitress asked him if she might serve him, he told her that he had not had a decent meal since he had left Marathan, in the Florida Keys. "I'm so hungry, I'll eat anything you'll set in front of me. So! Why don't you surprise me. All right?"

For a moment, the young counter waitress was speechless. She had never had such an order. Smiling at him she said, "What if you don't like my surprises?"

"Little girl," he told her positively, "as I just told you, I'll eat whatever you set before me, and while I think of it, make whatever you bring a double order and add a quart of milk."

The young waitress marched through the double doors of the restaurant kitchen to consult briefly with the chef, who grinned broadly.

"Point him out! He might be one of those drifters who hasn't eaten in a week and probably won't have enough money to pay for it."

"Not this young man," she told the chef. "Look at that brand new convertible in front of the door. Besides, he's staying here. He looks like a professional athlete of some kind..."

"Will you stop your yakking...point him out, honey!"

"Right there, next to that big recruiting sergeant," she pointed. "He's also very handsome. Probably has a girl in every town."

The chef evaluated the young customer. After another moment he told the girl, "He has a deep Florida tan. He's either a fisherman or a playboy. Let's throw him a couple of big steaks with all the trimmings. All right?"

"Now you're talking, chef," the waitress agreed. "If that young brute hasn't got enough money to pay for that ten dollar meal, I'll pay it and put a claim on him..."

Meanwhile the Army staff sergeant with six Vietnam ribbons, sitting on the next stool, carefully observed the young man on his right. At a glance he saw a rare potential recruit. "This one, doesn't even need a haircut," he thought to himself. "Probably some rich college kid."

With a proud grin, he extended his hand to introduce himself. "I'm Sergeant Dollarhite," he said clearly. "At the present I'm on a recruiting duty here in Charleston."

Raymond gave the sharp looking soldier a lengthy look before he accepted his hand. He never forgot what his father had told him some years ago that when a total stranger sticks his right hand in your face, better watch his left, because sure as hell he'll want something one way or another.

"How are you doing, sergeant? You getting your quota?" Raymond asked the man in uniform, accepting his hand.

"Speaking frankly..."

"Raymond. Raymond Heller. Just call me Raymond."

"As I was saying, not too well at the present. Too many radicals and drifters. The do-gooders see another world war, this time in Asia. If there should be a big war, we'll have to bring the youngsters in by force. Patriotism is a dirty word to them, and most of the media isn't helping. Actually, Vietnam is a real intimidation to them."

"I know it," Raymond told him, recalling that a Key West recruiter spoke to the seniors only four weeks before graduation.

"How did he do?"

"Two out of twenty-eight."

"Obviously, you weren't interested?"

Raymond laughed. "Sergeant! I come from a long line of sailors," he told him with much pride. "My Dad was a commander in the Navy during World War II. Grandfather commanded one of those old four stackers in World War I. I'm told that my great-grandfather was a buccaneer at the end of the 18th century. If I even suggest the idea of joining the Army, Dad would disown me."

The recruiter measured Raymond with a stare, trying to determine the worth of their conversation. "Raymond! I am not going to tell you that the draft will get you if I don't. We need strong, clean cut youngsters like you, who'll train today and lead tomorrow. But, I understand that father-son syndrome."

At that moment the charming waitress set a double order of New York steak, two large boiled potatoes, a double order of chef's salad and all the trimmings with a quart of milk in front of him. Instantly, Raymond stopped talking and started right in, piling on the food. "However, Sergeant Dollarhite," Raymond asserted between bites. "I'm spending the night here at this motel. Perhaps we can chat a little later. If you're not too busy, why don't you join me later at the pool? At home, I usually swim with my friends early in the morning."

"Boys or girls?"

Heller laughed. "Dolphins! Most people call them fish, but I tend to think that those beautiful blunt snouted animals with those great big teeth are almost human."

"I'll take your word for that," the sergeant remarked restlessly. "I have an appointment with my commanding officer. When I get through, I'll join you at the pool. All right?"

"Fine! I'll be on the lookout for you."

Several hours later, the recruiter arrived just in time to see Raymond diving from the highest platform in a beautiful swan dive. There was hardly a ripple when he hit the water. Without coming up for air, Raymond started cutting through the length of the pool, not once, but twice. When he finally broke the surface, like a submarine in need of air, Dollarhite could not believe what he had just seen. "This youngster really is a fish! And at least 200 pounds, irrefutably all man."

Five minutes later, the two husky men were sitting on soft-cushioned beach chairs, drinking cold Cokes and enjoying the torrid sun, not to mention that Raymond enjoyed watching the beautiful girls who were making eyes at him.

Again, the Army recruiter wasted little time getting to his subject matter.

"Raymond! Have you ever heard of the Green Berets?"

"Hasn't everybody? Even President Kennedy praised them before he was murdered in Texas. He started them on the glory road."

The sergeant cut him off. Since he had been one of them,

and since Raymond responded so well on the subject, he told him, "Raymond! If I had the pleasure of bringing you into our Army, I'd recommend you personally for that special breed of man."

"I suppose that's a compliment, sergeant. Are you one of them?"

"I was one of the first three hundred who volunteered for Vietnam, Raymond." The sergeant hesitated before he added, "as an advisor."

"What did you do over there? Give me some specifics!"

"We were sent there to teach the South Vietnamese to fight and survive...how to build and destroy...how to plant and how to harvest. We cross trained them in other skills like communication, operations and intelligence, demolition, weaponry and medicine. Those we trained," Dollarhite expounded further, "could serve their cause for freedom from the jungles, through the mountains, in combat, from the sky or from a frontal assault. Raymond, wouldn't you consider joining us? I know you'd meet our requirements mentally, physically and morally."

"I appreciate your compliments, sergeant, but I simply haven't thought about joining anything. The Army might be a real challenge. My Dad told me a lot about the Army. How the infantry moves in by night with special vehicles and drops them near their objectives."

"Don't forget the Airborne!" Dollarhite added quickly to keep things rolling. "It takes guts to step up to a C-130 exit door...feel the wind sting your face and body. Then there is the sensational free-fall, and you'll look up to watch the chute open and swell up with air. All of a sudden you realize you're on your way down to old mother earth."

"Sergeant! You're really giving me a candid look at the Army. I think if you're that honest some potential recruits may back out while they think about joining?"

"Raymond! I've gone completely overboard with you, because you're different from most young men. Tell you what," Dollarhite proposed. "Why not sleep on that. Meet me for breakfast at eight. You can tell me your thoughts. You might even call your Dad to let him know you're o.k.?"

"I'll do that," Raymond told him. "Remember, I'm not promising you anything. I might discuss our conversation with my Dad tonight," Raymond told him. "You see, since my mother died, the two of us have been inseparable...See you at breakfast?"

"Right! It will be on me."

At eight the next morning, Raymond and Sergeant Dollarhite sat in the far corner of the restaurant, eyeing each other. When the waitress came for their order, Raymond ordered six eggs, a double order of steak tips, hashbrowns, six slices of toast and a quart of milk.

After the meal Dollarhite was appalled as he leafed rapidly through his pockets only to find he had left his money, and his wallet at home. When Raymond saw the dilemma, he took care of the awkward situation.

"It happens to the best of us, Sergeant Dollarhite," he told him sincerely. "Besides, I couldn't expect you to pay for my breakfast. After all, I'm not in the Army yet."

"It's downright embarrassing," the sergeant shrugged. "I'll reimburse you later, o.k.?"

"Think nothing of it, sergeant. What is important is that I spoke with Dad on the phone last night. He was unhappy that I wanted to enlist in the Army, instead of the Navy. But, he told me that it was entirely up to me. So, sergeant, say no more. I now know what I wanna do with my life. I'm gonna sign on the dotted line."

Dollarhite was stunned with the news. He reached enthusiasticly for Raymond's hand and almost jerked his arm from the clavicle socket.

"When could you come to my office for routine paper work?" Dollarhite asked anxiously.

"Right now!" Raymond said positively. "And, while I think of it, you might just as well call Special Forces at Bragg and put them on notice that I'm coming to compete."

It took a major effort, preventing Dollarhite from laughing at Raymond's remarks. Finally, he humored him by telling him,

76

"Raymond! You'll do! You'll set your mark at Special Forces if and when you get there. I know it. It'll be a matter of time. When you finally get there, everything and everyday is a challenge, a contest, even a fight, if you will. Most personnel are eager beavers, in their early twenties. They are tough, robust, with what I call aggressive physiques, who train vigorously, like ruffians in a prizefight."

"I know that. I've met a few, including a pair of state troopers, yesterday."

"What? Why? You're not in trouble with the law?" Dollarhite inquired nervously.

After Raymond explained in detail how he met the two troopers and about their long conversation, the sergeant was amused.

"Raymond! I'll not question if you'll get to SF," he cautioned. "You should get to Bragg in about 18 months. This miserable Vietnam war isn't gonna disappear overnight. We've had a lot of casualties and, before this ugly war ends, we'll have many more thousands. My CO has told me to be honest with volunteers who are trying to beat the draft. As you know, Raymond, I've been over there. I see a helluva international entanglement, as long as the United Nations debating society in New York has anything to do with it."

"All the more reason why I wanna get in now," Raymond endured. "Just tell me where to sign. I'm in A-1 shape. I don't give a damn about those radicals who someday will regret that they should have pursued a career, instead of getting involved in things they know so little about."

"Very well, Raymond. I'll need a few important answers."

"Shoot!"

"When is your eighteenth birthday?"

"In three months. Dad gave me his consent last night."

"I'll call our Key West recruiter to get your Dad's consent in writing."

"Anything else?" Raymond questioned optimistically.

"Yep! Since you are an only son, Army regs state you'll see no combat unless you volunteer..."

"Stop right there, sergeant!" Raymond demanded harshly. "I'll never be a non-combatant!"

"All you have to do is volunteer," the recruiter restated clearly, raising his voice this time.

"I'll hold you to that," Raymond remarked slowly. "No problem. What else?"

"So let's get to filling out routine forms today. When I get your parental consent by phone, I'll run you up to Fort Jackson myself. As I've told you, we don't have the equipment or the manpower to enlist people here. Meanwhile, I'll put you up in my house."

"If you don't mind, sergeant, I'd rather stay at the motel 'til you get your call. Besides, when your wife finds out about my appetite, she'd probably throw both of us out..."

"As you wish, Raymond," Dollarhite agreed. "By the way, one reason I wanted you to stay at our house is because I'd like you to meet my son, Jimmy, who just made Eagle Scout."

Raymond was surprised. "You don't say, sergeant? I'm an Eagle myself."

"With that background, it'll make basic training a snap for you, Raymond. Being an Eagle Scout puts you way out front of everybody else, wherever you may go in the Army, or even in civilian life."

"That's good to hear, sergeant. I'm excited..."

"Good! Since I have to go to Columbia on recruiting business, I'll personally deliver you to Fort Jackson, by, say, Friday noon. How's that?"

"I'll accept that and your generosity," Raymond told Sergeant Dollarhite, after which the two men went to the recruiting office to start the processing.

Several days later Staff Sergeant Dollarhite drove his star recruit to Fort Jackson. Enroute Raymond received advice and answers to his countless questions.

"When you enter basic, " he told Raymond seriously, "Keep your mouth shut, your eyes and ears wide open! Follow instructions to the letter! Respect your superiors! It's YES, SIR and NO, SIR!" he emphasized. "Everybody in the Army must learn to accept orders in order to give them!"

Dollarhite explained further, "These are old cliches. They have become trite, although they express thoughts, ideas, opinions and courses of action. Some of us mention them, but fail to apply what they really mean."

"Well, well, sergeant! I didn't know you were a college professor? Let's have a for instance."

"The more you put into the pump, the more you'll get out of it. There's no easy road to education. The future belongs to those who prepare for it, and last but not least, he who dares to teach must never cease to learn. Raymond, as time goes on, I hope you will think about what I've told you enroute. You see, I care for my recruits. If you find it convenient, drop me a line now and then. I'm sure our paths will meet again, someday. Meanwhile, Raymond, maintain the highest standards of personal conduct and appearance. Recognize that you'll have your share of disappointments and frustrations. Recognize the brutal competition everywhere you go. In the Army, just as in civilian life, you'll experience a ruthless atmosphere of cut throat competition, which I know you'll handle when the time comes. But, my friend, watch those insincere apple polishing bastards, who'll try to do your thinking for you. The world and our Army is stacked right now with dissidents and freeloaders. But with your determination and confidence, I know you'll go a long way."

Raymond thanked the recruiter for his advice, and anxiously asked questions about Fort Jackson, which would be his home for the next eight weeks.

"First of all, Fort Jackson is a place in our history," Dollarhite explained at the beginning of his narrative. "I went through basic there, myself. When I reminisce and reflect to those priceless days, I think I learned there what I needed through my entire Army life. You'll see for yourself how big that military complex is. Got its name from General Andy Jackson, who was our seventh President... They called him Old Hickory. Anyway, Raymond, if my memory serves me well, the German Kaiser had plans of taking over all of Europe, when President Wilson told the War Department to find a camp big enough to start mobilizing and training our soldiers for eventual combat in Europe. So, in June 1917, the Congress designated the land donated by the city of Columbia and named it Camp Jackson. Shortly thereafter, the big camp trained aircraft pilots, artillerymen, balloonists, cavalrymen, wardogs and carrier pigeons. Back then, the camp spread out over 1,200 acres. Today, it's close to 52,600 acres."

While Sergeant Dollarhite wiped the sweat from his brow, Raymond recalled that his history teacher had lectured the class about Andrew Jackson who won a spectacular victory in the South at the Battle of New Orleans.

"Right on, Raymond. I guess history was one of your favorite subjects," Dollarhite judged thoughtfully.

"Go on, sergeant. Please continue..."

"By June 1918, the new camp had a compliment of more than 45,000 officers and men, who formed the 30th and the 81st Infantry Divisions. Since the Division did their training at Wildcat Creek, they were dubbed as the First Wildcat Division. That name remained with them throughout the war in Europe, where they fought and distinguished themselves with the American Expeditionary Force in France. My Dad, bless his soul, told me the Division saw action in the Lorraine and the Meuse-Argonne campaigns and that General Black Jack Pershing cited them for gallantry and bravery there. The 30th, the Old Hickory Division, saw action at Flanders and in the Somme offensive. The two Divisions had a lot of casualties. When the war ended in November, 1918, both returned to the States and shortly thereafter were deactivated. After that, 'til 1939, the South Carolina National Guard did their training at Camp Jackson."

"Then what?" Raymond prodded. "What happened when Hitler's Blitzkrieg overran half of Europe in '39 and '40?"

"The Army Chief of Staff, General George Marshall, by an act of Congress, activated the old camp again and named it Fort Jackson. From that time 'til now, it's been a permanent post. I guess after the Second World War, Fort Jackson became the largest construction project in the world, Dollarhite elucidated further. Since then the Army built over 100 miles of good roads, several thousand buildings, five or six thousand tent frames, and the National Guard kinda' took the place over again. They also installed a water filtration plant, which produces six million gallons of drinking water a day. They also built a 3,000 bed hospital, put new rail lines in and landscaped the gigantic training camp. It's said that over a million men and women had their training at Fort Jackson. President Roosevelt was so impressed with the camp, he brought Winston Churchill and other world leaders to see it. After WW II, Fort Jackson became a replacement center for a while. Now it's a full scale training center, with at least fifty firing ranges, twenty or more target detection ranges and about that many trainfire ranges."

"What's a trainfire range, sergeant?"

"That's where pop-up targets on natural terrain appear from nowhere, like an enemy soldier might appear in the field."

By that time, the two men were driving through the city of Columbia. Ten minutes later they entered Fort Jackson.

"Raymond! The road to success in our Army is hard work, something I'm sure you don't mind...probably be ice cream and cake for you. But...?"

"But what?"

"Raymond, I don't care who you are, or where you come from, getting up at five in the morning is tough to get used too. Agreed?"

"Agreed!"

When Staff Sergeant Dollarhite turned Raymond over to the corporal on duty at the reception desk, the corporal thanked him adding, "I'll take care of him as if he were my own brother." The soldier told the recruiter, "Thanks again for bringing us a real live one...I'd like to mention that the Brigade commander wishes to express his thanks for your personal effort, getting some of the best looking youngsters in your area to us."

After a final handshake between Dollarhite and Raymond, a corporal motioned Heller to follow him into a large processing hall, where he joined other recruits in what was the official Armed Forces Entering and Examination Processing Station.

"Hi," Raymond said with a friendly voice, hoping to get

81

an exclamation of response from the shabby looking, mostly long haired men, who had removed most of their clothes, and were obviously waiting to be called for whatever reason.

"What's your name, sucker?" the nearest of the lot mused. "I see they didn't have to shackle your legs to get you here."

Although recruit Heller was appalled by the uncouth and crude greeting, he offered a smile, trying to give an appearance of dignity and self-respect. He was about to say something, when another long haired hippy wearing glasses, with his chest exposed, revealing a mess of curly black hair, proclaimed, "I assume we're all draftees! We are all here because a draft board selected us for compulsory service. In other words, we are not draft dodgers! We are simply reluctant to accept that we are sacrificing our civil rights...Isn't that right, buddy?"

For a moment Heller recalled what Sergeant Dollarhite had cautioned him about "those apple polishing bastards, who'll try to do your thinking for you..." when the self styled punk spokesman remarked, "You, when you get your physical, tell the medics you've had asthma...you know...difficulty in breathing...you suffocate if you start running. Read letters that aren't on the eye chart. Tell them your hearing is bad. If that doesn't do it, tell them you've pissed in your bed since childhood, and," insisted the punk, "that will get you a ticket back home."

"What in hell is this? A teach in?" Heller demanded to know, springing to his feet, and towering over the little punk like an Alaska Brown bear would over a stray dog.

"Are you with us, or against us?" the punk asked Heller boldly, who remained perplexed for the moment.

"Neither!" Heller said emotionally between his teeth. "What bothers me is that you obviously think you're speaking for all these men. I don't believe you are. How about it?" Heller glared at the young man next to him.

"That guy ain't speaking for me!" the potential recruit grumbled with indignation. "I'll do my part for our country!"

With a wry grin, Raymond appraised the dissident.

"I'm gonna ask you to sit down and act like a man!" Raymond commanded the short man wearing sun glasses.

"Nobody needs your kind of advice!"

"Will you listen to this goon?" the punk remarked to those near him. "You men don't suppose he's a C.I.A. plant, or a spy? Or an M.P. in disguise?"

"None of those," Raymond told him calmly, watching his eyes. "I have a question for you?"

"Yeah? Let's hear it!"

"Are you a reject from the San Francisco student riots?"

The punk looked lethargically stupefied for a brief second. Suddenly he turned, grabbed an empty 16 ounce Coke bottle, knocked the bottom out in the same moment, then confronted Raymond with the sharp jagged end pointing at him.

"All right, mama's boy! Come get it!" the hairy self proclaimed spokesman glared aggressively at his challenger, who smiled and said, "I think you better drop the bottle before you hurt yourself," Raymond hinted, as several of the dissident's cohorts left their chairs to huddle around their spokesman.

When Raymond saw the welcoming committee, he grabbed the nearest wooden chair and easily ripped two of four legs from it.

"Come on you miserable troublemakers! All of you, or one at a time! Makes no difference to me!" Heller remarked calmly, confident in his ability and strength.

While the agitator's cohorts hesitated momentarily, their leader made several offensive moves toward Heller, who stood firm. The punk shifted back and forth. He feigned to slash Heller with the broken bottle, hoping to muster confidence and encouragement to his buddies, who had already decided this was not their day. When the punk realized he was alone, he mumbled and stuttered about the intolerable draft, which was flagrant and monstrous, taking his civil rights.

Heller anticipated the punk's next slash. In a counter stroke he intercepted the bottle with the chair leg, which splintered and broke. With lightning speed, Heller sprang upon the frustrated agitator, like a ferocious African cat upon a petrified gazelle, and crushed him to the cement deck, face down.

"Don't kill 'em! Don't!" somebody shouted. "The punk isn't worth it!"

But Heller would not be denied. Like the steel jaws of a vise, Heller's powerful hands cut off the punk's jugular vein as his eye balls protruded from their sockets. Abruptly Heller jerked the punk's limber body from the floor and hurled him flying throught the air, as if he had been shot from a mechanical catapult. He landed in a stack of empty wooden chairs near the exit of the hall. There was a crashing sound, the thud of impact of a lifeless object, suddenly hitting the deck, then all was quiet. Very quiet. The recruits, who had left their seats during the brief scuffle, quickly and quietly reclaimed them, without bothering to find out if their self centered egotist objecter, who demanded recognition, was still breathing.

At that moment the double doors of the hall swung open. A two hundred fifty pound sergeant and two six-foot five inch corporals in well pressed Army fatigues and spit shined boots, entered and announced, "Those of you who pass the physical will be attached to B company, 18th Battalion, of the 5th Brigade. Meanwhile, all of you sit quietly 'til your name is called." The sergeant paused briefly, as he noticed splintered chairs, the disorderly room, and broken bottle glass scattered about before he added, "And I mean remain quiet! Do I make myself clear?"

During the rest of that Friday and Saturday, there were written examinations, physicals, and vaccinations for smallpox, yellow fever and typoid. There were dental checks, haircuts, billet assignments, aptitude and classification tests, orientation meetings and clothing and dog tag issues.

Private Raymond Heller was amused watching how most of the recruits scrambled, scuffled and struggled to get fitted for their uniforms. Most had problems with the size of their shoes and their boots. "Two sizes too small, too narrow, or too large," were the most frequent complaints. When Heller's name was called the quartermaster leaned out of the tiny window to view the 200 pound recruit's feet.

"Well, soldier! What size?" he demanded. "Or, are you gonna keep it a secret?"

Heller looked down, then at the soldier in the window. "Fifteen, sir!"

"What? You mean thirteen, don't you, private?"

"No, sir! I mean fifteen!" Heller said positively. "Sorry about that."

While the clerk obviously went to find size 15 shoes for Heller, he removed his moccasins and waited. Several long minutes later, the clerk reappeared, motioning to Heller to come to the window for his issue.

"Try 'em, soldier! Maybe your feet have shrunk. Size thirteen is the biggest we have."

Heller shrugged. While this was a serious matter to him, everybody else laughed. He recalled that his father had told him "A good pair of shoes are necessary to walk tall, be he on a hike in the woods, or enroute to church on Sunday."

Nevertheless, Heller tried to please the clerk. Desperately he tried and tried again. "I can't make it, sir!" he pleaded. "I guess my big toe is simply too long, sir."

"Give them here!" the clerk ordered. "Wear your own shoes 'til Monday."

"Yes, sir!"

It was the same story with everything else. Nothing was large enough for Heller. "Damn it all!" the clerk blistered, thoroughly disgusted with his job. "I wanna see you bright and early Monday. If I can't find anything that fits you by then, I'll personally make you what you need."

After clothing issue, the recruits marched to their barracks on the hill. By this time Heller realized that the change from civilian to Army trainee had to be swift. He knew that for the next eight weeks, they would receive intensive training in the fundamentals of combat, which would undoubtedly be applied in defending the United States and preserve their own lives. Basic combat training was of profound importance.

Although reveille was at 6:00 A.M. that Sunday, Heller had already showered and shaved by then. By the time chow call went down, he was first in line. At the entrance to the hall, the mess sergeant scrutinized the recruits.

"Let me caution you," he announced, giving formal notice to the recruits, "take all you want, but you'd better be damn sure you eat all you take! I consider wasting food a major sin!"

Heller grinned. This was one breakfast that would not cost him a pile of money. When the line started moving, he really piled it on. Others, directly behind him, wondered whether or not their buddy, Heller, would leave something for them. Then he passed the mess sergeant, whose fixed eyes stared steadily and intently at the highly overloaded tray.

"Hey! Recruit! Tell me," he barked, "are you a chow-hound, or, do you have eight hotcakes and a pound of bacon, just because you love my cooking?"

Without qualms of conscience, Heller told him, "Sir! I thought I'd find out for myself, if it's really true that you make the best hotcakes in the Army. Right after I eat them, I'll set-tle that controversy in the barracks, sir!"

After Heller had moved on, the mess sergeant instructed one of his assistants to watch that recruit. "You! Watch him! Nobody in the world can eat eight big hotcakes and that much bacon," he presumed, "unless he's loaded with tapeworms."

After breakfast, all recruits returned to their barracks on "Tank Hill." Heller requested permission to take a walk around Fort Jackson.

"Permission granted," the duty NCO told him. "Bear in mind this is a big place. Don't get lost, Heller."

Heller thanked the man on the duty desk and turned to leave, when the NCO called him back.

"Yes, sir!"

"Heller! Yesterday, when you had that short conversation with that damn agitator in the classification hall, what did you mean when you said he must be a reject from the San Francisco student riots?"

Heller looked surprised. "I had hoped it would pass..."

"Some of the recruits, who think that your bowel movements don't stink, told of the brief encounter. Let me assure you that nothing will come of it. In fact you did all of us one hell of a favor. After the medics put that character's arms and legs in casts, we sent him back to his draft board."

"He should have been tarred and feathered."

"Right, Heller ! Now answer my question," the NCO in-sisted impatiently. "What did you mean, exactly?"

"Last May, at the University of California, Stanford, San Fransisco State and San Jose State, the left wingers and their ilk marched, rioted and signed petitions against the House Committee on Un-American Activity, among other radical things."

"Yeah! Now that you mention it, I heard about that."

"Well! It was another shameful propaganda maneuver," Heller related, shaking his head. "The strategy of the Reds to control our young people is no secret. That riot was a clearcut demonstration of a carefully planned operation by Red organizers, who worked through their agents, ultra-liberal professors, and other sympathizers on those campuses."

"Couldn't the law stop them?" the NCO asked anxiously. "After all, aren't those colleges and universities tax-supported institutions?"

"You're right on both counts. But, there were six hundred professors in those institutions who openly declared to abolish not only the committee, but also the Federal Bureau of Investigation. By doing that, they influenced the students under them. It is this type of classroom propaganda which induces many of our young people to get involved with problems about which they know little, and which has been bringing so much discredit upon our California Universities."

Heller continued, "Those of us who followed the outcome were baffled about the way the judge handled the rioters. . . Go home and behave yourself," he told them.

"If that ain't the damndest thing I've ever heard!" the NCO demured. "How come these big colleges allowed their professors to do that?"

"These 600 so-called untouchable professors and others from the intellectual community, under the guise of academic freedom to teach according to their personal convictions and without fear of reprisals from anybody, really let their hair down. My Dad told me, he heard from reliable sources that some of the more radical professors even threatened reluctant students that if they didn't take part in the riots they would see zeros on their test papers."

"So, that's what is meant by academic freedom?"

Heller elucidated further. "That's the way some of these professors did things. But, sooner or later, the entire intellectual community had better realize that they and schools, colleges and universities have obligations, too, especially if they're supported by the American tax dollar."

"What finally happened? Did the judge make them pay for their destruction?" the NCO asked with keen interest.

"No, the judge let them off with a warning. By doing this liberal and generous thing," Raymond emphasized again, "it encouraged other restless students and known radicals to defy authority. By coddling these people and by dismissing the charges for inciting a riot, others in the intellectual communities will probably get busy and do the same, until they simply go too far. Some of them will eventually get killed, one way or another."

"In other words, the radicals victimized them?"

"You hit the nail right on the head, sir," Heller told him, then added, "I'd like to get to the Post library. Can you tell me how to get there?"

The soldier laid a map of Fort Jackson in front of Heller and spread it. "The library is here, right here," he pointed. "Why don't you keep the map. It may come in handy some time."

Heller thanked the duty NCO, folded the map and left. Once outside, he noted that the clouds were very much the same as those above Key West. Although a cool rain fell gently upon the dusty grass, Heller walked briskly along the busy boulevard lined with trees, grassy plots and shrubs, which blended beautifully with athletic fields, swimming pools, service clubs, golf courses, a bank and a credit union. There was a commissary, a gigantic Army hospital, a hobby shop, a gymnasium, a fire department and a large, brick building which housed the military police. He noted it was 11:00 A.M. and that church bells were ringing at a small chapel close by. He wondered of its denomination as he walked toward it, then entered shortly thereafter. At the moment the congregation was standing, the organ resounded briefly, then a youthful choir in Army uniform led the congregation as they sang the extraordinary Navy hymn, "Eternal Father, Strong to Save."

Although there were neither seats not extra hymnals available, Heller joined right in, singing his father's most favorite hymn.

"Eternal Father, strong to save, whose arm hath bound the restless wave. Who bidst the mighty ocean deep, its own appointed limits keep: O hear us when we cry to thee, for those in peril on the sea."

Heller remained standing in the back of the church, and while the chaplain recited the *Affirmation of Faith* he prayed silently the same prayer he gave in his Valedictorian speech.

The subject of the chaplain's sermon was, appropriately so, *What is a church.* He had obviously tailored it for the numerous recruits there, for their basic training.

"My friends," he smiled. "Welcome. Welcome. Welcome to Fort Jackson. I prepared my sermon today, based on an old German proverb: A church is God between four walls. It is a house for worshiping the Almighty, All powerful, Infinite and Eternal. It is a house for prayer and a place for meditation. Indeed, it is hope, faith and love. A Church is people. People from everywhere and everyplace. Once, when I was on British Samoa, during World War II, I was fascinated to find the words:

I NEVER WEARY OF GREAT CHURCHES - IT IS MY FAVORITE KIND OF SCENERY

These uncommon words were carved on a sandstone over the entrance of a tiny Polynesian church above Apia, which is the largest city on Upolu Island. While I stood there with admiration, a little Samoan boy explained that it was Robert Louis Stevenson's last epitaph. He carved it himself, the little boy told me, before he died. My friends," the chaplain continued, "every chapel, or church has a soul. It breathes and vibrates."

Heller glanced at his watch. It was high noon. It was time for his first Sunday dinner in the Army. He turned and left just as suddenly as he had come into the chapel. After lunch, he soaked up the sun for a while, then he went swimming. Later in the afternoon he checked his first book out of the Post library. Later in the evening he visited the enlisted men's club, where he drank a bottle of beer, and had an interesting conversation with other recruits, who had been there most of the day.

"I say," Heller commented jokingly. "Which one of you is doing the buying?"

"Everybody is fresh out of money. We thought you might do it, Heller," one of the recruits said ambiguously, adding, "Heller, they tell me you're loaded with a competitive drive. Ever do any arm wrestling?"

Heller grinned emulously. "I've tried to pin my Dad for the last three years...never could quite make it...."

"How about it Heller? Loser pays?" remarked a recruit near him.

"O.K." Heller agreed, while his chest heaved with pride, as he recalled the enormous power of his father. "Let's go!"

It took Heller three seconds for the first encounter. Two seconds for the second and less than that for the final test of strength against a big muscular recruit. The large crowd which had gathered to witness the contest were stunned by Heller's successes. Heller simply smiled. "I'll see all of you on Tank Hill," he told them and left.

Reveille was at 5:00 AM. Since Heller shaved and showered the previous night before going to bed, he was first in the chowline. This particular morning, when the mess sergeant spotted his favorite chow-hound, he approached him, patted him on the shoulder and said, "I have hashbrowns and shit on the shingle this fine morning. Remember, take all you want, but eat all you take!"

Heller did not utter a word. He recalled that one of his father's favorite sayings was, "It is far wiser to be thought a fool than to open your mouth and remove all doubt about it." Nevertheless, Heller took his tray to get his ration. When he saw the semi-liquid, unappetizing mess and the recruit in front of him adding red catsup, he lost his ravenous hunger.

With a tone of enduring pain, he walked up to the mess sergeant, who looked distressed, and said "Sergeant! Here's my ration. You eat it!"

At eight sharp, Heller arrived at clothing issue. "I got

everything, including size 15 shoes. It took some special horse trading with one of our D.I.'s. Here, try em..."

Ten minutes later, Heller was back in his dorm, changing his civies for Army fatigues. Suddenly, all personnel were ordered to "fall out". When he tried tying his shoes, one had no shoestring and the other broke, as he tried pulling it together. "The hell with it!" he yelled and literally flew out of the barracks to join the formation, already at attention.

The robust, well tanned NCO wearing the campaign hat, could not believe his eyes. He scratched the side of his jaw, hesitated momentarily, then moved quickly to confront the straggler.

"Soldier! What's your name?" he exclaimed, his voice reverberated as if it came from a bullhorn.

"Heller, sir!"

"You mean Private Heller! Isn't that right?"

"Yes, sir."

"Say it! Say it!" the big NCO demanded loud and clear, obviously trying to implant and infuse some kind of positive sense of discipline in the mind of the new recruits.

Heller looked directly into the Drill Instructor's eyes, six inches from his own. "I'm Private Heller, sergeant!" he obliged loudly.

"I'm gonna remember your name, Heller!"

"Sir!"

"Don't tell me you have an excuse?"

"Yes, sergeant. I have."

"Make it loud and clear. I want all hands to hear why you couldn't get to your very first formation in this Army on time!"

"I had been ordered to report for clothing issue at eight, sharp."

"What? Why?"

"They didn't have my sizes last Saturday, sergeant."

"But, they had them this morning?"

"Yes and no, sir!"

"What?"

"They had everything, except my size shoe. The issuing NCO finally gave me a used pair.... He told me he guaranteed them

91

because they belonged to a drill sergeant. As it turned out when I tried tying them, one of the shoes didn't have a shoestring at all and the other busted in two. Sorry, sir!"

While the NCO examined Heller's shoes to convince himself that indeed he was telling the truth, there was considerable laughter down the line, which quickly subsided, when the big man turned toward them and displayed the look of a Bengal Tiger, who had just been shot in his hind quarters by a safari hunter in East Africa.

"COMPANY——AT EASE!" the sergeant finally ordered. After he paused for a long moment, he declared, "The company commander has instructed me to give you what we call ORIENTATION. But, first, I wanna introduce myself...My name is Sergeant Lawson," he barked under the distinctive World War I type campaign hat. "From this moment on, and for the next seven weeks, I will be your voice, your helpful hand and your watchful eyes, which will guide all of you through basic," he emphasized. "Every drill sergeant has acquired his knowledge through practical experience, and the school of hard knocks. It is our job to guide, instruct and encourage you in preparation and training you to become good soldiers. All of us are seasoned graduates from the tough Drill Sergeants School. The first thing we will do here is to build your body, sharpen your mind. You begin as a raw recruit, and you'll graduate as skilled soldiers. We will give you these basics in seven weeks, sometimes longer, depending on the skill of your choice. Meanwhile, you'll spend many hours on the rifle range, mastering your M-14 rifle, which, by the way, you will treat as your best friend. You'll be marching several hundred miles. You'll spend long days and nights on tactical training, bivouacing and patrolling. Sure, it's tough, but, we will not ask you to do anything others haven't done before. Nobody will pick on you, hassle or harass you. We are only doing our duty to get you through here and to make you one of a thousand recruits who go through here every week, and go on to schools of your choice, provided of course you qualify..." he explained further. "Soldiers, Fort Jackson is one sure gateway to the United States Army. A good soldier must be tough. Tough enough to stand a demanding routine. Tough enough to enter combat with a full measure of strength and skill. Tough enough to see the white in an enemy soldier's eyes and kill him, with or without a rifle, if the moment of truth should come. So, physical fitness will be a large part of your training, which Army professionals from the 'Point' have designed for your strength, endurance, agility and coordination. This type of training promotes self-confidence, aggressiveness and esprit. I want all of you to learn the four P's. They stand for Practice, Practice makes you Perfect Pro's.''

For the next seven weeks, recruit Heller and his company buddies learned that their drill sergeant knew the score. He guided them through rigorous, strict and severe physical training, drills and ceremonies. They learned military customs and military courtesy, nuclear, biological and chemical warfare, how to conduct themselves while on guard duty. They learned basic rifle maintenance, going through the hazardous confidence course, where rifle technique and marksmanship were stressed so profoundly, Heller and his buddies dreamed about them night after night.

There were nights when he heard the sharp commands of his instructors echoing in his sleep. In sequences of sensations, images and thoughts he had visions and aspirations of rescuing women and children from imminent destruction, of saving them during the clamor of battle, applying first aid by bandaging, splinting their hands and feet, then treating them for shock, snake and other bites and carrying them to bivouac areas to safety. When he told Sergeant Lawson about his pleasant reveries, Lawson told him how remarkable it was to have dreams of that type. "Mine," Lawson told him, "are mostly about catastrophes, barroom brawls, whores, and how I slipped and fell into a field straddle trench while bivouacing in Korea. The sad part of it was that I had just given a lecture to my company peons on how they should place a leg on either side of the narrow trench before nature would take its course."

Heller suddenly had an attack of spasmodic laughter over which he had no control.

After a while Lawson wanted to know if Heller ever dreamed about the technique of pulling the pin and throwing hand grenades at the 35 meter targets, or other crucial training.

"No! Never," Raymond told him. "I go to sleep with good thoughts and I awaken that way, I guess."

Toward the end of basic training, Heller and his comrades realized they were much tougher, more confident and much more responsible now than they were when they arrived at Fort Jackson. There was no question in the chain of command's mind that Sergeant Lawson had reason to be proud of his recruits. All had met the challenges. All had survived the tests. Most recruits had started lasting friendships. Many more had acquired an attitude of true comradeship.

At the end of the final three day bivouac, the company commander told all hands how pleased he was. "In all my days, I have never seen a more unified company of basic course graduates, with an ingrained habit of obedience and leadership. Never have I seen more spit and polish recruits from the firing lines to the reviewing platform...Never have I examined higher qualification results on final tests," the officer said in a nostalgic mood. "I'm proud, indeed, to inform you that Company B of the 18th Battalion will lead the 5th Brigade on the final review."

The entire company cheered at the news. Four or five husky recruits jerked Heller from the ground and carried him on their shoulders to nearby Wildcat Creek, where they lifted him high before casting him into the water.

Big Jim Heller had come all the way from Key West, Florida, to see his son graduate from Fort Jackson. For this rare occasion, he wore his navy commander's uniform, proud of his numerous medals and the gold he earned in WW II.

After the remarkable military review, recruit Raymond Heller was called to the commander's reviewing platform for a handshake and a special certificate for being the outstanding graduate of the entire battalion, which also granted him an automatic promotion to Private First Class.

Like all others, Raymond flew to his barracks for the last time to pick up his orders, which were posted on the dormitory bulletin board. Although he was not overjoyed that he would be assigned to Fort Gordon for Military Police training, he reasoned that "the Army knows best" and let it rest.

"Before you meet your father outside, Heller," the duty NCO said smiling, "don't you think you ought to sew your brand new PFC stripe on your uniform?"

"That can wait," Raymond replied. "I'm much too nervous to fuss around with a little ol' needle."

"Wouldn't you know it, Heller," the NCO insisted. "I happen to have a needle and thread right here on my desk. So, get your big ass over here and start sewing, or I'll cancel your ten day leave."

The stitching was over in less than five minutes. "My sincere thanks to the staff, especially Sergeant Lawson, who didn't get my hide at that first formation for being late..." Heller remarked, admiring his PFC stripe.

"I'll convey that," the NCO laughed, as Heller rushed through the barrack doors with his gear to join his father, standing in front of Raymond's car, which he had picked up where Raymond had left it in Charleston.

Both father and son literally roared an outburst of joy and affection as they embraced.

"Dad! Dad! You ol' walrus! Let me hug you..."

"How dare you call me an old walrus, you presumptuous young whipper-snapper?" Mr. Heller grinned with pride. "If you'll take that anaconda strangle hold off me, I'll show you that I don't have two tusks and still no mustache."

Their joyous reunion was without abashment. Nearby, the entire barrack's recruits stood and watched with admiration and inspiring feeling. They, too, wanted to meet Raymond's father before they parted, for indeed, they would remember Raymond with admiration and respect from day one, when he hurled that insurrectionist over their heads in the processing hall.

When Raymond realized they were surrounded on all sides by friendly troops, including Staff Sergeant Lawson, he was almost overcome with humility.

"Dad! I want you to meet the greatest bunch of soldiers I've met so far," he boasted, before he took Sergeant Lawson by his arm. "And Dad, this is Staff Sergeant Lawson, who made us look good after seven weeks. Dad! This is one helluva soldier!"

"Very happy to meet you, Commander Heller," the sergeant said with gladness in his voice, avowed with sincerety and with a strong handshake.

"Likewise. Likewise," Commander Heller echoed. "I've heard a great deal about you in Raymond's letters."

"I'll bet it was all bad..."

"On the contrary, sergeant! Raymond idolized you for seven weeks...especially after you gave him a pair of your size 15 shoes."

After an exchange of niceties, rehashing stories and numerous handshakes, the Hellers jumped into their vehicle and slowly drove from Fort Jackson toward Columbia.

In silence, Raymond had a pensive recollection of his basic training, which although rigorous and zealous to a most worthy purpose, was also pleasurable. He knew it prepared him for the task to come, for the days and nights he would give his all for God and country.

Chapter IV

STOP APOLOGIZING FOR BEING SOLDIERS

After basic training at Fort Jackson, PFC Raymond Heller and his father stopped long enough to get something to eat in the beautiful city of Columbia, SC. When Mr. Heller, still in his navy uniform, suggested that they might have a northern lobster with the big claws and all the trimmings, Raymond shook his head.

"Dad! I don't wanna be arbitrary or the slightest bit rebellious," he told him with a determined grin. "I'm hankering for a good, old fashioned, triple decker hamburger and a chocolate malted. After that, I'd like to see the North Carolina mountains before I report to Fort Gordon in ten days or less...How about it, Dad?"

"No big problem, you rascal," Mr. Heller smiled jokingly. "I happen to have a road atlas and a travel guide in the glove compartment. After we leave the restaurant, let's look at them?"

"You don't mind, Dad?"

"Of course not," he replied affectionately, pausing for a drink from a glass of ice water. "Actually, it would be nice to perpetuate and honor the memory of one of the greatest warships of all time..."

"The USS North Carolina?"

"Yes! I've always wanted to see what she looks like now that she can no longer ride the waves...?"

"As you've told me so often, Dad," Raymond reflected thoughtfully, "it's nice to remember where you've been, in order to plan where you're going."

"Tell me, how would you apply that, regarding the mighty battleship?"

"Why not face it, Dad? The battleship is like a prehistoric iron monster, and the 16 inch broadsides are past history," Raymond pursued stubbornly. "Today's technology and our enemy's sophisticated missiles would blow a 45,000 ton ship out of the water in less time than a shark could swallow a duck."

"Hold it! Hold it! Surely you know I'm not one of those old diehards, Raymond. You ought to know I'm an experienced realist constantly looking for progress, both visionary and imaginary. However, my concerns are always with practical matters, rather than wishful thinking..."

"Such as?"

"I wanna see the Navy reactivate a couple battle wagons and let them throw broadsides into Vietnam to support our Special Forces over there."

"We have B-52's for that purpose," Raymond argued with firm persistence.

"I know we have those old cracker boxes who must be replaced," Mr. Heller explained further, "Bombers simply can't deliver their payloads in bad weather."

"I beg your pardon, Dad," Raymond said apologetically, not wishing to continue the subject. "It's just that I'm in the Army now."

"Right!" his father smiled. "Let's get going. Let's see those long rolling hills and the tremendous mountains with their majestic beauty and peacefulness."

Raymond took the wheel, while Mr. Heller looked at the map. Minutes later they were headed north.

For the next four days, the two mature men from Key West were overjoyed with the beauty, elegance and panoramic symmetry on either side of the picturesque parkway in the deep Blue Ridge mountains. It seemed the earth embraced the clouds in the sky, with the tallest peaks penetrating heaven.

At Banner Elk on Beach Mountain, they stopped to see the play, "The Wizard of Oz." At Blowing Rock, they rode the "Tweetsie Railroad," which was Raymond's very first trainride. As advertised, there was an Indian attack, which even by Raymond's standards was remarkably real. While there, they also saw their first blacksmith shop, a real sheriff's posse, the ol' general store, the jail, and finally an old fashioned ice cream store, where father and son ate double cones of various flavors for an hour and a half.

Later, they visited the restored Daniel Boone cabin. The following evening, it was "Horn of the West" performed nightly from June through August of each year. The parkway itself offered the most colorful scenic views in all directions. The overlooks with their limitless views were incredible and magnificent, especially dazzling to the two men from Key West. Raymond was so impressed with Groundhog Mountain with its awesome beauty, a feeling of sentiment and reverence almost overwhelmed him. Barely above a whisper he said, "Dad! This must be the spot where the devil tempted Christ to fall on his knees and worship him. What do you think of this incredible beauty, Dad?"

Mr. Heller directed his eyes and attention at the hemlock, balsa and the colorful flowers and foliage, the spectacular handiwork of God and nature before he answered him.

"I agree. I agree, Raymond," he replied, gazing steadily in wonder and delight far beyond the earthly beauty. "When I see real beauty, I think of your mother and Katharine Lee Bates, who wrote 'America the Beautiful.' Surely, God's own works praise him."

Both men walked toward the swimming pool, where a party of guests dived, laughed and splashed in the cool mountain water and the warmth of a brilliant sun. While Mr. Heller looked down upon the American version of the numerous Swiss Chalets, with their glass enclosed frontages and open balconies, giving a sweeping view of the entire valley below, Raymond's eyes were on the bundles of femininity in the pool.

"They're real, Son. Real. Someday, please bring one of them home to me and make me a grandfather. Won't you?"

"Dad, you're still a hopeless romanticist," Raymond smiled. "As is, Dad, ol' boy, I have lots of time. I wanna see and do things first. Right now the Army has become my first priority. Someday, I'll catch one of those mountain gals and build us a good size cabin in the Blue Ridge."

"Speaking of mountains, Son, strange as it seemed at the time...I came home early one day from the submarine base and found your lovely mother in a hand crocheted, stretched out, elastic fitting bikini, just like the one you just saw on that young girl on the diving board," he smiled, pointing with his hand. "She insisted I see how lovely she looked at the time. Emphatically, she tried to explain that as time went on, while she was carrying you, her body would become stretched, and ugly, with varicose veins and possibly scars. I took her in my arms and assured her that I would never, ever stop loving her 'til the day I'd die, even if she became old, fat, or dehydrated. We chatted all night. Just before she went to sleep in my arms, she made me promise that the three of us--she never doubted that her baby would be a boy-would travel north to see the Blue Ridge Mountains someday, and spend a week in a little cabin near a trout stream. How happy she'd be if she could see us together. How proud she'd be to see you in your uniform. Raymond, your mother was obsessed with strong hemen in uniforms."

"I'm sorry, Dad," Raymond consoled his father in his distress and sorrow. "Surely, you know I, too, grieve and pray that perhaps we'll all meet again in that place called heaven."

Raymond wiped a tear from the side of his nose. He wanted to change the subject, since he knew his father might well display a complexity of feeling and emotion, unless he changed the subject.

"Dad! I hate to tell you but we had better start heading South. I have to be at Fort Gordon the day after tomorrow," he advised him.

"What's the rush? That's not what you told me before, Son."

"Sergeant Lawson told me if I could get down to Gordon in five days, I would stand a good chance of getting into the class which is already organized. Otherwise, I'll have to hang around for several weeks, waiting for the next class. I'm sorry, Dad. You know how I enjoy being with you again."

"In that case, let's get out of these mountains. Time's a' wasting!"

Enroute to Fort Gordon, via Winston-Salem, Greenville, SC, and Augusta, GA, the two men discussed Raymond's future in the Army, and why he was going to the Military Police School.

"Sergeant Lawson suggested it," Raymond told his father. "He also told me to see the world first before ending up in Vietnam. He told me that the next MP graduates would undoubtedly go to England, France, or Germany. Naturally, I've been thinking about Europe."

"What about getting to Special Forces at Fort Bragg, Son?"

"In time, Dad. It's like Lawson said, Vietnam is gonna be around a while. Meanwhile, I'll get myself qualified in every field of combat skills acceptable to Special Forces. I sure don't wanna be a neophite when I get to Bragg."

"What can you gain by going to Fort Gordon, Son?"

"I've studied the Army Occupational Handbook," Raymond said understandably. "Law enforcement will give me more of a generalized concept in such things as preserving military control, security, civil disturbances, prisoners of war and refugees. The MP's also fight with the infantry when the need arises."

"You got the handle on the door," his father said nodding his head again and patting Raymond on the shoulder. "How long will you be at the Military Police School?"

"Eight weeks," he told him, recalling how quickly the time at Fort Jackson had elapsed. "Actually, I can't wait from one day to the next. Each day is a challenge and a new experience. Like going to college to get a degree and playing major sports at the same time. I do know this, Dad, the Army is for me.

Someday, I might return to Key West and help you do a little fishing."

Mr. Heller's eyes, his facial expression and the silent nodding of his head provided a manner of approval.

When PFC Heller reported at the Military Police School at Fort Gordon, the duty NCO was surprised to see him so early. The soldier reread Heller's orders. Silently he scrutinized the PFC in front of him.

"Heller! You're either damn anxious, an orphan with no place to go, or, you're a damn fool," he commented, drumming his fingers on the desk. "Which is it, Heller?"

Heller grinned. "The first. I'm anxious and enthusiastic."

The NCO made a notation on Heller's orders and pointed out that since he was five days early, he could join the class already organized which would start at 0800, right after breakfast the following day.

"I'm real happy you told me that," Heller construed the soldier's interpretation. "I'll be there."

As the duty NCO showed Heller to his quarters, he remarked most cheerfully--"Heller! You are different! The Brigade commander will be pleased though to hear you sacrificed five days leave just so you can get started in an earlier class."

Raymond thanked the NCO, entered his room and looked forward to tomorrow.

At 0800, 75 potential MP's were patiently waiting to hear their orientation, familiarization and adaptation talk regarding special interpretation and training.

"Gentlemen!" expounded the officer-in-charge of training. "Law enforcement, be it civilian or military, requires individuals who can take quick and decisive action. Let me state here and now, strong communication skills, alertness, and the ability to adapt quickly and correctly on short notice, are among the primary traits the United States Army looks for. Leadership qualities are also significant and extremely important. It is essential that you gain the respect of others, whether you are writing a parking violation on the post, or escorting violators to a detention center. Other absolute qualities for MP work

102

and law enforcement are a pair of sharp eyes, good ears, and, of course, remaining in excellent physical condition."

The training officer took a drink of water from a glass then continued: "The work you might be doing could take you just about anywhere, from an intersection to a crime laboratory, from a maximum security site to a vehicle escorting a funeral or a military convoy. However, the predominant duty for most Army law enforcement enlisted personnel involves traffic control and safeguarding military personnel and equipment. You may also be assigned as special agents and find yourself photographing a crime, or making sketches of one. You may very well be involved in interrogating suspects, interviewing witnesses, or carrying out other aspects of criminal investigation."

At that moment, the lieutenant colonel lowered his voice and asked if anyone had any questions thus far.

"I have, sir!" Heller shouted from way back. "I have a question, sir!" he repeated.

"What is your name?" the officer asked sternly.

"Private First Class Heller, sir!"

"Your question?"

"What do MP's do during wartime operations, sir?"

"I was just coming to that," the officer declared. "If you'll sit down and listen, you'll hear your question answered. During action, such as a war, MP's guard and safeguard prisoners of war, civilian internees and detainees in special enclosures, on work details and during interrogations. evacuations and transfers. MP's will also process and search prisoners of war, internees and detainees, support rear area protection, fight as units in the infantry when required, collect tactical intelligence information, and handle refugees and evacuees."

During the next eight weeks, Heller remained fascinated with the Army, while he listened, learned and lived as a Military Police trainee. He learned Military Law, crowd control, more about close order drill and parade formations, how to use his 45 calibre service pistol for better effect, and how to field and detail strip it blindfolded. He learned when and how to use the billy club while apprehending, restraining or interrogating offenders, and how to confiscate unauthorized weapons and substances of drug offenders. He participated in practice police raids, and was taught how to assist in controlling domestic disturbances, apprehend and restrain violators of the law, advise individuals of their legal rights, conduct detailed searches and interviews of interrogatees and determine the worth of reports.

While at Fort Gordon, PFC Heller heard again and again *"First and foremost, an infantryman is a soldier's soldier! Be he with a strike team, or on a reconnaissance mission. Indeed, he is the real reason the rest of the army exists. All other combat and supporting elements have important missions, but, their main purpose is to get the infantryman to his objective, which he will defend, and die for the very ground he stands upon."*

Upon graduation from Fort Gordon, PFC Heller and Sergeant Pierre Zusette, who had recently returned from Vietnam where he had served with the 5th Special Forces, were assigned to the 202nd Military Police Battalion, headquartered in Inngrandes, France. Immediately after the ceremony, the two soldiers loaded their duffle bags into a friend's car, which took them directly to the Charleston Air Force Base in South Carolina. There, they boarded a C-141. Six and a half hours later, they landed at the Rhine Main Air Force Base in Germany. While they were waiting for their final transportation from the Paris train terminal to Inngrandes, Sergeant Zusette stated, "Heller! Did you know that your name is a household word back in Gordon."

"Come off it, sergeant," Heller replied.

"I'm serious, Heller. When the time came for the grades, your name was always on top, and when mental and physical achivements were on the line, you were first. Damn it, Heller," the sergeant wondered, "you're either an Army brat, or a college dropout...which is it?"

Heller was amused. "Neither," he said in a brief opinion of himself. "If you must know, I am an Eagle Scout, which I got long before I graduated from high school. Dad is a Navy mustang. He taught me everything known to man about pistols, rifles and shotguns, and how to maintain them. He taught me how to dive, swim, surf, pump iron, first aid, even the Morse Code, visual communication, like semaphore. Naturally, since Dad is a commercial fisherman, I learned to know fish. He and I used to swim with the dolphins in the Keys, early in the morning. They got quite used to us..."

"What in the world are you doing in the Army? Why not the Navy? You know-like father, like son?"

"It's a long story, sergeant, but I've heard so much about Special Forces, I thought I'd like to be one of them someday."

"Now you're talking! I was with SF in Nam. Damn glad to get out alive."

"Will you tell me all about your tour sometime, sergeant? Or, would you prefer not to discuss things like that with a brand new PFC?"

"On one condition..."

"What?"

"You tell me why we're in France, when General DeGaulle doesn't want Americans in his country?"

"You're on," Heller remarked, pointing in the direction of a coffee shop on the other side of the boulevard. "How about a cup of coffee for a start?"

Somewhat later, while they were drinking coffee, Heller explained that there was no mystery about United States occupation forces being in France, Germany, or anywhere else in Europe. "We are here to discourage another war. We are also here to respond quickly to so-called flare-ups between nations. We are in France and elsewhere, and everywhere, so that our enemies can see us. The Russians must know that the ol' U.S.A. is serious and is honoring our NATO commitment, defending our interests, as well as the interests of our allies and friends. We are also here to help preserve the cultures and ways of life which give each European country its own unique personality," Heller explained further in a scholarly analysis, and in detail. "Have you any idea what the Reds would do to the Eiffel Tower, which is the national symbol of France?"

"Use it for communication purposes, perhaps?"

"Possibly, or they might even dismantle it, strip it of the metal and someday throw it back at us in bullets and bombs, the same way the Japs did at Pearl Harbor, Hickham Field, and elsewhere in the Pacific..."

Sergeant Zusette lit a cigarette. After he exhaled he wondered where Heller got all his knowledge. "Your life is just beginning, Raymond...I guess your education started with your kindergarden teacher?"

"Dad got me going learning how to read when I was three. And eventually, while you were in Vietnam, I read everything I could get my hands on. While I think of it, can you tell me why the media never wrote or showed on TV how we shellacked the Viet Cong, all hours of the night?"

"I guess they just never got that close to combat. Heller! What would you say, if I told you that I was on stateside duty when I asked for a transfer to Europe?"

"I'd say you must have had a damn good reason--like maybe you tried to get away from a shotgun wedding..."

Both men laughed.

"I left because I love our country. I couldn't stand seeing it torn apart by subversives, one worlders and do-gooders who are destroying it from within."

"You're referring to those who clutter our field of education and those who praise the brutal Chinese, the North Koreans, Castro and now, Ho Chi Minh?"

"How do you feel about this damn war?"

"Right or wrong, it's our country, sergeant. We are committed and if and when the politicians keep their nose out of it, our generals can end this and any other war in less time than an alcoholic can kill a fifth of corn-whiskey. Like Decatur toasted under fire, May our country, in her intercourse with foreign nations, may she always be in the right, but our country, right or wrong!"

"I'll drink to that anytime," Zusette said setting his empty wine glass down. "Tell me, what other patriot are you reminded of?"

"Nathan Hale. As you may recall, he was a twenty-one year old schoolmaster, a patriot in an undeclared war, who volunteered to go behind the British lines to collect information. After they captured him, he was tried as a spy. Later, when his executioners knotted the rope around his bare throat, he broke his long silence and shouted the most magnificent words ever heard by men of all nations:

"I ONLY REGRET THAT I HAVE BUT ONE LIFE TO GIVE FOR MY COUNTRY"

There was a long moment of silence before Sergeant Zusette answered Heller. "You know, mon ami, I get lumps in my throat when I recall how my little ol' teacher, Miss Hazlewood stressed that in our history class."

Several hours later, the two soldiers were received by the first sergeant of the MP Battalion, who assigned them to their barracks and briefed them about their new assignment.

"Sergeant Zusette! Although you're a Public Affairs and Audio-visual career system specialist, the colonel wants you on a twenty-four hour standby, because you're one of the few French linguists in our outfit. You'll have your desk right next to mine in the personnel office. Your job is to be near the colonel at all times and to translate all communiques. He's most anxious to meet you."

When the first sergeant finished eyeing PFC Heller, he said, "You'll come directly under the Sergeant Major. Both of you will find out in no time at all that he's a soldier's soldier. He makes no bones that he believes all other combat and support elements are important, but," he went on, "their main purpose is to get the infantryman to his objective. So, regardless of your MOS, your special qualifications, your background in training, our MP Battalion will join and fight with the Infantry, if and when that time should come. Understood?"

For the next few months, Heller was engrossed with police reports, maintaining records, keeping battalion radio logs, processing evidence, helping prepare sworn statements and affidavits, collecting and reporting police information. Now and then, he had to testify in Military and French civilian courts. But Heller was happiest when the Battalion went on maneuvers and reconnaissance. He was even more elated when he read the coded communique that General Charles deGualle would review the 202nd MP Battalion at Chateauroux.

"Shaking hands with the General would really be something

to write Dad about," he thought to himself, while entering the sergeant major's office.

Heller handed the French communique with the English translation to Sergeant Major Cartwright, who thanked him, and headed directly into the colonel's office.

Since the door remained open to the commander's office, Heller could hear and see what was going on. First, there was a long silence. Then, suddenly the colonel stood up and asked whether the Sergeant Major Cartwright thought that the Battalion was ready for the formal review.

"Colonel Thompson! Our soldiers will make the boys in gray on the Hudson look like amateurs," his senior NCO told him sincerely.

"Good! As you know I depend on you, Sergeant Major Cartwright."

"Your orders, Colonel Thompson?"

"Get a battalion memo ready for my signature, and tell Sergeant Zusette to come in. I will want him in my official party because he's obviously the only real French linguist we have..."

"I beg the colonel's pardon..."

"Speak right up, Sergeant Major Cartwright!"

"I happened to be in the showers late last evening, when I heard a conversation between Sergeant Zusette and PFC Heller..."

"Go on?"

"For a moment I thought a couple of French diplomats were arguing about Nikita Khruschev and the Berlin Wall."

"Are you telling me we have another interpreter?"

"Yes, sir!"

"Heller, did you say? PFC Heller?"

"Yes, sir!"

"Before you bring him in, brief me about him."

"Colonel Thompson, this young soldier is a rare one. He's an Eagle Scout, earned 24 Merit badges and 5 Palms. He's one of the finest physical specimens in the Army. His ambition is to get to Fort Bragg. He says he's ready to give Special Forces troopers some competition. Besides that, sir, Heller is a performance orientated soldier, proud of his work, which he usually plays down. He made PFC in Fort Jackson, which as you know, sir, is next to impossible with a graduating brigade of over a thousand ambitious youngsters. Besides that, sir," he told the colonel, "Heller is also an expert rifleman, an expert with a pistol, and he can throw hand grenades like a big league quarterback throws a football. One of the rather remarkable things about Heller is that he is straight. No jargon of any kind. His vocabulary is like that of a teacher with an MA in English. As long as I've known him, sir, I haven't heard one four letter word..."

At this time, the colonel threw up one of his hands. "How come we haven't promoted him to corporal, Sergeant Major Cartwright?"

"He's on the approved roster as of today, sir."

"Bring that special breed of man in, sergeant major!"

Heller approached the commander of the Military Police Battalion. His garrison cap was neatly tucked under his arm. Two paces from the colonel's desk, he stood like a statue and rendered a snappy salute, accompanied with the appropriate greeting, "Good morning, Colonel Thompson! PFC Heller reporting as ordered, sir!"

The colonel returned the salute and said, "At ease!" At great length he told him what his senior NCO had told him about his uncommon performance of duty, his dedication, and his remarkable record and conduct. When the colonel asked him where he learned his French, he told him that he had been enjoying a worthwhile comradeship with Sergeant Zusette, who had been his teacher.

The colonel's eyes flashed at his sergeant major. "Most unusual...wouldn't you say, sergeant major?"

"Yes, sir!" Cartwright responded positively. "I happen to have corporal's stripes for PFC Heller's uniform and since our courier will be leaving for the Paris embassy at the conclusion of this...

The colonel finished the sergeant major's thoughts and remarks. "Give Heller and Zusette five days leave! Instruct the courier to drop them off anywhere they choose in Paris!" he ordered. "If that's all right with, Corporal Heller?"

"Yes, sir! Thank you, sir!"

Heller snapped to attention again. His right forearm was inclined at 45°. The tip of his forefinger touched slightly to the right eye brow. His thumb and fingers were extended and joined. His eyes remained fixed until the colonel returned the salute. Only then did he drop his arm. He executed about face and marched off.

Within fifteen minutes Corporal Heller and Sergeant Zusette boarded the Army vehicle for Paris. By the time they arrived at the outskirts of Paris, both were extremely hungry.

"Nouriture! Nouriture!" Heller hooted like a hungry owl. "I got to eat right now. See that gourmet cuisine restaurant we just passed?" he pointed, tapping the driver on the shoulder.

"O.K.! O.K." the driver agreed. "As long as you understand that once I stop you're on your own?"

"Right! Stop and let us out," Heller voiced with a big grin, while the vehicle came to a stop.

"I'll see you in five days at the American Embassy," the driver declared. "Meanwhile, enjoy yourself."

"Yeah! And thanks. We'll be looking for you around five PM on the fifth day," Heller announced as their driver gunned his courier vehicle and moved aggressively into the heavy Paris traffic.

"Cher ami! Allons!" Heller declared with great joy and laughter, pushing Zusette toward the restaurant.

"Damn it all, Heller! Can't you wait?" Zusette countered. "You're always thinking about filling your stomach..."

"Ol' buddy! Is there anything else so early in the afternoon?"

"Hell, yes! I'm interested in les filles," he said, anticipating getting together with one as soon as possible. With a big smirk on his face, he recalled how the boys have bragged about their encounters with the fairer sex of Paris.

"Let's flip a coin," Heller proposed. "Heads, we eat first, tails, I'll starve...unless you wanna split? We can rendezvous later."

"Absolutely not! There is what is called the buddy-

110

system...You go to town with a buddy and you had better come back with him, or your ass is mud."

"C'est a vous," Heller agreed in French.

After they crossed numerous bridges of the Seine River, they finally arrived in the middle of Paris. Heller spotted the Cafe de Flore on his left, which he remembered as having been Picasso's favorite. It was spring and many customers were sitting on chairs under the marquee projecting over the sidewalk. The tables were loaded with bottles of wine and food. The sidewalk was alive with ladies. Heller was certain a major Hollywood studio in France on location had stopped operation for the day. The youthful female stars, who were swinging and swaying like the palm trees on Hawaii in a noonday breeze, were, according to Sergeant Zusette, just ordinary hookers.

"Ordinary! What's the matter with your eyes? You must be getting blind," Heller told him. "Look at those inviting smiles, and those terribly high heeled shoes. O.K. my friend, let's get some food... *voulez-vous manger maintenant?"*

"Right now!"

"Good! I know now your stomach comes before those Hollywood rejects. But," he went on as they seated themselves under the marquee, "in the future stop your fantasies, forget your previous disappointments with your homespun girls. Everything is wide open here... wild!"

Heller disregarded what Zusette had said. *"Puis-je vous aider?"* a smiling young waitress said in French, looking at the nineteen year old soldier momentarily.

"Oui! Oui," he smiled back, adding, "Bring the menu, before I starve!"

The waitress turned her pretty head. "If you're in a hurry, I recommend our Roast Duckling *Au Poivre Vert,"* she told them in English with a pleasing French accent.

Heller and Zusette looked at each other. "I'll take a double order of the roast duck. My buddy takes a regular duck dinner. Understand, little girl?" Heller asked. "And hurry up before I eat your apron!"

While they were waiting to be served, Zusette explained the

French birds and bees to his buddy. "Remember we have five nights and four days. We'll get us a big room at the Fontainebleau Hotel first. After that we'll head for Montmartre. The place is loaded with cafes, shops and with *compaignons de voyage*. If we strike out there, we'll try Pigalle Square, which is the center of most night life spots. In the morning let's go sightseeing on one of those motorcoach tours. We might even have a look at Napoleon's Tomb."

Heller was curious about Zusette's earlier life. He asked him if he had been in Paris before.

"Yes! I've had a tour here before I went to Nam," he explained. "I married a mademoiselle with *savoir-vivre*. When my tour ended, I took her to Staten Island with me and everything was lovey-dovey. Eighteen months later I had to leave her, since I was headed for Nam. Yep! She wrote me every day. Sometimes even twice a day. When I got back three months earlier than expected, I found my wife in my bed with another man...a Marine, of all people."

"Did you kill 'em both?" Heller asked with humor in his voice.

"Nope! First, I locked them in the bedroom. Then, I threw all their clothes and belongings, including her douche-bag and the Marine's uniform out in the street. Next? I called the police and told them I just saw a couple of nuts running around the street in the nude. When I heard the siren, I unlocked the bedroom door. At the moment the Police drove up to the front door, I drove them out the back door. As I said, in the nude. After our divorce, Yvette married another American sucker, just like me."

After the two soldiers checked into a room at the Fontainbleau Hotel, they strolled leisurely down the sidewalk. The smell of perfume pervaded the air. At times they were literally surrounded by ladies, who were anxious and willing. Impulsively, Heller flung his arms around one of them, without serious intent.

"Another time," he told her in English. "Perhaps another time."

"Maintenant?" she insisted, hanging on.

"Non! Non! Heller smiled and pushed her gently from him.

Pigalle Square was very much like New York Times Square and 8th Avenue, or, like Waikiki's Kalakaua Avenue in Honolulu, where the tourist is king. They found topless clubs, massage parlors, burlesque, stage and sideshows of all kinds.

"If you wanna spend the money, you can have one helluva time. Here in Paris, pleasure is a way of life. I'm surprised the dope pushers and peddlers have not bothered us by now."

"I'll throw the first punk who approaches me into the Seine," Heller gestured tensely.

"No! Don't be an idiot," Sergeant Zusette barked. "Just say no, and let it go at that."

There was a long silence between the two. Zusette crushed his last cigarette under his foot on the sidewalk.

"Heller!" Zusette muttered, then changed his mind.

"What were you gonna say?"

"Can I ask you a personal question, ol' buddy?"

"Sure! Shoot!"

"Ever been with a woman?"

"If you wanna know if I've ever had an affair before, my answer is no. You see ol' buddy, I still haven't had my 20th birthday. I've come close a couple times, but," he expounded "when I hear, see and read the misery in the world, due to this sex revolution, I become a coward," Heller admitted frankly. "Sergeant Zusette! I'm hungry and tired. What do you say, shall we go back to our hotel? We'll most likely see others of your rank there, and I'm thinking you ought to kick up your heels with one of them."

"Okay, Heller. But, what about you? What will you do?"

"First, I'll get me something to eat. Then I'll call Dad in Key West. After that, I'll probably hang around the lobby and catch up on my reading...might make some plans for tomorrow."

Zusette agreed. Before he left he thought Heller ought to make reservations with a touring company for early morning.

"Right!" Heller told him. *"Bon chance!"*

On their second day, the two soldiers boarded a tourist bus in front of their hotel. The tour began at the 985 foot high Eiffel

Tower and ended that day at the wondrous Cathedral of Notre Dame on the tiny island, Ile de la Cite in the Seine River, which was once the heart of Paris.

On the third day, they visited the magnificent Paris Opera House. A small band of musicians was practicing and a would-be Helen Traubel was exercising her vocal cords during their visit.

Both men were impressed with the Arc de Triomphe de Carrousel with the bronze war chariot on top. At the time, Heller thought Zusette was in a hypnotic trance. He stood there in mental concentration without uttering a single word.

"Is it history or mysticism, buddy?" Heller asked him.

Zusette smiled. "You clown, for a few minutes I saw history all around us. I thought I saw Black Jack Pershing, leading his victorious American Army through the Arc into Paris. Then, I reflected to when Hitler brought his SS Legions through it after France surrendered. That's what I meant by saying I saw history all around us."

At the Louvre, most of the passengers in the bus rushed for the entrance. Heller and Zusette were too overwhelmed. When they finally entered Heller remarked that he had heard and read everything he could get his hands on about the contents of the famous museum which includes the Mona Lisa, the many Titian's and, among others, the Rubens' masterpieces. "I'm almost afraid to go in," he muttered. "But I will, of course."

Inside, Zusette took Heller by the elbow to slow him down. "I know how well read you are, ol' boy," he commented. "But, did you know the French Revolution, in 1789, stripped the Palace of Versailles of a considerable number of masterpieces and canvases, which suddenly appeared in the Louvre?"

"Name one!" Heller replied, enjoying this game of trivia.

"Well, the Mona Lisa for one and, the Titians and Rubens' canvases were some of the best known masterpieces that showed up at this place. You probably know that much was burned at that time and the gold and silver furniture was carted off and melted down to help pay for Louis XIV's war."

"If that's true, why doesn't the wordly wise Van der Kemp

of the Palace demand that these treasures be returned? Surely he can prove claims, legitimization..."

"My friend, a revolution almost destroyed Versailles. It would probably take another to restore it to its original splendor," Zusette emphasized truthfully, just as the curator approached and suggested they should join the rest of the tourists from their group.

When the curator pointed to Leonardo da Vinci's masterpiece, "La Gioconda" - the Mona Lisa - Heller and Zusette exchanged long looks.

"As you said, Zusette," Heller whispered, "it might well take a revolution to get da Vinci's masterpiece back to where it rightfully belongs. I'd like to tell you another thing," he continued, "regardless of the other countless paintings they have here, if they lost the Mona Lisa, they might have to close the door."

"Agreed," Zusette nodded. "Shall we go on?"

There was a carved statue of a simple Egyptian boy called "The Seated Scribe", which dated back to 2600 years BC. A mural ascribed "The Archers of a Persian King" on one of the enamelled walls.

Heller was emotionally moved when they stood near the "Pieta" depicting Mary grieving over the body of Jesus, after he had been removed from the cross. Raymond could hardly breathe thinking about his own mother, whom he never knew.

There was a portrait of Emperor Napoleon Bonaparte, crowning himself, while a petrified clergy and ministers of state stared with disbelief.

When Zusette saw the 16th century Francois Clouet painting of Elizabeth of Austria, who became Queen of France, he thought she must be the most beautiful woman of all time, including Madame de Pompadour.

"The official portrait of Louis XIV, looks kinda feminine" Heller thought, comparing the painting of Napoleon's triumphant pose, after the Battle of Eylau. Both men were particularly moved with the "The Raft" because it depicted the survivors of a wrecked ship, a scene both had seen in their time.

Landscapes of nostalgic beauty, such as "A Sea Port at

Sunset'' and classic works of lovely ladies by Jean-Auguste-Diminique Ingres were everywhere. However, the painting of ''The Death of Sardanapalus at his palace, depicting the slaughter of his many wives and mistresses'' and a large canvas by Meissonier of a tragic episode during the 1848 Revolution, showing the horror of a artillery bombardment in Paris, left many of the spectators in tears.

''I've had enough for today,'' Heller declared, after he had seen a painting of the ''Massacre of the Triumvirate by Antoine Caron'' of the 16th Century, depicting the gruesome inhumanities perpetrated in the name of religion, by soldiers butchering old and young alike. ''Let's get out of here!''

''Let's go!'' Zusette whispered in return. ''I need a stiff drink of cognac, whiskey, anything. . .''

''And I'm hungry again,'' Heller confessed loud and clear.

''What? Damn it, Heller! How could you wanna eat, after what we've just seen?''

''Partner! There's nothing wrong with my appetite, and a small glass of *pousse-cafe* would do just fine, if you don't mind,'' he answered.

On the final morning of their five day leave, Heller and Zusette decided to see the historic Palace of Versailles, recognized by art collectivists as one of the greatest repositories of worldly treasures.

''This feudal castle with its fountains, gardens and forests is so lavish and magnificent,'' Heller remarked. ''It makes the ol' Louvre look like a place where bodies of victims are being stored before cremation.''

''For chris' sake, Heller!'' Zussette blasted. ''The Louvre is like a common ordinary morgue!''

Heller was surprised by Zusette's ourburst.

''Isn't that what I just said?'' he countered in self-defense.

''I don't know what you said,'' Zusette said in anger, adding, ''I'd like to give you some free advice, if you don't mind?''

Without hesitation Heller said, ''Of course not. Shoot!''

''Many times you're too damn long winded, like the phonies at a society ball, debating who dances with whom. Heller, I'm telling you the Army has standards and procedures for orders

116

and commands. Cut out the wordiness. Get to the meat. I'm not referring to some outlandish specialized vocabulary, when I say that. Get to the meat! That way, there's no doubt or confusion. It may save your life in the field someday!''

After a long moment, Heller said without ill will, "I'll remember that!"

Inside the Palace, the twosome were intensely impressed with the splendid "Hall of Mirrors", the torches, the great works of the masters, such as the "Venus di Milo," the "Salon d' Hercule" and numerous other treasures of King Louis XIV.

When Heller kept staring in the direction of the Venus, Zusette suggested they move along with the crowd. "Come ol' buddy. What's so romantic about that old gal? Most of us know something about Roman mythology and that many years later the art experts identified her with Greek Aphrodite as the Goddess of love..."

"Now who's yaking too much? It isn't I! I was admiring the girl standing under the canvas, wondering who she might be?"

Zusette glanced at the girl, then at Heller. "That little snot-nosed society kid from Park Avenue in New York wouldn't give you or me the time of day."

Heller disagreed. "No! I'm gonna prove you wrong."

"How?"

"I'm gonna ask her for the time," he told him, as he approached her and Zusette just stood there and shook his head.

"I beg your pardon, madmoiselle," Heller said, bowing from the waist up. "Would you kindly tell us the time?"

"Of course," the girl smiled. "It's 11:31 hours precisely."

"Thank you," Heller said with satisfaction, loud enough so that his buddy could hear and see that he was right.

"Are you satisified now?" Zusette wanted to know.

"She gave me the time and a terrific smile. What bothers me is that she called the time like we do in the Army."

"That's the European way of telling time. Forget her! Remember our pass expires today. *Allons! Allons*!"

"I'm no ladies' man, Zusette. But, I have the strangest feeling that someday, I'll meet that little bundle again."

"Don't tell me that you've an *affaire de coeur?*"

"I'd say she's five five, weighs about 110 soaking wet, with one helluva curvy figure, kinda delicate, but strong and well rounded where it counts. Her legs? Ballerina's, I'd say. Sensational fingernails and barely a touch of mascara or lipstick..."

"Her face. What about her face? You know, eyes, nose and hair?" Zusette whispered with a grin, obviously realizing Heller was serious. "I think you're a romantic nut, Heller."

Zusette took Heller by his arm. "Let's go!"

"This little lady had *beaux yeux,*" Heller recalled.

"Cela va dire!"

"In English, Zusette, I'll always remember that the most beautiful girl I saw in Paris was probably from our good old United States."

"Cher ami, what color were her *beaux yeux?"*

"Her eyes? Blue. I mean kinda green. Bluish green."

When the two soldiers viewed Paola Veronese's "Christ at the House of Simon the Pharisee" the gentle hand of the lord and master of the Palace, the honorable Gerald Van der Kemp, touched them on their shoulders. In perfect English he said most pleasantly, "Gentlemen, this canvas is the most distinct victory painting of all Christianity."

Heller and his buddy bowed in recognition and respect. Once more they moved forward with other visitors to view with delight the marvelous works by da Vinci, El Greco, Gauguin, Goya, Homer, Manet, Matise, Raphael, Rembrandt, Renoir, Rubens, Titian, Van Gogh, Vermeer, Whistler, and Picasso.

The two soldiers stood astonished in Marie Antoinette's luxurious bedroom chamber, with miles and miles of breathtaking gold embroidery.

Much later, on their return trip to their post with the same courier who brought them, their conversation centered on the historic lady's extravagant bed. Heller, an admitted neophite on women and sex, thought out loud that "no woman on earth could possibly have enjoyed personal gratification with a lover in a monstrous bed like that."

"Besides," Heller went on before his companion could interupt his trend of thought, "I've read that sexual intercourse was rare and women's orgasm was unheard of at that time."

"Buddy! That's about the most ridiculous statement you've made since I've known you. Let me tell you something...be she queen or whore, all women with rare exceptions enjoy sex."

While Heller contemplated Zusette's sentiment, the latter added, "Heller! When in hell are you gonna let your hair down and plunge into what some call that earthly bliss all of us are living for from childhood?"

"If you're referring to sex, I intend to wait 'til I'm twenty-one, or 'til my wedding day. Both are a long way off, unless I have the privilege of getting near that little girl who gave me the right time this morning."

Heller expected a big laugh from Zusette. Instead, he said that it would not surprise him if sometime, someplace, he might see her again, which made Heller terribly happy.

After they had thanked the courier for the ride and had checked in at the personnel office, Sergeant Major Cartwright told them, "I'm glad you're back. So, let's get hot, bring your work up, then start getting ready for General de Gaulle's visit."

Yes, Sergeant Major Cartwright!" Heller and Zusette said simultaneously. "We missed you!"

"Get out of here, before I assign you some extra duty!" he shouted at the pair rushing from the office. Then he laughed.

From the day Heller and Zusette returned to their command, there was much excitement in the Battalion. General de Gaulle would first review the French Cadets at the Police Academy and somewhat later inspect the 202nd MP Battalion at Inngrandes.

Colonel Thompson, who had a distinguished record since graduating from West Point, looked at the Army like a priest looks at the Vatican. At 41, he was a full colonel, had led his battalion at the front in Korea, where he was severely wounded. Once in a while, Sergeant Major Cartwright would get in a talkative mood and tell his NCO's stories about his service with the colonel during that 'police action'. He told about how the colonel had threatened to courtmartial him, if he allowed the medics to evacuate him. "As long as I'm breathing, I'll stay with my troops! And that's an order!" he blistered before he passed out from loss of blood. "I often wonder why our media never writes about our real heroes?" Cartwright said frequently. "All I see is when we get the dirty end of the stick."

The colonel's steel blue eyes, his ruddy complexion and his crew cut made him appear ten years younger. He was six feet tall, weighed 190. His reputation was first to rise, first on the hikes, first on the firing line, even first to get vaccinated. Indeed he felt honored General de Gaulle would review his troops before his tour would end in Europe.

In order to implement positive action, Sergeant Major Cartwright summoned all officers and NCO's not actually on duty for daily briefings.

"The history of World War II shows clearly that General de Gaulle was regarded as one of the great architects of the destruction of Hitler and his cohorts. He was not just a general, but a statesman and Premier. Finally, in 1959, he was overwhelmingly elected President of France," wrote Corporal Heller in the Battalion news, with the encouragement of Cartwright and the blessing of the colonel. "Let us do our utmost to honor this great man."

During a battalion briefing, Colonel Thompson told the staff that he wanted no carelessness and no overconfidence. "All of you know that General de Gaulle has never wanted NATO troops in his country. Actually, he wants us out! But, since we are soldiers attached to NATO, let's assure our Commander-in-Chief and the French police, who've been looking at us for the last sixty days, that safety and total protection for the general will be our foremost priority..."

After hesitating for a moment, the colonel asked for questions.

The battalion medical officer raised his hand.

"Yes, Doctor?"

"Colonel Thompson, may I have your permission to explore the possibility of setting up a first aid station in that old Catholic Church, about two hundred yards from the reviewing stand?"

"Good idea, Doctor! Take Corporal Heller along to translate for you. It'll save you a lot of time. By the way," the colonel went on. "I want all of you to look at the general's intended route as soon as possible."

When there were no other questions, the colonel gave his usual flashy salute, did about face and marched off with Sergeant Major Cartwright. "Sergeant Major! Be sure Zusette will be an arm's length from me on the platform at all times!"

It was a blistering hot day when the father of France finally came. The small town of several hundred had swollen to many thousands. Many of the local people had gathered their children on the massive carved stone steps leading to a towering Catholic Church, built in 16th Century Gothic style, with twin spires, flying buttresses, steep roofs and pointed arches.

Many people were sitting in the grass near a large marble fountain, where most citizens of the town collected their water each day in buckets and plastic jugs. Countless others were on either side of the street, all anxiously waiting to see their hero, who would be in the very first car. Special troops were everywhere. Finally a French military band from the Police Academy with wind and percussion instruments appeared with the general in the official car directly following. After his vehicle had reached the reviewing stand, the general was greeted by Colonel Thompson, who escorted him to the platform. The band members had settled in their chairs directly in front of the reviewing stand and started playing the French National Anthem. Heller, who was stationed on the far corner of the platform, but in sight of Cartwright, observed how all the people had rushed toward the reviewing stand, except several small children who were sitting on the rim of the deep fountain approximately 100 feet from where he was stationed. For a moment he envied the little children, who were holding their hands up to catch the water emitted from the many spouts and nozzles. He wished he too could submerge himself to avoid the blistering heat. He recalled that a Spanish explorer by the name of Ponce de Leon had erected fountains like the one nearby, in the State of Florida and elsewhere. He was roused from his reveries when a weeping young boy of four or five came running toward him. Crocodile tears and dripping nasal mucus indicated to Heller that the boy's mother had obviously lost him in her desires to see the general.

"Mon petit... Mon petit... mon petit frere a tombre dans la fountaine!" he wailed in desperation, pulling and tugging Heller by his pants. At once Heller reacted. Within ten seconds Heller had reached the fountain. Miraculously, he spotted the little boy's brother in the deepest section of the marble basin reservoir, face down. In another split second he reached in, grabbed and lifted the child from the cool water and hurriedly, but gently placed him on the grass, face down, resting his cheek upon one of his arms. Quickly, he checked the little boy's mouth, placed himself in position and started applying steady downward pressure to force water from his lungs. Heller repeated the full cycle of resuscitation again and again for several minutes. When he felt certain his little victim was ready, he turned him over, tilted his head back with one hand, while placing the other under the back of his neck. Quickly, he sealed the little boy's nose and mouth with his own mouth and started blowing air in. After repeating it for several long minutes, Heller noticed exhalation. But he kept it up until the youngster opened his eyes and resumed normal breathing.

By this time, the Army medics who were stationed high up in the church had spotted the commotion. After they arrived, they took the child to their First Aid Station where they treated him for shock.

Meanwhile, Heller rushed back to his station without saying a work to anyone about the accident. He was certain the youngster was in good hands and that the boy would be returned to his mother as soon as possible. It was all that mattered to Heller and he was glad.

It was a day the 202nd MP Battalion would be proud of. It was a colossal event Heller would not forget in his European experience. It was truly something to write his father in Key West about.

Of the many things which Heller experienced while stationed in France, he learned what a "Senior Sergeant Major" was, and what he meant to the command and to the men. He was convinced that he had not met the man in the Army who could compare with that uncommon soldier. "Not Sergeant Dollarhite. Not his drill sergeant, Lawson, nor his good friend, Sergeant Zusette. None would make a good size pimple on Sergeant Major Cartwright's butt, regardless of their dedication, or their loyalty to the Army," he said to himself. "No wonder the colonel chose him as his top NCO while commanding a combat battalion in Korea, then took him along to France, and, now would undoubtedly try to take him to his forthcoming command in the States."

Suddenly there was a loud knock on the door of Heller's room.

"Come in!" he said clearly.

When the door opened and Heller saw it was the Sergeant Major, he came to his feet. "This is a surprise, Sergeant Major!" he told him. "Is there something important, sir?"

"Of course! That's why I'm here. Got a seat for me?"

"Take my chair," he smiled. "I'll sit on my bunk. Sorry, I can't offer you anything."

"First, you know you don't have to call me sir."

"That started during my early childhood, when I said, 'yes, sir,' and 'no, sir' to my Dad. I don't know if I told you, Dad was a commander in the Navy. It's been habitual ever since. Surely you know how I respect you, Sergeant Major Cartwright?"

"I appreciate that," the top NCO said seriously. "But, let's be man to man. Colonel Thompson and I have our orders. We'll be leaving for Washington in the morning."

"I understand that, Sergeant Major Cartwright."

"Heller! You've been with us for over 18 months. You've done a bang up job. If ever you need a favor, the colonel and I will do whatever it takes."

"Thank you, sir."

"Heller! The colonel asked me to find out what your goals and aims are? Would you be interested in going to the Academy?"

"Yep! West Point! It's the colonel's Alma Mater." he told Heller, adding, "he'll have his first star after he gets to

Washington. Rumor has it that he and I will be assigned to Special Forces at Bragg."

"Good! I hope to see you there someday."

"You still wanna get to Special Forces?"

"Certainly, Sergeant Major Cartwright. Whatever that takes."

"Very well!" Cartwright said sharply coming to his feet. "I'll cut your orders for the John F. Kennedy School for Special Warfare at Bragg, with TDY to Fort Benning, where you'll take three weeks of Airborne training. Is that agreeable with you, Heller?"

"That's great, Sergeant Major. Thanks."

Heller opened the door for his guest. When he attempted to say something, Cartwright shushed him with his finger.

"Soooooo, start packing! Shake a few hands, especially Staff Sergeant Zusette's. Tell your friends that you'll be leaving with the colonel and me for the Paris International Airport at 0500. We'll be airborne by 0800 hours."

Heller reflected on what his boss had said before he realized he called Buck Sergeant Zusette, Staff Sergeant Zusette. "Was that a slip of the tongue?"

"No! It wasn't a slip," he replied. "Sergeant Zusette meets all requirements. He has the time, the experience and since a vacancy exists, the colonel thinks he's earned it."

"I'll miss him. He's one hell of a soldier."

"I agree," Cartwright smiled. "My replacement is gonna groom him for first sergeant."

Shortly before the giant airliner landed in Washington, DC, Colonel Thompson, who was enroute to the Pentagon before going on to Bragg, reflected on his image of a soldier. Said he:

"Regardless of those pseudo-patriots, the false prophets and those who dare patronize Castro, Ho Chi Minh and their ilk, let the three of us remember we are soldiers. We are bound by our comradeship, our mission and our oath," he emphasized firmly. "We must fight, kill or capture our enemy before they do it to us! That is our primary mission and our final objective. No matter what our MOS is, our priority is to fight to win battles for our country and our allies, as quickly as humanly possible. I was an instructor at West Point when General George Patton told the cadets, 'Wars may be fought with weapons, but they are won by men! It is the spirit of men who follow, and of the man who leads, that gains the victory. To be a good soldier a man must have discipline, self-respect, pride in his unit, a high sense of duty, obligation to his comrades and to his superiors, with self-respect born of demonstrated ability."

The colonel measured Cartwright and Heller with his eyes. "Let us be even more proud of our purpose as soldiers. Let us who wear our country's uniform remain totally dedicated. If need be, let all of us sacrifice with our blood, guts and sweat, and," he stressed forcefully, "stop apologizing for being soldiers!"

Chapter V

THE CHALLENGE OF THE AIRBORNE

Fort Benning is located on U. S. Highway 27, approximately ten miles south of Columbus, Georgia. For regular Army personnel, Fort Benning has the distinction of being the "Home of the Infantry". It is named after Confederate Major General H. L. Benning.

At the beginning of the War between the States, officer Benning served as commander of the 7th Georgia regiment. Since Colonel Benning led his regiment from the front, was fearless, calm and daring, his loyal troops referred to him as "The Old Rock."

In 1861, he was promoted to Brigadier General, and shortly thereafter, committed his infantry in such historical battles as Manassas, Sharpsburg and Chickemauga.

At the Wilderness, a region in Northwestern Virginia and south of the Rapidan River, several Civil War battles were fought in 1864, between Generals Ulysses S. Grant and Robert E. Lee. Although General Benning's infantry gave a good account of itself, fighting gallantly and dying bravely, it was there that the South realized it was fighting for a lost cause. Like General Custer, who dismounted at Little Big Horn to stand bravely with his troops, General Benning, stood proud and tall until he fell, seriously wounded.

All through history, the infantry has been enthroned as the Queen of Battles. Its position among the combat arms remains preeminent. By blood and sweat, privation and hardship, perseverance and nerves of steel, and by heart and soul has this distinction been won. Down through the ages when kingdoms rose and fell, when civilizations sprang up and disappeared, the infantry has been at the heart of the physical contests to influence the outcome of history.

It has been acknowledged that the "Infantry is a fighting machine with a soul, an instrument of War created by God, which no man-made machine may excel." It has also been said, "When people have been strong and sturdy, with love for God and Country, its infantry will show its qualities. But, when ease, licentiousness, luxury and the madness for money have rotted the heart of body politics, its infantry will suffer likewise."

When Corporal Heller went through Fort Gordon, he had heard and read a great deal about Fort Benning, which is one of the United States Army's proudest posts. Later, during Heller's tour of duty in France, Sergeant Major Cartwright had told him that the famed Infantry School was the most influential infantry center in the modern world. The Fort and the school are so intertwined that it is virtually impossible to trace its history without recording the evolution of the school. "From 1918 until the present, the development of Fort Benning has been directly proportioned to the progress of the school." wrote a military historian who made a study of the huge military post. "Throughout the many years the mission of Fort Benning and the Infantry School has remained fundamentally the same— to produce the world's finest combat leaders."

When the military aircraft circled Lawson field, before landing, Heller was astonished with the enormity of the post. "Three weeks?" he asked himself, shaking his head. "It'll take me longer than that just to find the post library."

"Look at that 500 bed Army Medical Center," a senior NCO remarked. "Yep! The Army takes care of its own."

When Heller presented himself with his orders at the Airborne School, the duty NCO smiled, and while escorting him down the hall to the Sergeant Major's office, explained that he was expected, although his orders had not yet been received by the school.

"Come in! Come in, Corporal Heller," said the burly NCO with the short crew cut, courteously extending his hand. "I'm Sergeant Major Clark. I'd like you to know that your old boss called me from DC earlier."

Heller was surprised. "Is everything all right? Something wrong with my orders, perhaps?"

"No! Not really!" Clark explained, grinning. "You're the only soldier I've ever received who beat the mail."

"I hope that's a compliment, Sergeant Major Clark," Heller responded. "Now that I'm here, what can I do for you?"

"I wanna talk to you. Get yourself a cup of coffee, grab a seat and let's talk about my old gray-haired buddy. Tell me Heller, does he still lead the troops on those five mile runs before breakfast?"

"He's one helluva brown boot NCO. Seasoned and preserved, with pungent humor and wit. A real professional!"

Clark laughed and shook his head. "I've never heard anyone describe him like that."

"You and Cartwright served together in Korea?"

"Yes, we did. I'll tell you he's one of those unsung heroes the press forgot to mention. I know! He saved my butt more than once over there."

"Tell you what - how about having dinner with me this evening at the NCO Club around 1900?"

"Love to, Sergeant Major Clark," Heller said, adding, "Anything special on the menu, like steak?"

"Sorry. It's fish night. I hope you'll like snapper? Red snapper."

"Sergeant Major Clark, I grew up on fish," Heller recalled, licking his chops in anticipation for a good plate of seafood. "I am sure you've heard of the character who'll walk a mile for a Camel? Well, I'd run five miles for a red snapper dinner, day or night."

During their meal at the NCO Club, the two men exchanged ideas and thoughts. The sergeant major asked numerous questions, such as Heller's plans about staying in the Army, about women, about Vietnam and about his family.

Heller told the sergeant major that he intended to be a lifer like Sergeant Major Cartwright or himself, that his childhood sweetheart jilted him, that he intended to become a trooper with Special Forces and eventually hoped to get to Vietnam to fight the Viet Cong.

Suddenly the sergeant major's face became serious. It was obvious to Heller he had something pressing on his mind.

"What's the matter, Sergeant Major Clark?" Heller asked, looking straight at him.

"Oh! I wanted to know you better before I made you an offer," he told him. "When I told Cartwright in a letter that I was losing one of my best jumpmasters, he thought you might replace him eventually. The job is one of the best in the Army and there's jump pay and all kinds of privileges. You'll meet everybody who's anybody and if you do well in school here, I'll see to it that you get another stripe."

After pondering what Sergeant Major Clark had proposed, Heller thanked him, then asked, "Why me? I'm still on my first hitch and I've never been near combat."

"You don't need combat experience," the sergeant major told him with force, getting impatient with the youthful corporal. After measuring him inch by inch with his eyes, he added, "Heller! I like your attitude about the Army, but what I like even more is the fact that you'll see no actual combat duty, unless you volunteer, because you're an only child."

Heller realized that Clark could get whomever he wanted for his Airborne School. It was positively choice duty. After hesitating a long minute, he said, "I'm really flattered, but, I'd like to suggest that you wait and watch my performance for the next three weeks first. I might flunk the course. And then there are my orders for Fort Bragg. If I stay here, provided I qualify, I'll never be able to compete with the real pros. Actually, I wanna get to Vietnam."

"O.K., Heller! I've said enough. Let's wait and see what happens? You might flunk," he challenged him, expecting the possibility. "Jumpmaster duties are demanding. The requirements for the job are like a preparatory exercise of authority - an imperative concept to know, a demand for absolute obedience, and exact enforcement of even the most diminutive detail. Get a slight idea, Heller?"

"Tell me more, sir."

"Besides the pilot, the jumpmaster is the senior qualified airborne individual on board the aircraft. He must, among other important things, be a graduate of a jumpmaster course. He is specially trained and experienced in airborne techniques to perform his compelling and commanding position," he explained in detail.

"There's only one designated jumpmaster in any one aircraft. He has command authority over and responsibility for all airborne personnel in that aircraft. He is responsible for an inspection of the aircraft and the personnel, the enplaning and the jumping of personnel, and the dropping of special material or equipment. His responsibility includes assurance that all airborne personnel aboard observe flight regulations and comply with instructions from the pilot."

While Clark paused for a moment, Heller had one of many questions. "Does the jumpmaster jump with his men?"

"He does in a tactical unit," he answered Heller. "But not during parachute qualification training. There the static jumpmaster normally does not jump with the students. Heller, you're a week early for our next class. Why not explore the files at the museum? You will see our operation and how we function. Cartwright told me you're a naturally inquisitive soldier. How you scrutinize and analyze procedures, regulations and orders, your feeling about the army and the country at large."

"Thank you, Sergeant Major Clark."

"I want you to see our files going back to 1940, when the German General Staff first employed parachute troops in Holland, which really shook up the tranquility of the War Department in DC, not to mention the combined Allied War Council in England. The Nazi deployment of their airborne shocked and staggered everybody. The big brass was amazed at the aggressive German teamwork subsequent to landings, their infiltration tactics, their rapid advance and their fire support, before and after they landed their forces. If you read through our files, Heller, you'll see what Hitler's parachute troopers did in their invasion of Crete in 1941. Here," he explained further, "for the first time in history, airborne forces were employed en masse in a combined effort of gigantic proportions. The German air forces obtained complete aerial superiority, and isolated the island, while glider borne and parachute troops landed and stormed key installations. Within hours, they completed and occupied the Crete Airdrome. I could go on and on, Heller. But, as I've told you, explore the museum and my office, with the thought you might decide to stay as one of my team instructors."

During the next five days and nights, Corporal Heller complied with Sergeant Major Clark's wishes, browsing and viewing the incredible files of the Airborne School. He was simply fascinated with this uncommon privilege, actually holding War Department documents and directives from early airborne thinkers.

Heller was stimulated and excited to read about the historic German "Blitzkrieg Tactics," most of which were accomplished by parachutists dropped in the vicinity of bridges, which were then quickly seized and held, usually against light counterattacks. Thus, when the German Panzers, constituting the ground elements of their airborne ground teams, had pierced the defense lines and had reached their objectives, further advance was assured. This type of operation sealed the fate of Belgium and Holland before its defenders could mount a counteroffensive.

Heller viewed letters from the Adjutant General in Washington, from the War Department Office of the Chief of the Infantry, from Headquarters of the Army Ground Forces and the United States Army War College. There were letters and memoranda from colonels and generals and from advisors who had witnessed the need for landing infantry from the air on hostile territory, to seize and hold strategic positions, such as perimeters of landing fields and beachheads.

By the time Heller had seen troop training and school

organization charts, itineraries, bulletins, activations, designation data, requirements, qualifications data, and had had several long conversations with office personnel, he was ready to accept his clothing and equipment and make his first jump from the 250 foot tower. Later, when he told Sergeant Major Clark of his enthusiasm, he was told, "Good! I've reviewed your medical and personnel records. Everything is in order. I have no doubt you'll fly through this tough training like a bat out of hell."

That night, moments before Heller hit his sack, he noticed a copy of a War Department Memorandum pertaining to standard requirements and qualifications on the side of his locker. He started reading,

"(1) Selections for jumping personnel to be made from unmarried volunteers only.

(2) Men with good military records.

(3) Age - 21 through 30 (both inclusive).

(4) Maximum weight not to exceed 185 lbs.

(5) Minimum visual acuity of 20/40 in each eye.

There was more, but Heller stopped reading. His ruddy complexion turned white. "Good God!" he said to himself. "I'm only 20 and I'm 15 lbs. over the weight limit. How could Sergeant Major Cartwright do this to me? He knew my age and my weight!"

After a sleepless night, he took a quick shower before reveille. He followed it with 100 push-ups, and when he saw the graduating class running around the barracks, he joined them, hoping to lose a few pounds. Terribly self-conscious and confused, he had a warm glass of water for breakfast. At 0800 hours, he requested permission to see Sergeant Major Clark.

The sergeant major listened courteously as Corporal Heller demonstrated his genuine concerns. He was still living according to the Scout Oath, although things were somewhat different in the Army.

"You did the right thing, Heller. But," he explained, "the memo is over ten years old and has been modified several times. Better run down to the mess hall. Ol' pappy will stuff you like a Christmas goose. He understands what we call first day jitters, and that soldiers about to become airborne need lots of energy.''

Heller exhaled whatever air he had in his lungs and quickly made his way to the mess hall. After he gulped down six eggs, seven slices of bacon, toast and four large glasses of milk, his strength and self-confidence were completely restored.

The airborne class Heller was assigned to consisted of Navy Seals, West Point graduates, Cuban exiles and so-called freedom fighters. There were a few Vietnamese officers, some Marines and many NCO's from the 82nd Airborne stationed at Fort Bragg. All were volunteers. All were tremendous physical specimens, fully aware of the parachutist's requirements.

''You are here by choice!'' a sergeant blasted to the assembled group, ''with only one purpose and one goal, to become Airborne! Nothing else matters! If all of you'll remember that and work with us, we'll have the largest graduating class ever. I don't know if you, any of you, really know how tough it is to get through this school. You'll either make it, or fail. We had a 31% failure in yesterday's graduating class. You might keep that in mind,'' he concluded, ''and don't become a statistic!''

Since Sergeant Major Clark had briefed Heller on the many qualifications, responsibilities and demands of the airborne school he was far ahead of most other students right from the start. When Raymond called his father in Key West to inform him that he was at Fort Benning's Airborne School for jumpers, he was high in spirit, proud and happy.

''On the day of your graduation, I will don my navy uniform and personally pin the coveted silver wings on your chest, provided, of course, the Army will let me,'' his father boasted in exultation.

''It would make me a very happy soldier,'' Raymond told him in an expression of love and respect. ''I'll see you in about three weeks.''

The first week was called ground week. Reveille was at 0430 hours. Thirty minutes later and before breakfast, the entire class of 400 officers and men were assembled in front of the barracks for their first four mile run. "We separate the men from the boys, right after we get back," remarked a young husky from the sergeant major's office, adding "I want a volunteer to lead. Any volunteer?"

When no one stepped forward, Heller raised his hand and was ordered to the front.

"Let's move out!" the instructor barked, looking at Heller. "Hold it down to a steady trot."

Breakfast was at 6:00 AM. When the mess sergeant saw Heller up front as usual, he joked, "Please leave something for your buddies, Heller!"

After a big meal, it was time for the indoctrination and general instructions by a sharp, youthful training officer, whose eyes travelled over the soldiers in their fatigues. "I doubt if any of you knew I was running with you earlier," he said seriously. "I was pleased and surprised that all of you finished the run. Of course, as time goes on things will get tougher. Many of you won't make it! After lunch, around 1500 hours, we'll run again." he thundered. "And again, sometimes, before lights out at 2300. Tomorrow, things will really start popping. You'll see and feel rigid inspections, every hour of the day, by your instructors, 'til they come out your ass. As I constantly stress, at the Airborne School there are no short cuts. By the time you get through, the robust will be sturdier and the unfit may try to qualify another time, perhaps. All of you must be dogged with determination, overly aggressive and bold. But," he warned, "don't be foolish in this vigorous and almost brutal routine, which may save your life if and when you face the moment of truth, finally jump with full equipment and dangle like a toy balloon."

The training officer hesitated momentarily. "I'm getting ahead of myself," he agologized. "Before that moment of truth, you stand in the door of the aircraft, most likely a C-130, flying at 1250 feet, grasping and holding it momentarily. You'll feel the wind sting your face and body, tugging at your uniform and your equipment. Then, when the red light flashes to green, and I pat you on your butt, you make a vigorous exit. You will free fall briefly, then feel your harness jerk and pull as your chute feeds out and fills with air. At that moment you must look up and around your canopy to see where your closest fellow jumper is. Then and only then, you'll look down. Even at 1200 feet, people look small. But, let me warn you, don't look too long. Observe your fellow jumpers. Start maneuvering your chute. The field below will be getting closer. Stay loose. Try to relax. Keep your feet and knees together. Get ready for impact. Let your legs absorb the shock and roll. Collapse your chute. Release your harness." The officer paused. "When in combat, unsling your weapon and quickly move to your assembly area. Deploy into position. Bear in mind that in less than three minutes time, you'll have to put into practice what we teach you in three weeks, here at the Airborne School. Gentlemen," the young officer stressed with prominence and force, "that's the way it is every time you jump! It's the challenge of the Airborne! It's the challenge for life! Your life!"

That night, after the lights had been turned off, Heller met a platoon sergeant in the barracks latrine, where together they studied the "Glossary" of difficult and technical terms, and the translation of a new system of names used in the school.

"Have you ever heard of a breathing canopy?" Heller asked his classmate. "That's one of the words in the nomenclature."

"A breathing canopy? Come now Heller ol' boy," he wondered. "Are we gonna talk about airborne equipment or human anatomy?"

"It states right here," Heller pointed with his finger, "a breathing canopy is the pulsating or pumping action of an inflated canopy during descent."

"Let's see the glossary, Heller," the platoon sergeant insisted. After he had convinced himself Heller was correct, he remarked, "I'll bet the character, who invented that kind of terminology for a descending parachute, must have been a half-assed medical flunky. What do you think, Heller?"

Heller smiled. "We've learned two words and only got fifty-eight to go."

"What's the next word?"

"Ripcord. I guess everybody knows what a ripcord is?"

135

"It's the handle you pull to inflate the reserve chute. Right?"

"Wrong!" Heller told him. "It says right here that the rip-cord is the device that consists of a cable, locking pins, and a grip which activates the parachute when pulled or released."

"That's what I told you, Heller."

"In essense, yes. But, not in reality. Office personnel told me instructors want all of us to learn these technical terms verbatim. They want no hedging, and no hiding. We'll just have to learn them," Heller suggested seriously, before he mentioned the next word which was "malfunction."

"I sure as hell don't know what the book says, Heller. Right this minute, my arms and legs, my little tired ol' eyes and my charlie-horsed toes are all malfunctioning," Heller's classmate jested in good natured ridicule. "Unless I get some shut-eye, starting now, I'll guarantee you my mind will sure as hell malfunction. I'll say goodnight, Heller."

Again, reveille was at 4:30 A.M. Some students failed to make the early formation and missed the four mile run. Others staggered toward the assembly and squatted in the heavy grass with dewdrops of moisture as large as grapes, until three ruddy faced instructors shouted bloody murder at the crouching postures, which finally began to straighten up.

"All students, fall in for morning calisthenics!" somebody shouted.

Heller hit the grass up front.

While the exercise was strenuous and even disastrous for many, Heller did it with ease and pleasure.

After breakfast, Heller's company trotted obediently to a 12 foot high platform.

"Welcome to the Swing Landing Trainer," one of the instructors told the class. "So, without further ado we'll all slip into modified parachute harnesses now and practice parachute landing falls. Do I make myself clear?"

"It's as clear as Georgia mud," some soldier jested in the back of the platform.

"All right! Who's the wisecracker?" one of the instructors wanted to know, looking around.

When no one volunteered, he continued. "This apparatus

is also used to practice the last four of the five points of personnal performance, which give the students practical work in executing frontal, rear, and side parachute landing falls. It all boils down to proper mental and physical conditioning, which are essential to insure that all parachutists are psychologically and physically capable to jump with a minimum risk of injury. We place emphasis on development of mental alertness, instantaneous reaction to and execution of commands, and increase confidence in each of you and in the use of your equipment. We speak from experience and positive standards of training, including strict discipline, high standards of proficiency on each of our training apparatuses, and during each phase of training, a vigorous and progressive physical conditioning program. Last, but not least, there is a strong sense of esprit de corps and comradeship among all parachutists, which you will also have, if and when you prove yourselves."

After the very first few days, ten percent of the students had washed out for not progressing in physical conditioning. Some would be recycled while others were returned to their parent organizations. The rest of the class trained strictly and harshly, according to the rules and requirement to attain maximum perfection with the chinups, pushups, sit-ups, and a myriad of other Army exercises including road running, in cadence to 180 steps per minute. Ground week also included fitting and wearing the parachute.

Heller learned that there are five points of performance, or specific actions, an individual parachutist must perform between the instant he exits the aircraft and his recovery after landing. While soaring through the air, he must check his body position and count, one thousand, two thousand, three thousand, four thousand; check the canopy; keep a sharp lookout during descent; prepare to land and execute a proper landing fall. The performance conditioning at the mock-up apparatus, where a correct body position is taught to minimize the possibility of malfunction during descent, is also of very great importance. Heller heard the Jump Commands used for a fully loaded C-130 Hercules aircraft over and over until they were firmly a part of his thinking. *"GET READY! OUTBOARD PERSONNEL,*

*STAND UP! HOOK UP! CHECK STATIC LINES! CHECK
EQUIPMENT! SOUND OFF FOR EQUIPMENT CHECK!
STAND IN THE DOOR! and finally the command GO!"*

The 34 foot tower was the worst part of Airborne training.
It is in reality a short replica of the 250 foot tower. It is there
the student experiences falling through space from a static
height which will help him overcome fear, familiarize him with
the approximate sensation of his chute opening, checking his
canopy and so forth, before he faces the higher steel structure
with its four projections or arms. These arms are used to lift
and release trainees using a regular parachute. Because of wind
conditions, usually only three of the four arms are used at any
one time. The base area of the tower is frequently plowed to
minimize injuries upon landing of students while they are practicing and learning how to control their chute during the
descent.

During the final week, three medium range Army transport
C-130 Hercules stood near the main runway, waiting for
clearance for take-off from Fort Benning's Lawson Field. Their
powerful four turbojet engines were roaring. Inside each aircraft, sixty-four potential Airborne troopers were seated according to rigid jump procedures.

After the big birds ascended, there was absolute silence
among the students. Only the instructors, now serving as jumpmasters, moved about complying with last minute details.

At the 20 minute warning, the jumpmaster alerted all personnel to stand by. Bundles of supplies and equipment were
quickly moved to the vicinity of the aircraft doors, where they
were attached to the anchor line cables. Just seconds before
the 10 minute warning, the aircraft in which Corporal Heller
was the leading jumper, leveled off at 1250 feet. At that moment, the jumpmaster started his final inspection to insure that
all personnel had their equipment properly attached and that
the jump straps of their helmets were firmly secured under their
chins.

When the pilot turned the red light on six minutes before
reaching the jump zone, the jumpmaster started issuing his commands, at which time the 64 soldiers leaned forward and plac-

ed both hands on their knees. They positioned their feet with the rearward foot forward, prepared to stand. All eyes were on the jumpmaster. After each complied with the command *"STAND UP"* the next command *"HOOK UP"*, made most hearts pound considerably faster. There was no turning back now. The plane would go empty to Lawson Field and return with another load of fresh jumpers. Even Heller, who was now facing the moment of truth in the number one spot near the exit, had a squeamish stomach at this profound moment. After proper hook up, he inserted the safety wire through the hole of the snap hook and folded it down. The static line was grasped in his right hand, directly over his shoulder. As the commands were given, each was confirmed by hand and arm signals by the jumpmaster since the droning engines and the jump helmets made it difficult to hear them.

Upon receiving the command *"CHECK STATIC LINES,"* each jumper checked the line of the man in front of him, with the exception of the last man, whose line was checked by the jumpmaster. At the command, *"CHECK EQUIPMENT,"* each soldier checked his own equipment. After all were positive everything was accounted for, the "O.K." was confirmed by hand signal.

The command, *"STAND IN THE DOOR,"* echoed sharply ten seconds before the pilot's red light would turn green. Heller shuffled into the jump door. Simultaneously, he pushed his static line toward the rear of the aircraft. He assumed a good door position and now waited tensely for the word *"GO!"*, which came a moment later.

He thrilled at the incredible freefall before the harness jerked his relaxed shoulders and a sudden muscular contraction caused a reflex action. Heller lifted his head to see his chute fill with air. Although he knew he was first to go, he still looked about for other jumpers before he started maneuvering his risers. In less than two short minutes, he would have to be ready for impact on a hard field. When it came, he relaxed his legs, rolled with the chute, stood firm, collapsed his chute, released the harness and quickly made his way to the designated area, now watching his classmates floating to mother earth.

There were fifty-one failures out of the original class of 400 students. Although several jumpers had sprained ankles, no other mishaps or accidents occurred.

Relatives and friends were permitted to observe the final jump. It was a proud day for one particular member of the onlooking crowd, Jim Heller from Key West, Florida. He looked forward to pinning on his son's chest the sterling silver wings he had specially commissioned.

Although father and son were happy to see each other at Airborne graduation, young Heller looked upon the ceremony as one more step to qualifying for Special Forces duty at Fort Bragg.

Heller was a happy young soldier until Sergeant Major Clark called him to his office to congratulate him on his perfect performance at the school.

"You've been one helluva asset, just like my buddy Cartwright told me," he said without a smile. "Before we send you to jumpmaster school, would you like to take some leave?"

Heller's face became red with embarrassment. He attempted to make conciliatory excuses. "Being with you, Sergeant Major Clark, has been an adventure and an experience. I've learned a lot, and according to Sergeant Major Cartwright, this will qualify me even further for my next assignment at Fort Bragg."

"Don't be embarrassed, Heller," the senior non-commissioned officer injected quickly, without permitting Heller to express his regrets. "I know why you're so damn anxious to get to Bragg."

"It's obvious, Sergeant Major Clark. My orders were cut for Bragg, via your command..."

"That's true! That's true!"

"Well, sir?"

"Cartwright called me from Bragg last night..."

"Yes, sir! How does that concern me, Sergeant Major Clark?"

"Before I had a chance to tell him you graduated at the head of the class, he told me there were extenuating factors, over which he had no control, that required your presence at Bragg.

When I told the ol' goat to stop beating around the bush, he told me that General Yarborough of the JFK Center for Special Warfare is waiting to pin the Soldier's Medal on your chest."

Heller was surprised. "A medal? For me? A Soldier's Medal? There must be a mistake," he told him unassumingly. "I haven't even been near a combat zone."

"Damn it, Heller! Cartwright said you rescued a kid..."

"Oh! Now I remember," Heller recalled with sudden pride. "I managed to pull a little boy from a deep fountain in France and revived him. Anybody could have done that..."

"Heller! Anybody else would have hung around like a patron saint," the sergeant major said firmly.

Heller smiled and jovially asked, "So? Am I going to Bragg? It'll be real nice to get to see my ol' boss again."

"Yeah! If I keep you, ol' Cartwright would probably show up with some of his Green Beanies. . . Tell you what, Heller...give Cartwright my best, because he is the best."

"I will!" Heller told him with admiration and respect. "And thanks for making me a better qualified soldier."

"Good luck, Heller."

"Thank you, Sergeant Major Clark. I'll stay in touch."

At 0800 the following morning, the three Lockheed C-130 Hercules transports from Pope Air Force Base, on loan to Fort Benning for Airborne training, returned to their home base for routine basic maintenance, with 142 Airborne qualified soldiers aboard. If there were a decline in the moral philosophy on Army standards, personal conduct, loyalty and personal responsibility to their units, or to themselves, it did not show in these men. They showed candor, commitment, competence and courage, as their gleaming new silver wings indicated on their Army fatigues.

Enroute, Heller became engrossed in a conversation with the crew chief about Colonel John Glenn. The crew chief claimed that Glenn was the father of the forthcoming space flights.

"He's much, much more than that!" Heller declared clearly. "In World War II and in that miserable Korean Conflict, he flew over 150 combat missions."

"And that ain't all," a 82nd Airborne NCO sitting in the

next aisle added. "He's got five or six Distinguished Flying Crosses and everything else except the Medal of Honor."

"Can any of you imagine seeing four sunsets in three and a half hours?" Heller wondered out loud. "Or flying from coast to coast in one of those new F8U's in a couple hours? They tell me if it flies, with or without a motor, John Glenn can fly it..."

By this time, the transports were circling Pope Air Force Base, and within minutes the new paratroopers were marching toward waiting buses.

Heller was flabbergasted to see Sergeant Major Cartwright sitting in a military jeep waiting for him. Before Heller could open his mouth, the sergeant major's reverberating voice roared above the noise of the aircraft, "On the double, Heller! Throw your gear in the back! In fifteen minutes, " he stressed glancing at his wristwatch, "General Yorborough will pin the Soldier's Medal on you."

As the jeep rolled hurriedly from the field, Heller remained silent. Suddenly Sergeant Major Cartwright remarked in a controlled voice, "Heller! Don't you have a mouth? Say something, damn it!"

Heller scratched the side of his face. "My Dad advised me some years ago that it is far wiser to be thought a fool, than to open your mouth and remove all doubt, Sergeant Major Cartwright. I consider this is one of those times."

"I am sorry, Sergeant Heller," the senior NCO soothed. "After all these years, I got a little nervous waiting, wondering if you might stay with old man Clark at Benning?"

Heller laughed.

"That's better."

Heller quickly took the initiative. "Sergeant Major Cartwright! You referred to me as sergeant a minute ago. What's the joke?"

"It's relatively simple, Heller. When the command received the medal and commendation of your uncommon performance of duty, I confirmed that you were a coming lifer and a professional. When I told the General that you wanna fight with the Special Forces in Vietnam, although you'd never have to go because you're an only child, and of your record at Benning, he thought you deserved another stripe..."

"Thanks. Thanks a lot, Sergeant Major Cartwright. I don't think I deserve it..."

"What the hell do you mean? I know you deserve it!" the big NCO insisted. As their jeep rolled toward the administrative building, Cartwright added, "Bring your records! Leave everything else in the jeep. After the General gets through with us, I'll take you to the quarters you'll have while you're training with the Special Forces."

"Yes, sir!" Heller replied from sheer force of habit, and followed the sergeant major into the building.

"Sergeant Major Cartwright, may I ask you one question, before we go in? I never met a two star before."

"Act the same as you did when I took you to our colonel's office in France...General Yarborough has the broadest national military goals. He believes in loyalty up and loyalty down. He places a high value on all of his Special Forces men. Value, personal responsibility and military ethics are words he mentions frequently in his conversations. I know for a fact that he's gravely concerned about the rest of the Army's discipline and the combined value and responsibility which is necessary in the leadership structure, as I've said, from the top down. In other words Heller, General Yarborough is a team man, not just a coach. One who believes officers and NCO's should earn respect by setting examples."

Suddenly, the sergeant major stopped abruptly at the unmarked door at the end of the hall. "Here we are," he said seriously. "Heller! You are about to meet one helluva soldier. He's youthful, slender and stingy with compliments, and he believes in his job..."

"Something like our Colonel Thompson was in France?" Heller injected.

In another moment, the two soldiers were standing in the door of the general's office. "Come in, Sergeant Major Cartwright!" came the deep voice of the tall, unpretentious two star general. He stood behind a desk loaded with stacks of documents and records. On the walls of his office were murals and pictures of Special Forces action in Vietnam. "Bring your protege!"

Cartwright and Heller approached the general. Their caps were neatly tucked under their arms. At two spaces from his desk, they snapped at attention and saluted simultaneously.

"Good morning, General Yarborough! Corporal Raymond Heller reporting, as ordered, sir!" Heller said sharply.

The general returned the salute and said, "At ease!" A moment later, he flashed a rare smile at Heller, before he apologized about his heavy schedule, then simply approached Heller, who snapped to attention, and simply pinned the precious Soldier's Medal on his uniform.

"I'm proud to have you with me in Special Forces," he said solemnly, reaching for Heller's hand. "You can wear this medal and your new sergeant's stripes with pride. Congratulations!"

While at the John F. Kennedy Center for Special Warfare, Sergeant Heller and 49 other potential SF soldiers, learned very quickly that *Being good isn't good enough.* In their initial briefing they had Sergeant Major Cartwright's welcome.

"We challenge you. We dare you to dare!" emphasized Cartwright. "For now, I'll define what each of you will experience for the next four weeks in your rigorous training to augment that which most of you have already learned. To start with, gentlemen," he continued, "all of you have met the initial requirements for SF training. All of you had a score of 100 or more on your entrance examinations. You're all eligible for Secret security clearance, with no felony connections. Each of you can swim. All of you have a high school diploma, or better. All of you have passed the physical fitness test to meet Special Forces medical standards. You've gone through basic, advanced and Airborne training. According to your records, which I personally checked for flaws, each of you have at least eighteen months on your present enlistment remaining, after completion of training here. If you're serious about Medical Specialty training at Fort Sam Houston, twenty-four months of obligated service must be on the books." The sergeant major continued further, "None of you fifty have adverse personnel actions pending. None of you has lost time.

No one has overseas orders and none of you have terminated a previous Special Forces or Airborne duty assignment."

The senior NCO paused momentarily. "All Special Forces soldiers are highly intelligent, trained and motivated paratroopers. Most of you are multi-lingual. All of you are experts in at least one or more of five specialties, such as communications, weaponry, operations and intelligence, demolition and medical aid. You are in fact triple-volunteers, who chose to join the Army, became parachute jumpers, and met extremely high standards of our Special Forces. As you have heard, all of you will receive considerable training in geography, customs, local foods, animals, political history in the area in which you will serve. You'll train in jungle warfare, and high altitude-low opening parachuting called HALO for short. You'll get in some SCUBA diving and a considerable amount of hand-to-hand combat training. However," he cautioned, "it will be with cold steel, not with Boy Scout rubber Bowie knives. Gentlemen! In South Vietnam, Cambodia and Laos, the miserable peasants, the farmers and the montagnards, look upon Special Forces personnel as their saviours and friends. We can't let them down. We can't and we won't! Any questions?"

When there were none, Cartwright added, "I'll see you at 0500 hours in your working fatigues for a nice short five mile hike. You can clean up before you go to breakfast. At 0800 sharp, get back to this room for further instructions. Class dismissed!"

The four week Phase I was divided into two subphases. The first subphase of two weeks was spent primarily in the classroom and dealt with unconventional warfare subjects. Heller checked Webster's for its meaning and found it defined as a type of warfare that violates the rules or customs established by society. The second subphase was a field training exercise, which lasted fourteen days in the Uwharrie Forest, northwest of Fort Bragg. During the FTX, the soldiers applied all the training they received during Phases I and II and the first part of Phase III. They infiltrated by parachute in a HALO night jump and established contact with resistance forces on the ground. They then trained and directed resistance forces in the conduct of unconventional warfare against aggressor forces.

After completion of the course, with the students sitting in their final class, Sergeant Major Cartwright asked Sergeant Heller what he thought. Without the slightest hesitation he answered, "The toughest part of the course was those murderous runs at all hours of the day and night. And the SF confidence course has to be the toughest in the entire Army."

"What did you think of those obstacles?" the sergeant major wondered.

"I doubt if the war in Vietnam could be tougher than what we've gone through right here at Bragg and Camp Mackall," Heller supposed, while the rest of the graduating class nodded their heads in silent approval.

After the final phase had been completed, Heller and his classmates stood tall and straight in formation for a hearty handshake from the commander of the Special Forces school, the priceless skill identifier and the authorization to wear the green beret with the "flash."

At the suggestion of Sergeant Major Cartwright, Heller took another eight weeks weaponry course, which prepared him still further to operate anything from a musket loader to a 106 mm recoilless rifle. He also learned how to clean, fieldstrip and fire eighty different domestic and foreign weapons, as well as Claymore mines, hand grenades, and every kind and type of ammunition for the various weapons. In an eleven day FTX students had the opportunity to use the skills taught them during the course. Heller "live-fired" the Redeye guided missile, the Swedish K Submachinegun, the LAW anti-tank weapon from our own country, the AK-47 assault rifle from the USSR and the UZI submachinegun from Israel.

As graduates of Special Forces weapons course, they became specialists, qualified to train the forces of foreign countries in the use of small arms and the tactical employment in the defensive and offensive role. They could also train foreign forces in infantry tactics on the squad, platoon and company level, to include raids, ambushes, patrolling and map reading.

All Special Forces graduates are experts in guerrilla and counterguerrilla warfare, fire planning for infantry, direct and indirect fire weapons, and the security, maintenance and storage of weapons and ammunition.

When the time came for Heller to re-enlist in July 1966, he was ready to fight anything from Bengal tigers to Viet Cong, and he knew it. He was also left with fatherly advice from his friend, Sergeant Major Cartwright. "Regardless of what you hear about the erosion of military ethics of officers, practice loyalty up and loyalty down. I hope you'll spread that disease."

Chapter VI

A GRATEFUL ARMY COMMANDER

By midnight, Sergeant Heller and Doc Blanchard were waiting for instructions in the command bunker at Loc Ninh. When Colonel Outlaw and his staff arrived, including Majors Armstrong and Tieu, the two NCO's greeted them with a snappy salute. After the officers returned it, the colonel emphatically said: "Gentlemen! Let's get down to business. . .We have a job to do. I'm sure we'll give the Viet Cong a big surprise tonight. For one thing, my 1st Brigade is ready, willing and able. I'm counting on it. Now, check your men's weapons and verify our defensive positions that they are properly manned. If there're no questions, move out!"

According to his command sergeant major, Colonel Outlaw rewrote the book on the Infantry. The colonel had once told him that the Infantry was a fighting machine with a soul, that it was created by God and that no machine would ever excel it. Although he went to West Point, he once told his son that if he truly wanted an education in the Army, Fort Benning would have it all.

Later, when Heller spotted Colonel Outlaw's sergeant major inspecting the perimeter firing line, he asked if it was true that the colonel as a small boy shined Black Jack Pershing's boots?

The command sergeant major smiled and confirmed the rumor. "I know he did it. He told me he did and I have no reason whatsoever to doubt him. I visited his quarters at Fort Benning some years back and saw a personal autographed picture of General Pershing and his black stallion. I'll tell you this, Sergeant Heller—my colonel has served with Bradley, Patton and Clark and once was on General MacArthur's staff."

"In other words," Heller said seriously, "the colonel knows what he's doing?"

"You can bet your boots on that!" he told Heller.

At precisely 0030 hours, as was anticipated, the Viet Cong activated their attack with rockets, recoilless rifles and heavy machine guns. The moment the VC fire became sporadic, the most venerable "Spooky" was on station, droning continuously, dropping flares to illuminate the area between Camp Loc Ninh and the nearby jungle brush. When the new defenders of the camp saw what was estimated as a battalion of black clad VC guerillas advancing en masse, they were ordered to hold their fire until the enemy actually approached the barbwire. "Then, and then only, will we start blowing their heads off!" Colonel Outlaw had ordered.

Heller and Blanchard were in the heavy machine gun pit close to the west wall. It was upon this flank that the howling mass of disciplined communist hordes advanced, screaming and expending their ammunition, even before they reached the outer perimeter.

"Hold your fire! Hold it just another 20 seconds!" the fighting Colonel shouted.

When the most forward VC dropped their wooden ladders over the barb and concertino wire, Colonel Outlaw blew a whistle and the fire fight commenced.

As the Viet Cong mortar fire hit the wall with mysterious precision, ripping man-size holes therein, the defenders were either killed or wounded by shrapnel fragments. When Heller and Blanchard heard cries for medics, they both ran from position to position to encourage the defenders. "Spread out!

Spread out! Keep down! Back off from the wall; hit the ground; fire your weapons from a spread eagle position. Don't fire unless you have a target!"

The VC kept advancing. When they reached the wire, most hesitated for a brief second, wondering if they should go over it, under it, or through it. Ladders or no ladders, they would get entangled and torn, if not by bullets, certainly by the barbwire. They knew either would rip the flesh from their body. This was the moment bullets would slam into them.

During the height of this night combat, the soldiers in the forefront saw Colonel Outlaw was there with them, firing his light weight AR-15, firing it from positions vacated by casualties. The bird colonel also offered encouragement, reassurance and advice, like a typical gunnery sergeant on the firing line. During this time, he inspected his troops, evaluated their accuracy and their courage. Now and then he would speak to a soldier calling him by his first name. A moment later he would pat them on the shoulder, "Keep up the good work, John or Jim or Henry, whatever. Watch that right front. . .Use your grenades when they get too close! Don't try to be heroes! Do your job and survive."

Even though the noise from gunfire, grenade explosions, and the cries from shrieking wounded soldiers of both sides was constant, the deep voice of the colonel reverberated like a sound wave on a mountain lake in Maine. Only when a runner appeared from the command bunker, did the colonel leave the front. "I'll be back, boys. Remember the reputation of the Infantry is at stake." he shouted at his soldiers, running by them in a crouch.

Then he was gone.

Suddenly, when an enemy bugler sounded what obviously was a call to withdraw, the Viet Cong stopped advancing. Like puppets on a string, controlled by the puppeteer, they simply turned and ran through the holes of barbwire, and in the direction from whence they came. At this point many defenders were jeering. At least for the time being they had scored a victory, giving them a chance to draw more ammunition, get a cup of coffee, a cracker or two, or relieve themselves.

At that moment a tall young Army captain appeared at the west wall and eyed the situation. In a crouch, he made his way by Heller's machine gun position to the wall, just as the last flare from Spooky had died out. When the captain noted that the relentless defensive fire had almost ceased, he poked his head cautiously over the wall to see the fleeing VC, leaving their dead and seriously wounded in the darkness. In another moment there were more flares from another Spooky on station. Once more it looked like daybreak, revealing countless VC bodies entangled in the barbed wire. Several were still alive, obviously pleading for help. Some were bleeding profusely, their eyes staring. Torn VC bodies littered the ground.

Without thinking of the consequences, the captain ran back to Heller's machine gun pit. "Hey! You two guys! Are you asleep? Let's go after them! We got them on the run! I say after them!"

Heller and Blanchard exchanged looks. Not only were they confused, but neither of them had ever seen the captain before. "But," they reasoned, "he is an officer." His uniform so indicated with two shining silver bars on his collar.

Heller shrugged. He was positive Colonel Outlaw would not have ordered pursuit of the disorganized VC, who would regroup in the woods and return for another assault.

"Is this an order from the colonel, sir?" Heller questioned. "I beg the captain's pardon..."

The aggressive young officer could not believe his ears. Enraged, he jumped into the machine gun pit. "You what? Damn it! I gave you an order! Follow me or I'll have you court martialled for cowardice!"

"Sir! I was present in the command bunker..."

"Let's go! And bring all those CIDG's up front, who're relaxing!" the captain ordered further. "We'll chase those humpbacked gorillas right back to the Ho Chi Minh trail!"

"You've heard the captain's order!" Heller finally shouted loud and clear. "Let's go! Take your ammo and whatever you're firing and head for that big hole in the west wall. Move!"

A buck sergeant from the 1st Brigade questioned Heller's order. "Going after them is suicide! We'll be cut down like flies! Just supposing the colonel has ordered an air strike, like he should? The pilots couldn't tell the difference between us and the VC..."

"The order comes from an officer. I know it's irrational and utterly illogical. But it's an order. Let's move it!"

"Yes, sergeant!"

When the last of the reluctant Brigade soldiers stumbled near Heller, he grabbed his arm. "Soldier, this is an order! Our lives depend on it! Run to the command bunker! Tell Colonel Outlaw that a young captain ordered the troops on the west wall to pursue the fleeing VC! Run!"

The young soldier took off like a bat out of hell.

"Here's hoping," he thought to himself, as he joined the rest of the small force, who were now approximately 25 feet behind the officer who was leading them.

Spooky continued droning high above, dropping flares, spitting bullets at the VC near the edge of the jungle growth. Suddenly he veered off as if he inadvertently had overlooked something and was now positioning his aircraft to make another run.

"The colonel got the word from the runner," Blanchard thought aloud. "I'll recommend you for a good cigar, Heller..."

"Damn it, Heller!" remarked a CIDG NCO, who spoke English like an American. "We'll follow you anywhere, but, this, this officer...where in hell is he from anyway?"

"Pass the word up the line to consolidate when we get to the brush. If the officer is still alive by then, tell him I want a conference. Spread out! Go! Go!" he ordered. "Stay close to the ground and snake forward!"

"What do you want me to do, Heller?" Blanchard asked. "Just name it."

"Crawl from man to man. Find out how much fire power we have and try to find our rambunctious captain," Heller persisted. "I'll wait to hear from you right here, say, in five minutes. All right, buddy?"

"Right, Here I go!"

In less than three minutes Blanchard came back on all fours.

"That hot shot officer is dead. So are four CIDG's, who were with him. The VC surrounded them...Here's their dog tags. The wounded are helping each other. All of them know that the VC will launch another assault. We had better get back and out of their way.

"Thanks, buddy! I'll recommend you for a chocolate milkshake," Heller said jokingly before getting serious. Let's move up. You take the lead. I'll stay ten yards to your right, slightly behind. Go!"

Two American soldiers came crawling toward Heller. "Both of us are slightly wounded, sergeant," one of them said with contempt. "Really nothing to worry about."

Heller smiled at the two and patted the nearest on the shoulder. "Crawl through the grass to the wooded area for consolidation. Then we'll make it toward camp."

"We'll make one sweep for wounded. If you find one not breathing tear his dog tag off and move on."

"Right, sarge!"

"Pass the word to those you find in one piece, that we'll take a short rest, then high tail it back to camp. I'll lead..."

"That stupid captain!" the soldier groaned. "We might all get killed."

"True!" Heller acknowledged. "Right now we'll have to make a move and make it fast. I can feel another VC assault in my bones..."

Suddenly an enemy phosphorus shell flashed like lightning in an electric storm when it hit near Heller's position. Recoilless rifle and vicious small arm fire raked the grass where Heller's comrades were clinging to mother earth, trying to seek cover behind blades of grass.

At the first lull, Heller instructed the buck sergeant to move up. When he failed to respond he stabbed him with his forefinger. "Move up!" he told him once more. "I'll cover while you try to get some of the men back to camp."

When the NCO still didn't move, Heller took a closer look. The young American sergeant's entire head and skull were split in half and his brain was hanging out over his nose.

"That idiot, captain!" Heller said between his clenched teeth, as he removed one of the sergeant's dog tags and put it in his pocket with the other five.

Heller remained dispassionate. His attitude of controlled alertness under such critical circumstances surprised the few soldiers close by, who looked to him for guidance and direction.

"We'll go from here!" he ordered thoughtfully. "Anybody left with grenades?"

"We have four between the three of us..." the nearest soldier responded.

"Pass them to me...all four of them. I think I can reach the low brush, where VC may be waiting. When I throw the grenades, stay low and rush close to the exact spot where they land. You can be sure you'll have no contact with VC there. On your way, cover the forty or so yards as quickly as possible and take anybody still alive along. After you consolidate, stay put 'til I get there."

Heller laid the grenades carefully on the ground. "One more thing, men. If you spot any grenades on any living or dead, take them along. If possible, grab any loose weapons and take them along, too."

"What about ammo? Suppose there isn't any for those weapons, sergeant?"

"If you see ammo, take it along too, if you can. At least take the weapons. When the guns are out of ammo, we'll throw them at the VC! Understand?"

"Yes, sir!" the small group answered in unison, giving the young Heller the respect normally rendered a seasoned combat veteran.

"Stand by! Here we go!" Heller confirmed, pulling the pin from the first grenade. He raised his head for a split second to note the terrain and the brush approximately forty meters to his straight front. Then, coming to a kneeling position, he hurled the first projectile to the edge of the brushy growth. After the explosion, a screaming jibber-jabber began which obviously had a startling effect on other VC. They could not tell the source of the grenades. When Heller threw a third and finally his last, several soldiers rushed over the dead and took from them what they could carry. They picked up the wounded and quickly, but cautiously took the edge of the brush, where surprised Viet Cong guerrillas were overwhelmed by a desperate small group of soldiers who were not ready to die. Blanchard was among them. He had been seriously wounded in the chest and in the legs. "Where's Heller?" he mumbled in obvious agony. "Did he make it?"

"Make what?" Heller asked, approaching Blanchard on his belly.

"You big clown, you...You're still the best grenadier in, in, in the Army," he uttered feebly but with admiration, before he was overtaken by unconsciousness.

Heller began tending his friend's wounds as he ordered the six kneeling troopers, "You guys throw those grenades you picked up as far as you can in the direction of the jibber. Form a semicircle around me. Ya got it?"

"Yes, sir!" replied the nearest trooper.

Heller counted the grenade explosions. There were six, then all seemed quiet for a moment. Suddenly, the VC launched a short mortar attack at the surviving Special Forces detail. But the projectiles overshot their mark. The VC still weren't sure where their enemies were located.

Heller found that Blanchard was still breathing. He was shivering and quivering and his teeth were chattering. "Shock!" He knew it well. He knew he had to keep Blanchard warm. "One of you take the jackets off the dead VC and cover him. On the double!"

Heller ripped the leather shoestring from one of Blanchard's boots and tied it above the bullet wound to stop the loss of blood from his thigh. Pulling it tight, he placed his green beret under the string to insure pressure. When he was positive he had stopped the bleeders, and Blanchard's body was relatively covered with enemy clothing, he summoned what was left of the patrol to give them instructions.

"I want each of you to fire everything you can muster in rapid fire to let the VC think we have a strong force right here. Then, I want you to spread out, stay low and try to get back to camp. You will stop for nothing! I'm certain the colonel has somebody out there by now, looking to rescue what's left of

155

this stupid lost patrol. Any questions?'' Heller asked a soldier closest to him.

"What about you? Don't you need some help with Blanchard?"

"Hell, no! One of you count to fifty...then go!"

In less than a short minute, Heller watched the survivors zigzagging through a hail of small arm fire coming from the brush.

Heller laid his buddy on his back and prepared to pick him up. He took a deep breath and exhaled as he lifted the almost lifeless weight of his friend to his own back.

At that instant Heller started an incredible journey out of the brush. Before he took his first step, he froze to a sound he thought he heard. It came from a short distance to his left, perhaps fifteen to twenty yards, he estimated. Then he spotted them. There were four Viet Cong, slowly making their way directly toward Heller.

Heller dropped to his knee and quickly, automatically pulled his 45, but changed his mind. He was alone and there were four, or more, of them. He suddenly spotted a single grenade on Blanchard's belt. He unhooked it, pulled the pin and threw it at the VC, who never knew what hit them.

Knowing it was a matter of minutes before other VC would follow, Heller adjusted his buddy over his shoulder, like a farmer does a sack of potatoes, and started running toward open terrain.

A VC saw the movement and, after taking a few moments to assure himself that it wasn't another VC, he came to his knees and threw a grenade toward the moving Heller and the soldier he was carrying. Both men went down in a heap. Heller was seriously wounded, but he was mentally alert. His head was spinning. Although he was physically as developed as a professional wrestler and could move like a big league fullback, his strength began to wane. His vision became faint. For a second he thought he saw a VC coming toward him, but he waved it off as an illusion. When he heard the crackling and sudden sound of grass and branches being crushed by somebody's feet, he took a long look. His vision cleared and he saw a VC in black, coming toward him brandishing a machete.

Heller threw his Jim Bowie knife with a fifteen inch blade with as much force as he could at the VC's chest. The man grunted with pain, gave Heller an astonished look and then fell forward, as the knife had penetrated up to the hilt in the guerrilla's heart.

With super-human effort and with excruciating pain, Heller raised Blanchard onto his back and started crawling out of the heavy jungle grass toward the open field. He knew his left leg was almost useless, that he was weak from loss of blood and that his once enormous strength was deteriorating. Still, he kept pushing and advancing, like a slow moving, tree dwelling sloth.

"Sooriee," Heller implored the Special Forces recovery team, who found them. "Ta tak e caarr ooofan bb bbud dyy. Weeee, aarree oonly on lefftt..."

After Sergeant Heller had made that and other incoherent sounds, he sank into total unconsciousness.

He did not know that his buddy Blanchard died on his back. He did not know that Colonel Outlaw's recovery patrol combed the brush and found four dead Viet Cong guerrillas in one pile and a short distance from them another who had a Jim Bowie knife in his heart, which had his initials thereon. Nor did he know that the patrol found some seriously wounded CIDG's still breathing among the dead VC's, who eventually told the full tragic story of an inexperienced young officer who should have listened to his team sergeant, instead of ordering him and the soldiers on the west wall to pursue the fleeing Viet Cong.

Neither did Heller know, or care, that the colonel recommended him for the Silver Star, and that he dispatched a helicopter to fly him to the nearest Field Hospital at Saigon for further evaluation and an emergency operation at the 93rd Field Hospital in Long Nien.

Chapter VII

DESPAIR WITHOUT FULFILLMENT

After several operations at the 93rd Field Hospital in Long Nien, where many pieces of shrapnel were removed and bones were set, and where Sergeant Heller's entire abdominal cavity and lower extremities were totally immobilized with a plaster cast, he was transferred to the Third Field Hospital in Saigon. After another brief evaluation there, Heller and fifty other critically wounded casualties were flown to the Central Medical Evacuation Center.

Another flight took the wounded to Travis Air Force Base. There, a special evacuation hospital aircraft took them to Womack Hospital at Fort Bragg, the home of Special Forces.

By the time he and the other casualties had arrived at the huge military hospital, the Patient Administration Division (PAD) had sent telegrams to next of kin, announcing their condition and their arrival. When Big Jim Heller got the call, he threw his overnight ready-bag in Raymond's convertible and headed north. Later, after driving through the city of Marathan, a State trooper stopped him, driving 75 in a 55 mile zone. When the trooper asked him where the fire was, he explained that his son, Raymond Heller, who had been fighting in Vietnam, had arrived at Womack Army Hospital in Fort

Bragg, North Carolina, in critical condition. "I got the Army telegram..."

"Never mind, Mr. Heller. I recognize you now," the officer said calmly with a big grin on his face. "You're the one who threw those college hippies off your boat out in the Gulf Stream..."

Before Mr. Heller could comment further, the trooper told him that he would escort him over the next five bridges and would also notify every officer on duty in the Keys, all the way to Miami, to clear the right-of-way for him.

"Good luck, Mr. Heller. Give my best to your son!"

Fifteen hours after receiving the telegram, Mr. Heller arrived in Fayettville, NC. Ten minutes later, he entered Fort Bragg, where a sympathetic Army MP escorted him to Womack. When he attempted to enter his son's room on the sixth floor, several Army nurses with a team of assistants were preparing him for surgery.

"Sergeant Heller is due in OR this very minute," one of the nurses informed Mr. Heller curtly. "If you're a member of his family, please join the others down the hall in the waiting room. Besides," she explained further, "he's so heavily sedated, I doubt if he would recognize his own mother."

"Please! I'm his father. Just one look?" Mr. Heller pleaded. "I've driven almost a thousand miles, all the way from Key West."

"All right, Mr. Heller," she agreed reluctantly. "One fast look! No attempt at any conversation, while the gurney is rolling by. Let me assure you, sir, the Army takes care of its own. He's in good hands. His vital signs are stable and all our surgeons will do their best."

Suddenly the vehicle was pushed near Mr. Heller and he managed a glance at his son's weary face.

"Thank you, madam," Mr. Heller sighed, nodding his head vigorously. "I'll be in the waiting room for news."

"After surgery, the chief surgeon will speak with you," the nurse added stiffly, ushering him toward the other anxious relatives and friends.

Mr. Heller thanked the Army nurse once more, then slowly

entered what he thought could not possibly have been the ward waiting room. It was densely packed with numerous bemedalled and decorated, suntanned combat veterans. He was flabbergasted with the soldiers' loud voices and he thought that perhaps the Army was conducting a military critique.

"I must have gotten into the wrong room," Mr. Heller said loudly to a senior non-commissioned officer, who appeared to be distressed also.

"I don't know why you're here, sir?" the grayhaired, muscular NCO remarked. "We're all Special Forces, waiting to get the word about one of our illustrious comrades, who's in the operating room, right now."

"Would that be Heller? Sergeant First Class Heller?" Mr. Heller wondered, watching the NCO who appeared astonished. After a pause, Mr. Heller proudly announced, "You see, I'm Sergeant Heller's father."

The noisy room suddenly became a hushed motionless stillness.

"I'm Sergeant Major Cartwright, Mr. Heller," the NCO told him, with sympathy and apology in his voice. "All of us here have an affinity with your son of whom we're so damn proud. But, Mr. Heller, let me introduce you to some of the best combat veterans in the Army. Gentlemen! Meet Mr. Jim Heller, who's our favorite sergeant's father from Key West."

In spite of the enduring pain in his heart, Mr. Heller grinned and raised his right hand in a semblance of a civilian salute.

"Gentlemen! I'm impressed. I never dreamed of your kind of loyalty for each other. When my son gets out of OR, he'll really appreciate your concern."

"Perhaps we can all have a beer at the NCO Club?" one of the younger NCO's suggested, looking and waiting for a reaction. When none came from anyone he said, "Pardon me! I'm just a little thirsty. . .dryness in the mouth."

"Close it, Moose," Cartwright said distinctly. "If you can't wait 'til we get the surgeon's report, I'll get you a glass of water myself."

There was a long period of quiet stillness, which Mr. Heller broke. "Sergeant Major Cartwright! How was it that you practically beat the hospital aircraft here? It's beyond my comprehension, how fast you got the word about my son."

"It's really quite simple," Cartwright spoke softly. "The old colonel who whipped the VC's at Loc Ninh told his sergeant major to send me a message. Another Special Forces NCO called me from Travis by telephone, which he confirmed by letter several days later. I might tell you, Mr. Heller that your son has been recommended for the Silver Star. He's an incredible, unbelievable hero, which doesn't surprise me," he explained. "I had an ardent admiration for him in France. At the time, when the colonel wanted to recommend him for West Point, he declined. He told me then that he wanted to fight with Special Forces in Vietnam. Well, sir, with that in mind, I cut his orders myself that same night and brought him back with us. I guess you saw him get his Airborne wings at Benning?"

"Yes, sir! I was proud to have had that privilege," Mr. Heller recalled with pride. "I pinned his wings on his chest."

"Mr. Heller! Let me tell you a little more," Cartwright insisted. "At Camp Mackall and again with SF at Bragg, he was either the top man in all his classes, or the next one down. As we all know, he had to volunteer for combat in Nam because he's an only child. On his very first mission, he lead a recon patrol and found all kinds of weapons, and at the same time his volunteers killed five VC guerrillas without losing a single man. Somewhat later, while on a 48-hour pass, he killed a VC guerrilla pimp wielding a knife with his bare hands. I'm real proud to have had my hands on his mold. No telling how far he might have gone in our Army, if that idiot, over anxious officer hadn't got him into trouble, which cost him his own life, plus eight or ten CIDG's and your son's best friend. Yet, he accepted that order to show that when a superior officer gives an order it has to be obeyed. He led by example!"

The room again became quiet. The silence lasted almost thirty minutes before Sergeant Major Cartwright said, "Men, let's bow our head for one short minute and say the Special Forces prayer..."

As the soldiers bowed their heads, Mr. Heller could feel a

161

strange vibration. Emotionally, he joined silently with the Lord's Prayer, as the group around him recited,

Almighty GOD, Who art the Author of liberty
and the champion of the oppressed, hear
our prayer
We, the men of Special Forces, acknowledge
our dependence upon Thee in the preservation of human
freedom.
Go with us as we seek to defend the defenseless and to
free the enslaved.
May we ever remember that our nation, whose motto
is "In God We Trust," expects that we shall acquit
ourselves with honor, that we may never bring shame
upon our faith, our families, or our fellow men.

Grant us wisdom from Thy mind, courage from Thine
heart, strength from Thine arm, and protection by Thine
hand.
It is for Thee that we do battle, and to Thee belongs
the victor's crown.
For Thine is the kingdom, and the power and glory,
forever, AMEN.

When the soldiers had finished their prayer, the Chief Surgeon entered the waiting room with several dozen restless professionals. When they saw the medical officer in the white smock, all hands including Cartwright jumped to their feet and encircled him.

"Which one of you is Sergeant Heller's father?" he asked with a happy smile on his face.

"I am he, sir!" Mr. Heller said quickly. "What about my son? Please tell all of us. Please, sir!"

"Gentlemen! Most of my news is good," the doctor explained. "We were able to pin his hip bone and the upper femur together. But..."

"But, what, doctor?" Mr. Heller and Cartwright asked simultaneously.

162

"Severe casualties, such as your son, will usually acquire psychosomatic affects later on. Trauma and delayed stress are the other half of the battle. We'll just have to wait and see."

At this point Cartwright raised his hand.

"You have a question, sergeant major?"

"My question is - - when can we visit our young hero, sir?"

"Leave your number with my office. I'll call you. . ."

"Yes, sir! Thank you, sir."

"What about me, doctor?" Mr. Heller wanted to know. "I've come a long way, doctor. Raymond is all I have. . ."

"From Key West, I believe?"

"Yes, sir."

"I assume you were an officer in the Army in the second World War and undoubtedly belong to the AUSA, the Association of the United States Army?"

Mr. Heller smiled for the first time in three days. "No, sir. I was in the Navy. I was a mustang, mostly in the Pacific. When Raymond was born, my wife died. . ."

"Very sorry, Mr. Heller. But in spite of your loss, you obviously raised one hell of a fine youngster? I know he'll come through the depression, exhaustion and the nervous tension. But, it will take time," the doctor explained. "As is, your youngster's driving force and incentive impulse makes me almost positive he'll leave this hospital in five or six months at the most."

"Anything I can do. sir?"

"I'm counting on you, Mr. Heller. Tell you what," he said. "Why don't you go down to his room and wait for him to wake up. I'm Dr. Markham. I'll keep my eyes on him."

When Mr. Heller got to his son's room, a young Army nurse in a flawless, starched white uniform with a slight smell of antiseptic was just leaving.

"I'm Captain Rogers, Mr. Heller," she smiled beautifully. "I see no reason why you couldn't wait in your son's room."

"Thank you, Captain. . ."

"I presume the sergeant is your son?"

"Yes, mam. He's my only son. How is he?"

" If you haven't heard, the operation was remarkably successful. But, we'll have a special watch on him, just in case he has nightmares."

"I'm grateful, Captain Rogers. Thank you."

"For what? I haven't done anything yet."

"For being so informative and for what you may be doing in the future."

"Why don't you go in, Mr. Heller? But, try not to rouse him. Please wait for him to open his eyes. Will you?" she suggested, adding, "By the way, Mr. Heller, it may well be my imagination, but I think I've seen your son before somewhere."

Mr. Heller grinned at the gorgeous nurse, and tiptoed into the room. Quietly, he moved the only chair closer to his son's bed. He sat down, facing him, while his lips started to move in silent meditation, reflecting upon the very first time the navy nurse brought him into the nursery at the Naval Hospital, and gently lifted a tiny corner of the baby blanket, so he could get his very first look at him.

"That was 22 years ago," he said to himself. "A lot of water has run over the dam since then!" His mind wandered back as he sat quietly in the dimly lit hospital room.

The day before he arrived at the Key West Naval Air Station in 1944, all of the base naval activities had received copies of his orders. Thus, as was customary, there was an official welcome for him by the commanding officer and his staff, first at the aircraft and somewhat later, at the air station officers' club.

There numerous officers and their wives or companions were patiently waiting to comply with the rules of decorum for a returning hero.

"Big Jim Heller," as he was called before he enlisted, cared little for festivity at the time. His thoughts were about his wife of four days, who knew he was finally coming home to do a normal tour of shore duty.

"Surely," he thought, "everybody knows Kitty is expecting me. How in the world can they drag me into the club?"

When Captain W. I. Lewis, Jr. and his staff entered the club ballroom with Lieutenant Commander Jim Heller in their midst, the officer of the day thundered, "Attention!"

All hands in their spit and polish vernaculars rose, except those of flag rank and their ladies, until the official party was seated. At that moment, Captain Lewis, standing close to his vivacious wife Marlene, nodded his head toward the duty officer, who instantly gave the command, "Carry On!"

Minutes later, the bemedalled commanding officer rose and proclaimed, "Ladies and gentlemen! I am positive all of us are proud and happy to honor a former enlisted man, who has returned to us this day. To the neophytes, let me say that Lieutenant Commander Heller is a product of 31 Knot Arleigh Burke, who dared to tangle with the Tokyo Express in the Solomon Islands. Therefore, ladies and gentlemen, let us drink a toast to a fighting man's home coming."

The celebration was festive, hilarious, joyful, but short. After numerous toasts, many junior officers almost mobbed Commander Heller with handshakes and questions. All of them wanted first hand answers. None wanted to hear more myths, mysteries, or surprises. Admiral Ingersol of Anti-submarine fame, was sipping scotch at the next table. Abruptly, the stalwart naval officer leaned toward the commanding officer's table and suggested that Lieutenant Commander Heller should give an account of himself and of his experiences while with the Pacific Fleet. A brief moment later, the youthful Navy captain came to his feet again.

"Ladies and gentlemen!" he announced clearly, but smiling, while waiting for the noise to subside. "Ladies and gentlemen!" he repeated once more. "Commander Heller will honor us now with a short critique. If all of us will listen, we may indeed learn something we don't already know..."

Compulsively and intelligently Heller rose from his chair. Bowing slightly like a gentleman should toward the Admiral and his ladies, he said with confidence, "Admiral Ingersol, Captain Lewis, ladies and gentlemen! Before I begin I'd like to propose a special toast to Stephen Decatur, who was one of our greatest naval patriots..."

"Granted!" echoed through the officers club. "Granted!"

"Let us lift our glasses high," Heller urged with pride. "As Stephen Decatur said—'Our Country! In her intercourse of time with foreign nations, may she always be in the right. But right or wrong, our country!"

The robust Admiral jumped to his feet. All others in the large officers' club did likewise.

"Let's drink to Admiral Decatur and to a very fine young officer, who knows his history," he proffered with propriety, while Heller waited patiently to start talking.

Ultimately, Heller cleared his throat and leisurely addressed his peers and the ladies. "On December 1st, 1941, I received my orders for the Battleship *USS Arizona.* After a three day honeymoon our aircraft approached the Hawaiian Islands and most of us tried to get near a window to see the paradise of the Pacific. As our D.C. 6 flew over Diamond Head and got near Pearl Harbor, the pilot dipped his wings for all of us passengers to see the big naval base. Well, as it was, ladies and gentlemen, I sat next to an old Army colonel, who suddenly jumped to his feet and shouted: "My God! My God! What in hell is the matter with Kimmel and Short? They must be idiots, or mad to ignore rumors that the Japs might attack Hawaii, whenever they think it's advantageous to them! Why, the whole Pacific Fleet is sitting below!"

The club loaded with several hundred officers was now as quiet as a morgue. Lieutenant Commander Heller had made his point with effectiveness.

"Go on! Go on!" somebody shouted near the bar. "What happened next?"

"Like everyone else aboard, I rushed to the window. At a glance I had to agree with the colonel," Heller went on. "Our entire Pacific Fleet was at anchor below," he persisted nervously. "It was 0600 Sunday morning the 7th day of December when we arrived at Hickham Field and shortly thereafter I had coffee with the distinguished Army officer at the BOQ. When I asked him who Kimmel and Short was, he simply told me that Kimmel was the Admiral in charge of the naval base and that Short was the General responsible for our entire Island chain and in overall command of all Army personnel. After I left that angry colonel, I grabbed my luggage and caught a ride with a sergeant, who was headed for Pearl

Harbor. As luck would have it, the miserable old vehicle got a flat tire five hundred yards from Hickham. While the driver changed to his spare, I noticed what a delightful warm and sunny morning it was. Churchbells were ringing in the distance. Seagulls were gliding gracefully, like children playing in a school yard. Suddenly the gulls disappeared and I wondered why. Abruptly, I heard the sound of approaching aircraft, shattering the peaceful environment. In another short moment I saw the roaring twin-engine bombers with the round red balls painted on the fuselages. They were in tight formation and I wondered why. In another second I realized they were Jap warplanes, now attacking Hickham Field with heavy demolition bombs, levelling and demolishing everything above the ground. The explosions rocked and trembled the ground I was standing on. It seemed as if an underground volcano had erupted, throwing monstrous geysers of boiling lava over the entire airfield, swallowing the aircraft parked wing to wing and the living and the dead soldiers and airmen. Ladies and gentlemen," Heller went on. "There was nothing for me to do, other than to crawl behind a pile of cut coconut trees. I watched helplessly as the incendiary and demolition bombs rained down. When I actually saw the smiling profiles of the Sons of Nippon pilots strafing whatever was left standing, I took refuge in a deep man-hole in the middle of the highway."

Heller stopped long enough to take a swallow of water, then continued. "All of you know what happened to other Army and Navy facilities and Pearl Harbor. In that blatant daylight attack, my ship, the mighty Battleship *ARIZONA* went down with 1201 officers and men. At the time many of us wondered why the Imperial Jap Fleet didn't invade Hawaii," Heller propounded, lowering his voice, sweating from remembering the grotesque sight of the flaming bodies he saw running from Hickham Field, screaming, rolling like sticks of firewood near their aircrafts, heroicly attempting to save them.

"The Japs wanted to cripple the Fleet and as much as possible of the Army," a young Army officer thought aloud, in the back of the club.

Heller wondered if indeed he ought to continue. After all

167

it had been almost two long years since the relentless attack, which had cost the United States over three thousand dead and an untold number of men mangled, maimed and mutilated.

The hushed stillness in the club suddenly ended when one of four Army officers rose and declared, "Gentlemen! Let us drink a toast to the gallant soldiers of Hickham and Schofield, and to those men who survived to fight another day! Let us hope and pray that General MacArthur will wipe out the Jap bandits from the Pacific!"

At that profound moment the flashy commander of the submarine base stood near the Admiral's table. "Please join me in a toast to the sailors, soldiers and to General MacArthur!" he suggested so forcefully, it sounded as if he was giving an order.

Heller set his empty glass down before him, desperate to get home. "Surely they'll let me go now," he thought when Captain Lewis shouted, "Go on, Heller! Go on!"

Heller nodded. "Sir! I could go on and on. I could eulogize an untold number of Army and Navy heros. . .But, wouldn't you have a heart?" he begged, with a serious face, standing erect and debonair. "I would like to get home and give my beautiful wife her first order. . ."

Once more the club vibrated spontaneously with laughter. After things had quieted down, one of the officers boasted, "Did you say you're about to give your brand new wife her first order?"

"Yes, sir!" Heller told him, pleading with his eyes and his voice. "May I have the privilege to leave, gentlemen?"

The distinguished commanding officer smiled at his beautiful wife. He chose his words deliberately. "Commander Heller! You have our permission to leave, provided you'll tell us what that first order to your wife will be. Will you share it with us?"

"Yes, sir!" Heller replied quickly. "I'll share it. . . When my wife comes to the door, I'll pick her up, carry her to our bedroom and order her to deliver a ten pound baby boy in nine months and twenty-seconds. . ."

This time the club members really roared with laughter. Most of the ladies stirred emotionally, some with tears in their eyes.

By the time Heller got his hat near the exit of the club, the bartender lifted a giant glass of beer high above the bar and literally shouted, "Ladies and gentlemen! Let us all drink a special toast in honor of Commander Heller's first son. As he told us so eloquently, in nine months and twenty seconds, we may well have another potential sea captain in our ever growing fleet."

After the final toast, the club became alive with laughter, shouts and meaningful advice from well wishers as Heller stood near the exit. He raised his right arm high. His hand touched the visor of his hat. Suddenly, he sliced with expertise, in a salute not routinely seen except at Annapolis and West Point.

Ten minutes later, officer Jim Heller arrived at his home on Simenton Street in Key West. The very moment he raised his hand to knock, the door opened and Kitty stood there in her wedding gown, with arms out, reaching for him.

"Kitty! Kitty! Kitty, my love..."

"Jim! Oh, Jim! My precious husband," she cried joyfully, while tears were running freely down her lovely cheeks. "Jim! I've missed you sore...ly."

After Jim Heller had literally drowned his wife with passionate kisses, he swept her off the floor and carried her into their bedroom, where she clung to him with affection, desire, need and love.

" I love you. I love you, Jim," Kitty whispered to her husband. "War or no war, I need you," she rambled on as if she were in a trance. "Darling, I want a baby. A little boy, who'll look like his dad..."

"You little darling. You must have a sixth sense," he told her grinning from ear to ear. "I hope you don't mind. I kinda mentioned at the club that in nine months and twenty seconds from the moment I land on the front door, you'll be delivered of a ten pound baby boy..."

"Darling," Kitty laughed. "Please put me down and help me out of my gown. We've already wasted fifteen precious seconds..."

"Oh! Of course! Of course!" he stuttered, as he put her on her feet, then assisted pulling the long zipper of her dress, going down on his knees to remove her satin slippers. In another moment he stood fascinated. He watched and observed her every move, remembering their hasty wedding at the Air station chapel and their three day honeymoon, 20 months earlier. He watched her completely and finally disrobe, trying to recall the reasons why she kept the wedding dress for this moment. Jim remained motionless, bewitched, captivated by Kitty's delightful qualities and femininity. After she had disrobed, she looked at her husband's fixed face. At the moment she appeared emotionally vulnerable, shy, covering her firm breasts with her arms, reassuring him that indeed, she was real.

In dismay, she asked him, "Darling, aren't you gonna take your uniform off? We are married you know..."

"Oh! I'm sorry. I've fantasized this bewitching moment every hour of the day...Now, that it's here, I still find it hard to believe."

"Please, Jim," she urged. "I've been waiting for so long. My body is yearning for yours. I thought you would overwhelm me with love and affection. Instead, you brag at the club, then stand around wasting..."

Jim Heller, finally came to life. He tore the uniform from his body. Seconds later, he lifted Kitty from the floor and laid her gently on the king-size bed.

For another brief moment he feasted his eyes upon Kitty's sensational figure, her slim waist, her flat tummy, her long creamy thighs, her long blonde hair which covered her breasts, and the radiance of her glowing face.

"You're sensational, delicious, darling. You're the epitomy of what us poor frustrated men at sea dream about," he whispered in her ear as he embraced her. At first, he held her tenderly, afraid he might hurt her. Finally, he took her passionately in the ultimate phenomenon of love, the most noble and wondrous exultation, humanity's greatest triumph. Married love was indeed in fidelity with God and man.

From that moment on, lovely Kitty Heller knew that she would be with child. Being married and being together, sharing pure joy, contentment, gratification and ecstacy in endless streams of fullfillment was now a complete reality. Rights, obligations and needs were now positively joined, imbued with utter humility and pride. It was a total commitment, spiritual and holy, conceived in human dignity, faith and love.

There was never a day that Big Jim Heller failed to bring candy, flowers, and numerous other presents, including a 14-karat gold eternity ring with six diamonds and an equal number of sapphires, to his wife who was expecting her first child.

"Darling," she told him one morning at the kitchen table, "You're spoiling me rotten. How can I possibly repay you?"

"I'm trying to bribe you, Kitty," he told her, placing his hand on her abdominal cavity and giving her a meaningful good-by kiss. "Remember it has to be a ten pound boy."

"Ah! I see it all now. I see what it's all about," Kitty smiled. "I knew you had a motive. Well, my darling husband, you can stop trying to bribe me with presents. I promise you it will be a ten pound baby boy, even if it kills me."

Jim Heller turned white. He turned toward her and grabbed her roughly by the arm. "You beautiful idiot!" he said harshly, staring into her eyes. "Don't you know saying things like that is a bad omen?"

"I'm so sorry, Jim," Kitty said irreproachably. "Surely you don't believe in omens?"

"Of course not, Kitty. It's just that I feel some things are better unsaid, that's all. Please kiss me. . .see you after school."

As the days passed into weeks and the weeks into months, Kitty followed her prenatal instructions to the letter. Her obstetrician was her husband's best friend at the Key West Naval Hospital. He tailored her pregnancy to her individual needs and prescribed a complete and well balanced diet for her and her son.

" You can relax, Kitty. It will be a boy," he assured her. "In all my years as an obstetrician, I have never been more positive."

"You wonderful man," she smiled at him. "I think I'm gonna kiss you on the cheek. . ."

"Please do," her doctor urged her. "I'll promise I won't tell anybody, certainly not my wife. . ."

"I'll do it for you, doctor," she told him with glowing happiness in her eyes, as she hugged the navy medical officer and kissed him on his brow.

"By the way, Kitty, as you know my wife Becky is with child, too. Why not get together with her? Start doing a little shopping. Think about little things...little blue things, for boys. Think about ten dozen diapers, little blue cotton shirts, blue crib blankets, blue nighties, blue diaper pins and perhaps a dozen baby bottles..."

"Oh! You dear, dear man," Kitty remarked with pride, always smiling. "I'll breast-feed mine. No bottles for us."

"That's good. That's very good," the doctor nodded affirmatively. "Breast-feeding is best for mother and baby. The mother's milk is far superior during the early months of life because it offers a full range of nutrients for growth and health. Nursing your son benefits you physically an well as the child. Also, nursing your son hastens the return of the womb to normality, as well as your weight and your shape," the doctor concluded, in his informative chat with his favorite patient. "Kitty, please follow my instructions," he indoctrinated her further. "Take long walks with Jim. Gets lots of fresh air and take deep breaths. If you experience any discomfort, such as bleeding, persistent headaches, nausea, persistent vomiting, unusual swelling of feet, hands or face, fainting spells, etc., please contact me at once. Otherwise, I'll see you in sixty days. All right?"

"Thank you, doctor. Thank you," she repeated several times, her green eyes sparkled and her face was radiant with expectation and happiness.

Meanwhile, Jim Heller was enormously happy at home and while teaching at the submarine school, where most enlisted men patronized him against his wishes. Jim Heller never failed to tell them at least one true story of navy combat action, stories about General MacArthur, Stilwell, or about men and fighting ships, stories of United States Marines, the courageous Army nurses on Guadalcanal, the powerful Tokyo Express and last but not least, the awesome power of the battleships.

During his shore duty at Key West, Lieutenant Commander

Heller was best known for special assault gunner training and how to use the multible "hedgehogs and mousetraps" when fighting German U-boats. Among other critical requirements, Heller insisted that all instructors must have had actual combat experience aboard a warship, preferably with newly perfected sonar equipment. Heller and his handpicked instructors were knowledgeable on sophisticated electronic, supersonic echo ranging equipment, graduating approximately 10,000 officers and enlisted men. Without exception these men were positive that the terrible U-boat menace was being slowly, but surely, eliminated.

There was great joy, when word was received in Key West that General Mark Clark and his fifth Army landed in a flanking movement at the seaside resorts of Anzio and Nettuno, about 30 miles south of Rome. The general sent a personal letter of thanks to the Chief of Naval Operations lauding the personnel deployed on Army and Navy supply ships, who were coming and going to Italy and the new African front. They were sinking a large number of German U-boats in the middle of the Atlantic.

Veterans of rank, who were familiar with the war effort in Northern Europe, especially in England, acknowledged that ships with "Killer personnel" aboard, were in fact greatly responsible for getting critical supplies for an eventual European D-Day.

That June, 1944, the GI's General, Omar Bradley, in the Battle Cruiser Augusta, directed four Allied armies sweeping ashore on the beaches of Normandy. Not a single U-boat was encountered. The Stutka dive bombers were being eliminated by a numerically superior fleet of American fighters in support of the stupendous armies, which swept across France and, in due time, into Hitler's Germany itself.

General Eisenhower's command was "Attack! Attack! Move forward on all fronts."

It was no longer a secret that the German Grand Admiralty could no longer risk their dwindling number of U-boats roaming about the Atlantic without fixed goal and territorial range. The massive American convoys in the North Atlantic enroute to Murmansk in Russia, via Reykjavik in Iceland, feared neither U-boats or Stutkas.

Although Lieutenant Commander Heller was promoted to full Commander and had his orders to command a brand new super coast guard cutter to work in coordination with the Atlantic Fleet, he respectfully declined the assignment. When his superior officer confronted him regarding his decision against commanding the new ship, Heller explained that his wife Kitty was with child and that he had reasons to believe she was having complications. "Sir! I might not perform well in critical situations while aboard," he told the officer, who understood the seriousness and regretted not having Heller's combat experience from the Pacific. "Jim! You are still on rotation shore duty," he told him. "When and if your personal problems subside, a command assignment will be waiting for you. As is, I'll assign another qualified officer, who'll consult with you regarding the Caribbean Islands where German U-boats are still lurking. Jim, keep up your wonderful work at base and give my best to Kitty and her forthcoming son..."

"Thank you, sir! You're very kind to understand," Heller told him with regrets. "It'll probably be over in six or seven weeks."

At home, Heller recognized the ongoing complications for Kitty. During the day he kept a constant vigilance by calling her from the naval base at all hours. At night, he watched her in silence. He was appalled to observe how his son kicked so terribly hard within her. It appeared that the youngster wanted out of his mother's womb right this very minute. Two weeks before Kitty was due to deliver, she was diagnosed as having mental depression. Although Heller insisted she must stay at the hospital and must have a day nurse at home, she refused both. "Please! Please!" she cried. "Please be patient with me, Jim! My time has not yet come."

Jim Heller was desperate. To ease things at home, he took two weeks leave to be near her. There were more complications and Jim begged her, "Kitty! If what you tell me is true, you obviously don't have labor pains...you don't even have minor cramps. You couldn't possibly have contractions...So, for

God's sake darling, please let me take you to the hospital, if it isn't all ready too late..."

Even though Kitty would not hear of it, Jim Heller called a Navy ambulance, which appeared in a matter of minutes. By the time Kitty arrived at the hospital with Jim by her side, her temperature was 104. Her throat, lungs and all her joints hurt her painfully. At first the young medical officer at admission thought Kitty had rheumatic fever. When she started bleeding from her mouth and nose, and they spotted blood in her urine, he called the head of surgery, who summoned the chief of obstetrics. A further examination revealed there was an enlargement of the liver, the spleen and the lymph nodes. The laboratory specialists found that leukemia cells in her peripheral blood smear had obviously penetrated the bone marrow. The lady was also hemorrhaging from her womb. The team of medical specialists diagnosed her illness as acute leukemia and placed her on the critical list.

When the commanding officer of the hospital received word that Kitty was terminal, he handpicked the finest surgeons, including her own obstetrician to take the child by caesarean delivery.

"Gentlemen!" the Captain said clearly. "We'll have to have Jim's consent to take the child...Is he with her?"

"He is, Captain," came the sad voice from a surgeon in a white smock, simultaneously announcing that the operating room was already on standby, except for scrubbing.

At that profound moment, Jim Heller stormed into the Captain's office. With a strong outburst of emotion, he verbally assaulted Kitty's obstetrician, calling him a Quack, firing unceasing questions at anyone who would listen.

The Captain of the hospital stepped forward and took him by the arm. "We're doing all we can, Jim," he told him with compassion. "Jim! We'll have to have your consent to take the child by caesarean section. Please, Jim. Every second counts..."

"You have it, sir!" he shouted, pleading for them to save Kitty if there was a choice.

"What hurts so badly," he rambled on, "is that I had to

hear the OR Nurse discussing Kitty's critical condition as I was making my way through the hallway! Tell me, Captain, is it true? Is my Kitty terminal?''

Jim Heller was completely vanquished, stunned and in a state of trauma, after the Captain informed him that the diagnosis was confirmed and irreversible. The Captain was solicitous. He looked troubled, searching for words of encouragement. With a heavy heart, he suggested that they call on the Divine Creator in the chapel and pray for a miracle.

When Heller and the Captain arrived at the entrance to the chapel, Heller changed his mind about entering.

"Captain! I wanna see her! Please, sir! I got to!" he begged, virtually writhing his wrists from his powerful arms. "Please, Captain! Please, sir!"

The Captain nodded. "We'll have to run for it. They ought to be entering the OR just about now. We'll wait right here..."

At that very moment a white covered gurney and a team of nurses and corpsmen were coming down the hallway. Two of the ladies in white were carrying IV bottles with whole blood. When the vehicle started to move past the two officers and Heller saw the numerous needles and tubes attached to Kitty's arms, legs, nose and mouth, he turned pale. His eyes stared at the Captain, who ordered the team to stop.

"Please let Commander Heller see his wife for a brief moment!" he ordered gently, much to the surprise of the team.

"But, Captain!" a nurse objected bitterly. "Every second counts."

"I know, nurse," the Captain judged solemnly and with great seriousness, as the frustrated Jim Heller leaned over the gurney and wailed like a wounded prairie wolf.

"Darling! Darling! I'm so sorry you're suffering so terribly...Please don't die...I couldn't live without you...Our life is just beginning...I need you," he begged with earnest humbleness, imploring some kind of a response, which did not come.

"Jim! Kitty is so heavily sedated," the Captain pointed out, patiently, "she's totally unconscious."

At that moment the gurney rolled through the swinging OR doors, and the Captain led Heller back to his office.

While the surgeons and their crews labored diligently and painstakingly on Kitty in the OR, the CO reassured the expectant father about the fiducial professionals, with their skill, faith and their special magic.

"I'm positive you'll have a normal child," the Captain insisted, "except..."

"Except what, sir?" Heller shot querulously, staring into the symphathetic eyes of the Captain, now sitting behind the heavy mohagony desk. "Except what?"

"Jim," the Captain explained further, with a smile on his face, "come to think of it, our chief obstetrician, who I've heard is a personal friend of yours, personally told me that Kitty's boy is so immense and is of such superhuman size, he actually anticipated having to take him by caesarean delivery....."

Heller almost smiled. "Skipper! I think you're just trying to amuse me. Aren't you, sir?"

"It's the gospel truth, so help me, Jim," the Captain insisted, glancing at his wristwatch. "But, as is, Jim, the child will be no problem at all. It's the mother, Jim...."

"What is this Leukemia thing, sir? Is it some kind of a cancer? Can they save her? At least prolong her life? Will she regain consciousness? See and hold her son?"

The CO intended to explain one question at a time. However, his secretary suddenly entered and informed them both of the baby's birth. Heller rushed to the hospital nursery where he met an OR nurse carrying a large bundle of blue baby blankets.

"Captain!" the nurse smiled delightfully. "Under these blue blankets is the Heller baby boy. He weighs in at eleven pounds, eight ounces. If you gentlemen care to have a look at the largest and healthiest child ever born in this hospital's history, I urge you to do it.

The CO of the hospital was overjoyed, while Heller looked mummified.

"And besides all that, he's got green eyes and blond hair," the nurse added with disbelief, looking at the Captain.

The Captain smiled and thoughtfully said, "This is a special child. What do you think of your son, Jim?"

Heller suddenly came to life, as if someone had given him a "polynesian hot foot."

"You mean my son is under that bundle of blankets?" he managed to say, slithering toward the nurse holding the brand-new bundle of humanity.

"He sure is," the nurse added. gently lifting the tiny corner of the baby blanket, and Jim Heller finally got his very first look at his son. A feeling of euphoria came over him. Joy flittered through his bloodshot eyes. When he found his voice again, he innocently shouted, "Thank God! Thanks, Captain! Thanks to the doctors, the nurses and the corpsmen. Thanks! Thanks! What can I say, nurse?"

"Well! While you're thanking everybody," the nurse proclaimed with pride, "I'd better get this bundle to his stall and feed him...Just look at him. He's eating his whole fist..."

"Hold it, nurse!" Heller ordered. "Just as soon as his mother comes out of sedation, she'll breast feed him..."

The nurse glanced at the Captain, covered the child's head again, and quickly left without another word.

After the nurse had departed with the baby, the Captain put his arms around Heller's massive shoulders and ushered him down the long corridor, toward Kitty's room.

"Count your blessings, Jim. You have a fine, healthy son." The Captain paused there, trying his words before uttering them. "Jim, I've been a realist all my life," he stated plainly. "As is, Kitty's problem is ominous...Let's hope and pray that the Divine Creator will hear and favor us, and that the boy will not be afflicted..."

"Yes, sir," Heller replied. "I feel so helpless, futile, small..."

"Jim! I've left word for someone to come-a-running to get you in my office, if and when Kitty regains consciousness. Meanwhile, my secretary will keep you supplied with her delicious coffee," the officer explained. "I have an important inspection at the submarine base. So, relax and pray. It's a matter of time...all right?"

"I'll comply with your wishes," Heller told the remarkable Navy career man. "I'll stay with your secretary 'til I'm called."

Two long hours later, Commander Heller was finally ushered into his wife's spacious room. Eleven dozen roses adorned the numerous medical accessories, enhancing the appearance of the room. IV bottles were standing and hanging everywhere. Some with whole blood. One of the three nurses was wiping Kitty's face with an alcohol sponge. Another arranged the pillows under her head and fluffed them with her hands. A third nurse carefully laid her baby boy next to her and uncovered him. Heller stood motionless. He was afraid to breathe. Suddenly the baby started to wail and Kitty opened her green eyes. The man she loved was but inches from her face. "Darling, aren't you gonna kiss me?" she asked in a soft whisper, trying to smile, now looking at her eleven pound, eight ounce boy.

Heller looked at the nurse close to him. "May I kiss my darling little mother?" he inquired of her.

"Yes. By all means," she told him. "Please be gentle."

"Kiss me now, my precious husband," Kitty whispered, barely strong enough to keep her eyes open, "and hold me in yourrr arrrmms...I, I lovvv youuuu..."

"Kitty!" Jim cried softly into the bed sheet, complying with her wish, to cuddle her in his arms. The beautiful young mother flashed a tired smile, closed her lovely eyes, turned her head toward the child and stopped breathing.

The doctor and one of the nurses who had been monitoring Kitty's heartbeat, stormed into the room. One of the other nurses grabbed the child and rushed from the room toward the nursery. One of four surgeons told Heller to wait outside, while another nurse pushed him through the open door.

Heller saw a team of doctors rush into the room. He knew they would do everything possible to keep his precious Kitty alive.

However, the doctors failed to re-establish the heartbeat. Kitty Heller had died.

Outside, Jim Heller recognized the naked truth. Precious Kitty and his beautiful dream had come to an end. With determination, dignity and love, he would remain monogamous and loyal to his Kitty. He would rear his son and would name him after one of his favorite Admirals of the Navy, until he too, some day and in time, would join her at the place where the angels live forever.

As "Big Jim Heller" sat there, facing his son in Room 600, he bent slightly over the bed and folded the sheet several inches to watch his son's face. While he waited patiently, bearing and enduring his son's obvious pain, he thought about President John F. Kennedy, who had been assassinated in Texas, and, how Lyndon Johnson inherited the responsibility of trying to convince a divided country that Vietnam had indeed become an undeclared American war. Mr. Heller thought about the waves of dissent, which rocked the United States and how college professors and other intellectuals spearheaded student riots and those who espoused, preached, even praised the Viet Cong, and collectively organized deserters and draft-dodgers, who fled to Canada and Cuba. He remembered how members of the clergy and radicals from college communities encouraged burning draft board offices and draft registration cards, desecrated and defiled the American Flag. He recalled how the Students for a Democratic Society organized leftists, radicals and their ilk, literally espoused Marxism in major colleges and universities, and, how black student union supporters rampaged through buildings, leading to Martin Luther King's march on Washington, D.C.. Last but not least, there was Jane Fonda and her frenetic radicalism, in frank support of Hanoi, while irresponsible and incompetent public officials, pseudo experts and self-seeking windbags stood silently in the wings of Congress, wondering what side of the bandwagon to get on.

Big Jim Heller had known a small number of deserters, who used the war as an opportunity to get out of the country, due to their personal problems. Most of those he knew had financial difficulties, marital and family problems and many other personal reasons. He knew some had deserted from military service, not necessarily because they were afraid to die, or because they hated their military superiors for their own weaknesses. Many of those who evaded serving thought that the draft boards were unfair, allowing the wealthy to remain in colleges and universities, while the poorer class were forced to fight 9000 miles from home. There were those who received financial assistance, council and assurance that once the war was over, the politicians would get them unconditional amnesty. "They will do it gladly for votes the next time around," they were counseled, when they asked their leaders what would happen to them after the war.

When Mr. Heller sat alone in his son's room, waiting for him to come out of sedation, he reflected on 1965, when the news from Vietnam was appalling. Indeed, there was no unity internally. It was a country of misery, rivalry, division and constant defeat. According to information at hand, most of the old South Vietnamese leaders in the country had been liquidated. There were grisly stories of death and torture by Viet Cong guerrillas, who had taken considerable territory and were multiplying in number and strength by the hour.

Jim Heller and his friends never doubted what they heard from Army and Marine Corps personnel, who had served in Vietnam, that the despicable Viet Cong and their allies practiced acts of barbarism on American prisoners of war. He never doubted that they inflicted unbearable pain to force information and confessions in what they called psychological warfare. To those who survived and were eventually returned, the mental and physical pain, the agony and anguish, the violent distortions, under abominable circumstances, were beyond comprehension. There were numerous G.I.'s, who fought and died, while brutal men and their warlords watched with eyes drunk with hatred and revenge. The echo of the politicians, who would commit the youth of America to "Wars of Attrition," with never a clear cut victory, started to reverberate. The spread of the communist religion, far beyond Adolph Hitler's dream, spread forcefully over the land and had to be stopped.

"The Vietnam War is a repeat of the Korean War," a friend of Jim Heller had told him. "Life in Asia is cheap. War is a way of life there."

Those were Mr. Heller's silent thoughts, as he waited for his son to awaken. "Dear God," he whispered solemnly, lifting his eyes toward the ceiling, "please let Johnson's War, the numerous executions, the wholesale murder, the grisly stories of death and torture by the Viet Cong, who time and time again flee into their designated United Nations sanctuaries to rest, regroup and attack American fighting men in a struggle that can bring no victory...please let it end soon..."

Suddenly there was movement in the bed. Patient Heller was regaining consciousness from his state of deep anesthetic sleep. As his eyes cleared gradually, he shifted his head. Finally he seemed totally aware of his father's presence.

"Dad! Dad!" he whispered from impulse. "How long have you been waiting?"

"Not very long, son," he told him, beaming with intense love and pride. "I thought you'd be glad to see me when you opened your eyes?"

"Oh! Dad! Dad!" Raymond smiled in emotional helplessness. "You'll, you'll never know how I've missed you...Please tell me, Dad...have you forgiven me for deserting the Navy syndrome in our family?"

Mr. Heller ignored his son's questions. Instead, he bent over him once more and kissed his forehead. At the same time, he squeezed his hand. There were numerous words of affection before Mr. Heller reminded Raymond that, "That first mate job on my new shrimp boat is yours for the asking. It pays well..."

Raymond's eyes glistened with tears. "I might have to take you up on that, Dad. My Army career may well be over."

"Don't worry about it, Son. All of Key West and even Brownsville, Texas, is asking about you," Mr. Heller stumbled. "I've been a lonely father, especially when I didn't hear from you while you were in Vietnam."

Raymond struggled with words. His voice lacked strength and firmness. Nevertheless, he had to know if his father had truly pardoned him for joining the Army.

"There's nothing to forgive, Son," Mr. Heller said, trying to console and comfort him, as his chest swelled with pride.

"Dad! ...I wanted to do something on my own for a change, I guess. Shouldn't all of us try? Rather than keep hanging on to that ol' apron string, people mention so frequently?"

"Son, you've been independent since you were three when you told your babysitter you didn't eat spinach..."

For the moment the seriousness of their conversation turned to laughter, although Raymond was dead tired. Nevertheless, he tried to continue.

"Dad! I'm pretty well fouled up. I'll probably get a medical discharge. I know the Army takes care of its own, but, I am concerned about leaving here. You know how hostile many people are toward soldiers. The media has successively called us baby killers, rape artists and God only knows what else..."

"You haven't got a worry in the world, Son. If they discharge you, and you have a problem getting around on your feet, you can pilot one of our shrimpers. You can do that from a sitting position."

"Not so fast!" remarked Dr. Markham coming into the room, holding a sphygmomanometer and stethoscope in his hand. "Before you take off, please let me check your blood pressure."

In spite of the pain and misery, Raymond and his father smiled. "After you get Raymond's, take mine, Dr. Markham," Mr. Heller joked, as the medical officer wrapped the rubber cuff around Raymond's upper arm and inflated it.

After he had determined the systolic and the diastolic pressure, Dr. Markham recorded his findings in the chart at the foot of the bed.

"Well, doctor? Does he, or doesn't he have blood in his veins?" Mr. Heller said seriously.

"He's loaded. Now, let me check yours, Mr. Heller..."

"Please don't waste your time on an old horse like me, Dr. Markham. I was just kiddin' you. Just get my son back on his feet."

"I will, Mr. Heller," he confirmed. Do you have any questions?"

"Yes! Please give us some details on that four hour operation. I bit my nails for the first time in 40 years."

"There's nothing significant about the time," he explained. "We had to go deep to implant a durable silver bar into the upper femur - that's the upper part of the upper leg bone. We also implanted a strong silver pin to hold the hip-bone together, for more strength and quicker healing purposes. It took time to graft tendons and tissue and to reconnect muscle fibers. The rest was routine, except for the cast, which took another hour."

"How long will it be before we'll know everything is healing?" Raymond injected, sipping from a glass of water a corpsman was holding in front of him.

"Observation and X-rays will do that for us," the doctor emphasized. "But getting Raymond on his feet will take time. First, he'll be in a cast for 7-8 weeks. After that, there will be many sessions with our top flight physical therapist, who'll prescribe exercises and eventually will establish his physical limitations, if any."

"That doesn't sound too complicated," Mr. Heller said optimistically. "What else can you tell us, doctor?"

"All our war casualties will have sessions with the Army psychologist, who'll help them understand themselves better, and to achieve a more complete and satisfactory adjustment."

"What can I do?" Mr. Heller wanted to know.

The ward medical officer's face became momentarily grim. "I want you to stick around as long as you can, Mr. Heller. From what I can see, your presence will hasten Raymond's recovery. Since you were a commander in the navy and probably still have your I.D. card, you might be able to get a room at the officer's club. If not, there's a guest house with every convenience close by. In fact you can walk to it from here."

"Great!" Mr. Heller said thankfully. "I'm relieved."

He rushed toward the medical officer as if he were about to attack him and once more shook hands. "Now that I've met some regular Army personnel, I'll forgive my son for joining the Army," he told him. He was now certain that Raymond was in good hands.

For the next ten days, Mr. Heller stayed at the Fort Bragg Guest House. During his stay in the hospital room, the two men discussed the malodorous, noisome and putrid Vietnam war. "There's a lot many of us combat soldiers can't understand," Raymond told his father.

"Cambodia and Laos protect the VC by giving them sanctuaries. The guerrillas from the north, usually in small teams, hit us at their convenience, overrun towns and people, murder and ravage the countryside. Then, when we counterattack, they haul ass to their sanctuaries. We respect the borders, so the Ho Chi Minh trail is flourishing, in spite of massive bombing runs by our heavy bombers. Also, South Vietnam recruiting is a sham. Their new contingents of raw troops are mostly in their teens, from thirteen on up, who learn war by trial and error. The VC destroyed the Pleiku airbase, which was the largest one in Nam, with hundreds of bombers, fighters and helicopters, sitting there like our Pacific Fleet did when the Japs mauled Pearl Harbor.''

''All I know is what I read in the papers,'' Mr. Heller told his son. ''T.V.? I swear I saw the same scene of destruction three days in a row, but from a different angle and by a different correspondent. What bothers me more than anything else, is that T.V. news crews never show pictures of our troops winning or being victorious. All we ever see is our losses, our casualties and our suffering. I think the only encouraging news on T.V. was about the Gulf of Tonkin, where the North Vietnam mosquito fleet harassed our patrol ships. I am glad Navy firepower sent them down ol' Davey Jones' locker.''

''Most of us in Special Forces were wondering what was going on back home?'' Raymond complained. ''Some of us couldn't believe that President Johnson had such a hard time finally agreeing that North Vietnam must be bombed into submission. Surely retaliation was justified. In any war, it's an eye for an eye, a tooth for a tooth.''

''You and I believe that, Son,'' Mr. Heller confirmed, adding, ''I think that was the time our bombers finally started dropping their payloads on selected targets in the North...''

''I recall Special Forces started training South Vietnam so-called 'Terror Squads,' who were parachuted into the North to destroy and harass them. But, as it turned out, most, if not all joined the VC instead.''

''Last year and this, antiwar sentiment continued loud and clear. One day a small group of anatagonistic students from some college were sounding off while they were on one of our small fishing boats. They made no bones about how they felt, what they called the "Vietnam Civil War," in which we had no business. I listened to those phony sophisticates discussing how they agitated ROTC students in their classes until I could stand it no longer."

"Dad! You didn't?"

"You guessed it, son. I asked those creeps if they had ever learned to swim? When they told me they were on their college swimming team, I threw three of the four over the side. 'Swim you lousy punks,' I shouted after them."

Raymond laughed so loud it hurt him all over. With a wry grin on his tanned face, Mr. Heller added, "No! None of them drowned. You see, I threw them over the side near the Sombrero Light. And, Raymond, you should have seen those characters cut through the water, when they weren't sure if those big fins nearby belonged to sharks or porpoises?"

"Please, Dad!" Raymond wailed, weak from laughter. "Let me catch my breath. . .and could you get me a glass of water?"

Big Jim Heller poured the water in a glass and handed it to his son with a straw. A moment later, he showed a small flask of *pousse cafe*. "It's for my throat," he told him seriously.

Raymond stirred. *"Pousse cafe?* If I recall my days in Paris, I can tell you *pousse cafe* is a strong drink, but not for medicinal purposes. Where did you get it, Dad?"

"From a neighbor, Raymond. He can't wait to meet you."

"Did he tell you it's very popular in Paris?"

"All I've been told by him is that its good for my larynx, my pharynx and my trachea. You wanna swig, Son?"

"Not now, Dad. Thanks anyway. I would like to know how those three punks got off the Sombraro Light? Please tell me."

"I really don't know, Raymond. I do know that after they did get back in, they jumped into their fancy Cadillac and took off like greasy demons. One of our troopers gave four long-haired hippies a ticket for going 75 in a 50 mile zone, and I assumed it was them."

"Oh! Dad! You're still my hero," he told him with affection. "You know, Dad, I often wonder why the media never mentions that word 'hero'? I've known hundreds of them in Nam.''

The ward medical officer and the nurses were encouraged with Raymond's prognosis and his healing. When the medical officer discussed Raymond's profound progress with his father, he was pleased. "I do have bills to pay. There's insurance, I need a new set of nets, and I can see my youngster is coming along," he told the doctor. "If it's okay with you, I think I'll head for home. What do you think?"

"If you'll leave your telephone number with me, I'll call once in a while," the doctor told him.

Mr. Heller removed one of his business cards from his wallet and handed it to the doctor. "If you and your friends ever wanna go fishing, let me know. I know how to get the big ones."

"You know something, Mr. Heller?" the doctor said, grinning, "I might take you up on that..."

Chapter VIII

THE MAGIC
OF
FLORENCE NIGHTINGALE

Before Big Jim Heller departed from Room 600 at Womack, there was a tender embrace of affection, sprinkled with compassion and love. "Raymond is in good hands," he mumbled to himself, now without doubt and anxiety.

However, that same night Raymond needed a urinal. He became restless when he rang for a nurse and no one came. "I'll be damned if I'll let it loose in my bed," he thought to himself, as he attempted to get up.

The ward nurse, who had been engrossed with another patient when Heller rang for her, found him on the hard deck near the bed, delirious and in shock. Emergency X-rays revealed additional fractures of the femur. By the time orthopedic personnel had carefully cut off his casts, Heller's upper leg and his entire hip had turned black and blue. Nevertheless, after a three hour operation, the surgical team was highly optomistic that Heller would recover. Later, when the ward medical officer investigated, he discovered that a young student nurse had given the sergeant a bed bath and subsequently failed to replace the bed rail.

At four in the morning, Doctor Markham called a staff meeting and ordered a twenty-four hour special watch.

"I want an entry in his record, every hour on the hour!" he said with anger in his voice. "I want a notation on his chart, even when he emits gas from his anus! I want the A.O.D. to personally check the special watch, just in case somebody falls asleep! Am I making myself clear?"

There was an obedient "Yes, sir!" from everybody and the doctor seemed satisfied. However, when he made his morning rounds, he decided to see the Chief of Nursing Services to get a nurse who had experience handling serious Vietnam casualties.

"I'd be most grateful to you, madam," the ward doctor told the chief nurse, "if I might be able to acquire the special nursing qualities of Captain Pamela Rogers. I knew her at Tripler in Hawaii."

The chief nurse was happy with the doctor's request.

"But," she asked, "may I ask you why you're specifically asking for Pamela Rogers, Major Markham? I'm under the impression the nurses on your floor are most capable."

"That's true, madam. However, I have a special patient, who distinguished himself in Vietnam. He could well benefit from her personal and professional abilities."

"Isn't that the nurse Tripler Hospital nicknamed Florence Nightingale?"

"The same!" Doctor Markham confirmed. "But, Pamela Rogers has much more to offer her patients than that old nurse in England did during the Crimean War. Captain Rogers is totally dedicated, warm, friendly, compassionate and very pretty."

"You don't say?" the Chief of Nursing Service speculated. "Are you sure you want her taking care of your patient, or are you shopping for a bride, doctor?" she inquired with a big smile on her face.

Dr. Markham continued, "Pamela Rogers is strict with patients. And her father is a practicing psychiatrist in Charleston, South Carolina, who taught her a heck of a lot more about war casualties than we teach our nurses..."

"Say no more, Dr. Markham. Captain Pamela Rogers will report to you for a briefing about the patient within the hour, if that's agreeable with you?"

"It is! It is!" Dr. Markham repeated. "Thank you."

With great anxiety, Nurse Rogers reported to Dr. Markham, who simply pushed Sergeant Heller's medical chart toward her and suggested that she review it with her usual meticulousness.

"Pamela! Sergeant Heller in room 600 is positively one of our unsung heroes of that stinking war in Vietnam. I am confident you will handle him and all his visitors with your habitual sensitiveness..." Dr. Markham told his favorite nurse, then abruptly left the office.

At 1800 hours, Nurse Rogers assumed her duty. When she knocked on the door of room 600 and no one answered, she pushed it open with her knee. Her hands held a small hospital tray with two glasses, one with medication, the other with water. Although her patient was heavily sedated, he was well aware that a new nurse had shoved a thermometer under his tongue and was observing his breathing and counting his pulse. Moments later, she took his blood pressure, which was normal.

"Sergeant Heller! I'm Captain Pamela Rogers," she told him almost in a whisper. "If you are fully conscious, please take your medications."

With his eyes closed, Heller shook his head. "I'll take your pills later nurse," he told her without opening his eyes. "Right now, I really don't need them."

"Doctor Markham insists you take your medication every four hours. They are pain killers and I know you've been in pain. Is that not so, Sergeant Heller?"

"O.K. I'll take them. Would you please put them into my mouth and let me wash them down with a glass of water?"

After Heller had taken his medication, he opened his eyes just long enough to see the nurses nimble fingers, tapered and soft to the touch, as she patted the pillow.

"I am sorry about what you're going through," Captain Rogers told him. "If there's anything I can do for you, ring your call button," she said with compassion. "Perhaps some good soup will give you strength."

"Please! Please! I'm so tired," he told her.

At this time, the chow wagon stopped at room 600 and the

190

food service orderly brought a small tray with chicken soup and crackers.

"Please!" he begged. "Just let me rest. My head is spinning. You just got through saying if there's anything you can do for me...well, I'm asking to please let me rest..."

Captain rogers finally agreed. "But, we'll keep your plate of soup warm for you 'til it's time for your medications, all right?"

"Yes'm."

"May I do anything else for you, Sergeant Heller?" she asked, wishing to please him. "Anything at all?"

"If you really mean it, I'd appreciate if you'd kindly read to me from Balzac on the locker. Dad brought it."

The nurse was surprised. No one has ever asked her to read a novel to them, expecially while they were on the critical list. Captain Rogers picked up the only book on the bedside locker, glanced at it for a second, "Where would you like me to start?" she asked.

"Where everything starts, mam," he replied. "At the beginning."

"Of course!" the nurse replied, moving the only chair in the room closer to her patient's bed and started at the beginning. By the time she had reached page seven, Heller was snoring.

Although Heller slept soundly until midnight, Pamela kept on reading. She thought it was a fascinating book by a French literary giant, who marvelled at everything, expecially the delightful spinster mademoiselles he met in the turbulent city of gay Paris, where he revelled and wrote about his rapturous encounters.

At midnight, Heller ate the warm soup, which the nurse fed him with a spoon. He accepted his medications, and reluctantly accepted a urinal without looking at her. "It's down right embarrassing and painful to ask a woman for a urinal," he thought. "Surely, there must be a way to get around that."

Nurse Rogers was relieved at 4:00 in the morning by the regular night nurse, who gave Heller his medications and stayed with him long enough for Heller to go back to sleep.

Nurse Rogers was right on time the next working day. "How are you this evening?" she smiled pleasantly.

"Lousy!" Heller replied.

"Sorry to hear that," she told him honestly. "Please open your eyes and take your medication."

"Please put them on the locker," he growled, grabbing the pillow from under his head and covering his face and neck with it.

"What? What did you say?" the nurse gasped frantically.

"Sergeant Heller! The ward medical officer prescribed these medications. . . Please take them now," she pleaded patiently, standing very close to his bed and still holding the small glasses.

"I don't need medications!" Heller countered from under the pillow. "You people keep me doped up with these damn narcotics that keep stupifying my intelligence. . ."

"It's for your pain. We don't want you to keep suffering," the nurse soothed him.

"I can take the pain. But when you deprive me of my mind, I'd rather have died with my comrades in Nam. . ."

Captain Rogers decided she had had enough. "Your conduct is rude and shocking," she told him with prudence and caution. "If you refuse to take your medications, I'll call the A.O.D."

"Call him!"

"Let me remind you, Sergeant Heller," the nurse told him with professional calm. "You're still in the Army and, whatever your reason, don't you think you ought to accept orders from your superior officers?"

"That's it!" he countered and tried to move. "I'm in this critical condition because I consciously followed what you just said, a superior officer. In fact he was inexperienced in battle. Actually, he didn't know his rectum from a hole in the ground. When I questioned his order which countermanded the existing, he threatened me with a courtmartial for cowardice."

"You wanna tell me the rest?" she asked with compassion.

"We walked right into an ambush which we knew was waiting for us. So, he gets himself killed, along with seven others, not to mention those who were severely wounded, including me. My best friend, Doc Blanchard, was killed."

"I'm sorry to hear you tell the terrible experience," she told him, as she set the glasses containing the medications on the locker, wondering what she must do next. "I can't possibly let this patient dictate what he does or does not do," she thought.

"Once more," she pleaded with serene tones in her voice. "Please don't trifle with me and take your medication."

"Not now!"

"I'll warn you for the last time. . .please take your medication willingly, or I have no choice but to call the A.O.D. He might put you in a straight jacket and shove them down your throat," she exclaimed.

When Heller did not answer, the nurse took the telephone off the hook.

"The A.O.D., please," she said clearly. "This is Captain Rogers in Room 600!"

"All right!" Heller chuckled. He opened his eyes and noticed the beautiful nurse with a determined look, her head high with the pride of a true professional, "I'll take your pills. Hand them to me."

"Too late!" she told him to achieve an understanding once and for all. "I have the A.O.D. on the line. If you take your medications and let me see you swallow them right now, I'll ask the gentleman to forget this call."

"But, I can't reach the glasses. . ."

"Try!"

Somehow, Heller stretched his arms and managed to get his fingers around the small glass with the medication. After he had it in his hand, the nurse smiled with relief. "Put the pills in your mouth!" she ordered.

"I have to have water."

"It's on the locker."

Heller made a conscious attempt but failed to reach the glass of water. Nurse Rogers put the telephone down and pushed the glass within range. With maximum effort Heller finally swallowed the pills and washed them down with water.

Nurse Rogers picked up the telephone once more and apologized to the A.O.D. for the call. "I heard your remarks," he replied. "If you ever need me, whistle!"

After thanking the A.O.D. she replaced the telephone, and made her entry on Heller's chart: "Administered 1800 medications."

At the end of her special watch, nurse Rogers left room 600 with a sense of satisfaction. Now that she knew she penetrated Heller's defensive armor, she would continue tomorrow where she left off the first night.

From that day forward, Heller's behavior remarkably changed for the better. He even started shaving himself and brushed his own teeth. Since he resented bitterly having to ask for a bedpan, the nurse stored one of them close enough for him to reach it.

The next evening when the chow cart arrived and the orderly set Heller's tray on the bedside locker, Heller stared at it. "I don't want it!" he objected.

"Why do you object, sergeant?" nurse Rogers asked politely, stirring the bowl of rice soup.

"I had rice soup 'til it came out of my ears in Nam," he answered.

"I don't blame you," the nurse nodded. "Tell me, sergeant, what would you eat if I could get it for you?"

With force, he said, "I grew up on meat, fish and potatoes. You people are starving me to death! I've lost sixty pounds and I'm weak."

"I'm sorry for your soft diet," nurse Rogers told him with compassion. "I agree with you, and to let you know that I mean it...If you'll give me a few minutes, I'll run up front and discuss it with the ward doctor who has the duty tonight."

"Mind? I'd kiss your feet, if you'd let me."

"That won't be necessary," she smiled and rushed from the room. When she returned within minutes with a tray containing three pieces of chicken, a boiled potato, bread, butter, and a green leaf of lettuce with cottage cheese, Heller felt like jumping out of bed.

"Captain Rogers!"

"Yes, Sergeant Heller?"

"May I tell you what I think of you?"

"Is it nice, sergeant?"

"You are not only beautiful," he told her between bites, "but you're also producing the desired effect with a minimum of effort. Besides, would you believe me, I dream about a girl like you now and then?"

"Some high school sweetheart, perhaps?"

"No. I've only seen this girl once in my life."

As the days and weeks went by, the intensive efforts of both doctor and nurse paid off. However, Sergeant Heller still remained evasive and in partial retreat.

"I can't quite put my finger on it," she told Dr. Markham. "Heller wanted to make a positive contribution to the war effort, and he earnestly distinguished himself. I guess he thinks that his Army career is at an end and it's hard for him to accept that."

"We'll cut his cast off in the morning, Pamela. I want you there. Perhaps you can help him take his first step."

"Have you discussed Heller's condition with physiotherapy, Dr. Markham?"

"Thanks for reminding me, Pamela. I'll do it right now, over a cup of coffee. Meanwhile, give Heller the word that his cast is coming off in the morning. I'm positive he'll be glad to hear that."

Several days later, Heller started physiotherapy. Nurse Rogers was so impressed with his progress that she recommended Heller be removed from all medications, unless he asked for them. "But," she told the doctor, "I'd really like to keep my eyes on him..."

"Say no more, Pamela. It so happens that one of my other nurses has her orders for Walter Reed. I'll see the Chief of Nursing Services again. I think we can manipulate that ol' gal into what we think is most advantageous to us," he said clearly.

"There's no doubt in my mind, doctor, that we've embarked in the right direction with Heller. In fact, every time I get near him, I get a feeling I've known him before. He's the kind who grows on you, I guess."

Dr. Markham pulled a chair out and motioned the nurse to sit down. "It may well be that you're falling for that big brute of a heman. Or, you may be discovering that you have perfectly normal instinctive feminine desires..."

Captain Pamela Rogers blushed, while her heart pounded in a syncopated rhythm. "I'm just trying to prove to you that I'm a good nurse and I'll make every deliberate attempt to get that big brute of a man back on his feet. That's all," she told her favorite Army medical officer, who simply smiled with approval.

"Pamela, you're like a beautiful daughter to me. So stop your medical rhetoric, and you certainly don't need artificial eloquence with me. The way I see it, Heller is something very special in your life of challenges. With some extra effort, properly channelled, you might even get him on the dance floor. But," he explained still further, "you'll have to be honest and accept that ever since time began, men will go through hell and high water, if a beautiful woman is waiting ashore."

The nurse was utterly surprised at Dr. Markham's inference. "I don't quite understand, doctor?"

"For heaven's sake, Pamela, you're not just a damn good nurse. You're ambitious, beautiful, intelligent and single. Personally, I guess I classify myself as a hopeless romantic, trying to promote an affair between an officer and an enlisted man. Lord knows I'm certainly no neoclassic nor a liberal. But," he went on, "on feelings of the heart? That's something I'm for. With your remarkable assets you could easily resolve, even expedite, Heller's recovery and get him back to active duty. The other day I gave a staff sergeant a ride from the Fort, who told me he had been in Heller's outfit and that he would lay his life on the line for him. "If it hadn't been for Heller, I would have died a grotesque death," the soldier told me, without elaborating about the details. I think he was one of the survivors from the Battle of Loc Ninh. He told me the story of Heller's conspicuous gallantry and intrepity in that final action. He said his colonel had recommended Heller for the Silver Star. The soldier told me that Heller could never have been taken alive by the VC."

"Dr. Markham! What is it you'd have me do?"

"I'm glad you asked, Pamela. Heller suffers from mental depression. Why don't you act out his spontaneous impressions and situations? You see my dear, you and Heller are much alike. You're both fiercely independent, strong willed, loaded with integrity, and sound moral principles. You're honest, virtuous and chaste."

"I don't know what to say, Dr. Markham. I, I..."

"Good! Just listen to me..."

Pamela nodded. Without uttering a word, she leaned back in the upholstered armchair, as the medical officer continued.

"As I was about to say, you are a rare, beautiful human being, who can reanimate Heller's courage, his strength and his will. That is, if you'll give him the right signals, and don't tell me he hasn't noticed you?"

"If you don't mind, Dr. Markham," she smiled momentarily, "Heller couldn't tell you the color of my hair, or, for that matter, the color of my eyes."

"I doubt that, Pamela," the doctor said clearly. "He's undoubtedly had some bad experiences with girls and the fact that his mother died giving him life, not to mention that his childhood sweetheart jilted him for a young West Point Cadet four weeks before high school graduation. That tremendous young trooper probably has had other let downs with the fairer sex. It could very well be the true reason why not a single female has come to visit him..."

"What bothers me more than anything else, doctor, is that whenever I come into his room, he pretends he's sleeping..." she remarked casually, commenting still further, "It could be that Heller simply doesn't care for girls?"

"Hold it, Pamela. Heller is far above average in intelligence. In spite of his wounds and his mental depression, he's showing emotional stability. One of these days he'll jump out of his sack..."

"And what?" Pamela smiled, as they were interrupted by the ringing telephone.

Dr. Markham picked up the receiver. "Dr. Markham!" came the clear sounding voice of the operator. "This is the long distance operator from Key West, Florida. Would it be convenient for you to speak with Mr. Jim Heller?"

"Sure! Certainly! Right now," he replied, giving his favorite nurse the word that Sergeant Heller's father was on the line. "Mr. Heller calls me by appointment every other day..."

During the long conversation between doctor and his caller from Key West, Pamela Rogers attempted to leave. However, Dr. Markham urged her to stand by. After he hung up the phone he directed his attention once more to his very special nurse.

"I've wanted to have a straight talk with you since the day I met your father in Hawaii."

"Really? Dad never mentioned your meeting," she injected with astonishment. "Wanna tell me what your chat was about?"

"You, of course. I'll assure you nothing surreptitious. I'll confess your loving father hopes that you'll find yourself a mate for life and someday soon thereafter, make him a proud grandfather of a pretty little girl; just like you were...according to a picture he has in his wallet."

"Oh, no! He wouldn't," she laughed. "I know how exhaustive my dad is where I'm concerned. Was it...?"

"Yes, it was," he laughed. "You undoubtedly were the most beautiful three year old little darling displaying your talents and child-like beauty, twirling a Hula Hoop around your tiny hips..."

"Dad is such an old fuddy-duddy," she said, while her eyes sparkled with tears of laughter. "And, I had better check on our patients, Dr. Markham...Don't you agree?"

"Indeed. But, do think about what we've discussed. I'm counting on you."

"I'll keep it in mind, Dr. Markham, now that I know I have another dad." After taking several steps toward the office door, she turned. "Dr. Markham! Would it be appropriate for me to visit Heller in my civies, this evening?"

"Yes! Yes! You might rattle his cookie jar," the doctor grinned, adding, "the Army wants our Vietnam casualties who leave Womack happy and healthy."

Nurse Rogers waited to see if the doctor had anything else to say. When he had nothing to add, she told him what a wonderful humanitarian he was. After they had a good laugh she wanted to know if he would like to see her before she visited Heller.

"I'll be looking for you, Pamela...say around 2000?"

"Yes!" she agreed. "2000 will be fine."

At eight that evening, nurse Pamela Rogers presented herself to the man she revered and respected like her own father. When he saw her, he stood silent, his mouth was open, but this particular moment the brilliant doctor, indeed a true disciple of the Hippocratic oath, failed to come forth with words. The stunning lady was wearing a brand new seductive point d' esprit outfit, shaped into a minimum constriction jacket, with a narrow skirt. The sleeves and jacket opening had a doused hemline with flounces of gilt-encrusted lace. Her hair was long and blonde, groomed back far enough to reveal diamond earrings. Her cosmetics were audacious and devastatingly feminine. When she turned like a model on the stage, her youthful and sophisticated figure was sensational from any angle. The contour of her breasts looked lovelier and sexier than the doctor had ever dared to dream about.

At last when he found his voice, he nodded his head, while his fingers drummed the stack of records on his desk.

"Captain Rogers?" he managed to say. "I presume?"

"You were saying, Doctor Markham?"

"Pamela! You are the living characteristic of the woman so rare in America. I, I, I," he studdered. "What can I say? You're too beautiful for words."

"What you're saying in general terminology is that you think I am the epitome of the perfect Army nurse, I hope," she smiled. "You think Heller will be impressed, seeing me in civies?"

"Will he be impressed? Come now," he laughed, pausing a moment. "If he doesn't jump out of his sack, I'll...I know it will be a long while before he's ready for discharge, if ever."

"I hope so, doctor," she said flirtatiously. "What some of us nurses will do for our patients."

Several minutes later, the gorgeous young woman made her

way through the long corridor on the first floor. When she moved toward the elevator, there were whistles. Some looked, others stared at her. "I have never seen such effortless rhythm in all my life," a Major in uniform whispered to his associate.

"She looks familiar," his colleague replied. "I guess she's probably one of those U.S.O. flames...might even be in pictures?"

After nurse Rogers had entered the elevator, a young sergeant asked her to autograph the cast on his broken leg. "It'll heal much faster just thinking of your beautiful hands," he told her.

After she reached room 600, she knocked gently, waiting to hear Heller's voice. When he did not answer, she knocked again. This time she was positively amazed. Heller yelled, "Come in, Captain Rogers! Come in if you must!"

The lovely nurse made her grand entrance and approached the bed. "Sergeant Heller! Would you mind telling me how you knew it was I who knocked?"

"My conscious intuition, nurse. Besides, you're two hours late," he told her casually, without opening his eyes. "If I were able tonight, I'd serve pink champagne. Your chemistry is..."

"Please open your eyes. I might surprise you," she said softly, brushing her tongue over her luscious lips.

"I don't need to open my eyes to see you looking like a princess. It may surprise you. I have a sixth sense...power of perception, you call it. I know you so well I don't need my eyes to become aware of you, your perfume and other things, which suggest your presence. I see you in my dreams. I fantasize about you. I know when you tip-toe into or out of my room, with your head high, your little french nose tilted toward heaven. And how you rustle when you turn and move."

Nurse Rogers was flabbergasted. Speechless. When she regained her voice, she bent over him and shouted - directly in his ear - "Heller! I think you're a coward! That's what I think!" she blistered. "I've had enough of your insults. Open your eyes, or I'm leaving!"

"Please don't leave," Heller said quickly and opened his eyes in admiration. "I'm real glad you came. If I weren't a prisoner in this bed, I'd be tempted to find out if you are real. You know, real flesh and blood. The facts are that you have been an illusion, like a tumbleweed in the wind of time. I know Army regulations, even better than you. I know my place. You're an officer and I'm enlisted.''

"You big ox, have you finished?"

"No!"

"Damn you!" she countered with sardonic mockery in her voice, determined to attack his sarcastic remarks. "Heller! You are stuffed so full of self-pity, you really don't need a nurse or a doctor for that matter. As I said," she continued, "What you really need is a wet-nurse! One who will suckle and fondle you like an infant! Well, let me remind you that you are in a United States Army Hospital, not a nursery!" she challenged him further. "If you ever get up enough guts to get off your back, I would hope you'll go down to the lobby to see Private First Class Bryant Womack's portrait."

"Why should I?" Heller asked suddenly and forcefully. "Why should I look at a little ol' private's picture?"

"I think you ought to see what a real hero looks like! Womack received the Congressional Medal of Honor posthumously for conspicious gallantry far beyond the call of duty. He died from loss of blood," she related impulsively, now that she knew she had his attention.

Heller took a deep breath of air and exhaled it. "Captain Rogers, there's a lot of truth to what you threw at me just now," he told her in a subdued voice, repressing his real emotions. "If you would wheel me down, I'd really like to see Private Womack's portrait."

"I'll wheel you down," nurse Rogers volunteered.

"When?"

"In the morning."

"Why not now?" he insisted. "I'm anxious to see - as you said - what a real hero looks like...So, please bring that wheelchair over."

"I'd love to." she told him with assurance and gladness in her voice. "But," she cautioned, "perhaps we had better wait 'til morning?"

"No!" Heller insisted. "You started this thing and like my

dad tells me -- never start anything, unless you intend to finish it."

Heller turned and let his legs hang over the bed, while nurse Rogers got the wheelchair. "You sure are a complicated man," she told him, as he tried to get out of bed. He held on to her for dear life, with one leg on the wheelchair, which suddenly took off across the room.

"Please, let's forego it tonight," she begged him. I want the doctor to be present. How about after morning sick-call instead?"

"I guess you're right," he said with disappointment in his voice. "We'll do it in the morning."

Sergeant Heller x-rayed his very special nurse with penetrating eyes. "As we both know, Army regs don't permit officers to consort with enlisted personnel. Isn't that so?"

"True!" she answered affirmatively. "True!"

"I'm real sorry I gave you such a bad time, when I should have kissed your hand to show my appreciation for visiting me tonight," he told her. She came closer to rearrange the pillow and pat it, as she had done so frequently before.

"You know something," she remarked. "You can be quite nice. Most of the time you're a true gentleman, and if you'll let me, we can become good friends, on our nurse-patient relationship. What do you think?"

"Do I have a choice? I think I'd have to ask for sleeping pills if you didn't stop in to see me after hours," he told her. "Which makes me think how nice it would be if some of my SF buddies would stop by for a chat. I'd be glad to see them, even if they have never been in Nam before. I realize now, I was way off base when I said I didn't wanna see anybody. It's been real lonely around here, after dad left for home."

"I know that," she smiled.

"So, what else is new?"

"I don't know if you are aware that Sergeant Major Cartwright inquires about you each day, then, posts your prognosis on the bulletin board with other regulations and notices. He'll be happy to know, and," she added, "would you like me to call your dad, whom I met, while..."

"Really? Would, would you do that for a poor, lonely, miserable Special Forces sergeant?" he pursued further, hoping to arouse sympathy from his special nurse. "Dad gave me several personalized cards... if you give me a moment?"

Heller pulled the drawer from the bedside locker, removed the wallet and quickly extracted several cards. "Take an extra card for one of your friends, who might want to hire a guide, or a boat, to go fishing."

The beautiful nurse thanked him, examined the cards critically, then added, "My dad goes fishing in the Keys once a year. He'll be glad to have the information."

"Oh! When you call my dad, tell him I feel great and I hope to be on my feet in another couple weeks or so. One more thing, Captain Rogers..."

"Yes?"

"Reverse the charges."

"Is that all?" she asked softly, almost in a romantic whisper.

"No! I,I,I'd like to kiss your gentle hands..."

Captain Rogers' delicate face turned crimson. After a long moment she said cleverly and with witticism, "Sergeant Heller! You are in a rare and gallant mood. Somehow, your disposition and temperament are amusing."

"How about it, Captain Rogers? May I kiss your hand?" he said, refusing to give up. "Please?"

Nurse Rogers made several steps toward Heller's bed and offered her right hand to him, which he held gently for a moment, then kissed it with noble politeness and restrained sensuousness.

"Please don't tell anyone," she said romantically, but with humor. "Pleasant dreams."

"Pleasant dreams to you, Captain Rogers," Heller said gently. "May they all come true."

Captain Rogers found sleep impossible that night. When she arrived at 0745 in the doctors office, he was not there. She dialed Sergeant Major Cartwright to inform him that Sergeant Heller would be glad to have visitors from now on. The big NCO at Special Forces Command Headquarters was delighted with the news and gave Captain Rogers some of his own.

"As a matter of fact, at 0930, the Commander of the XVIII Airborne Corps, the Commanding General of Special Forces and the Commanding Officer of Womack will be in room 600 to honor Sergeant Heller, give him a citation and a hero's medal - the Silver Star - to be exact."

Captain Rogers was surprised. "Does Dr. Markham know that?" she asked anxiously.

"I believe they wanted it to be a surprise to everybody, including Heller. So, Captain Rogers, since you are in charge on the 6th floor, I'd like to suggest that everything be in ship shape...You know...clean pajamas, sheets...Heller ought to have a shower and a shave...The works!"

"I assure you that Heller will be ready," she told Cartwright.

After she replaced the telephone, she started running from the office, when Dr. Markham intercepted her.

"Hold it! Hold it, Pamela!" he commanded her. "Do you realize you are completely ignoring me, and without even a good morning?"

Captain Rogers faced her superior officer without her usual morning smile. "I assume you haven't heard, Dr. Markham?"

"Don't tell me Sergeant Heller fell out of bed again?" he joked good naturedly.

"No, sir! I just got the word from Sergeant Major Cartwright that a Lieutenant General, a Major General and our hospital commander will be in room 600 at 0930 sharp, to bestow the Silver Star medal on Heller."

"How come you got the word from Cartwright?" the doctor wanted to know. "We get our orders through our own command channels."

"Heller asked me to call the sergeant major to tell him that he'd welcome visitors from now on. That's when he told me, sir."

"That's good news, Pamela. Meanwhile, please do what you must," he told her. "We'll discuss Heller's progress later."

At 0930, the long hospital corridor from the elevator to room 600 swarmed with MP's and VIP's. But only a handful of people were permitted to enter room 600. After an MP NCO shouted attention, Heller was surprised. He had no knowledge that two generals, four colonels, and Sergeant Major Cartwright were coming into his room.

Sergeant Major Cartwright read Heller's citation, after which the three star general pinned the Silver Star on Heller's p.j. top. This was followed by a short word of praise, a well wish and a handshake from all officers present, then just as suddenly as it started, all ceased.

When all visitors had left except Captain Rogers, Heller remarked, "So! I got another medal. This makes it an even dozen, I think. Sure I'm honored, but after I'm kicked out of the service, medals won't mean much. What makes all of this so despairing is that I can feel in my bones I'll be discharged, when, in fact, I wanted to stay for life."

"You're not out yet," she said thoughtfully. "Wait 'til you're out of the cast. I know what a miraculous job the surgeons did."

"Well! I'm a realist," he told her glancing at his cast.

Later, when nurse Rogers entered Dr. Markham's office, he greeted her at once, with a big grin. "Come in! Come in, and good morning!" Before she could reply, he asked, "How did things go in 600 last night? Surely Heller flipped his cords with your sophisticated personality, your splendid clothes, your long shiny hair, all that gilt-encrusted lace, not to mention your delicious cosmetics. Let's have the details?"

"Doctor! The truth of the matter is, at first he wouldn't even open his eyes," she explained truthfully. "When I threatened to leave, he finally opened them. I might tell you, Heller tried not to be surprised with me or my civies, but he was in a talkative mood. When I mentioned that this Army Hospital was named after Private Womack, who won the Medal of Honor, he hung his feet out of bed and almost ordered me to wheel him down to the first floor to see Womack's portrait and citation. He also let me know that he's been lonely since his father left and hoped some of his Special Forces buddies might come to visit him. He asked me to call his father in Key West. Sergeant Heller expects to be out of bed in another couple weeks."

"Wonderful, wonderful," the doctor responded. "Keep it

up, and keep me informed. Dress any way you like after working hours. Get his confidence, his trust. Talk to him about his life before he enlisted. I think he's ready to open up. Watch his reactions carefully. Sympathize with him, but show no pity, Pamela. This is a sharp Vietnam veteran, who laid his life on the line. He's highly decorated, as you know. He believes our generals could end this war of attrition in 96 hours. Let me emphasize not to let him listen to those news doom-merchants, who report nothing but defeat for our forces in Nam," Dr. Markham suggested further. "Sergeant Heller wants no special favors. He believes in his dreams of a brighter tomorrow, certainly that the American people and their elected politicians will back those who accept fighting so far from home. It's all mental for Sergeant Heller. Perhaps seeing his comrades again will get him over the hump."

Shortly after Captain Rogers had been dismissed by Dr. Markham, she returned to room 600, which was a beehive of Special Forces troopers who had known Heller from previous commands. As the nurse entered unnoticed by the callers, Heller had their attention. Said he, trying to answer a question candidly, "Truth is seldom pleasant! Journalism has become a monster of double standard derelicts, who have buried sacrifice and virtues. Some seem determined to pursue an age of anti-heroism, instead of upgrading our Army and the other services."

"What you're saying is," interupted one of the NCO's near Heller, "is that the media is, in fact, molding the minds of the people at home?"

"That's the naked truth and all of you know it!" Heller insisted dogmaticly, offering himself as evidence. "Right now, under General Westmoreland, we have leadership and front line Army discipline, which always starts from the top and radiates down. As Sergeant Major Cartwright stresses, "Respect must be earned! Personal responsibility and selfless duty has to meet the challenges of the day, be it in combat or on the firing range..."

"Hold it! Hold everything," Captain Rogers suddenly spoke

206

up. "I abhor interrupting, but, it's almost chow time. Why not return during visiting hours?"

The soldiers looked at each other as if they could not accept the nurses sense of reasoning. "Madam!" remarked a sergeant first class, who had his orders for Vietnam, "Those of us who are heading over there can learn first hand from Sergeant Heller, rather than learn things the hard way. All of us are pleased Sergeant Heller came out of Nam without stigma, or resentment..."

"Please!" the nurse insisted patiently, looking at Heller for approval. "Please come back at visiting time."

That evening, nurse Rogers, still in her spotless uniform, returned to Heller's room with the 2000 medications.

"And how is my little princess?" Heller mused. "You think these tranqualizers are necessary this evening?"

"The ward doctor thinks so, sergeant!"

"What I need is more visitors. Like those this afternoon, and someone like you in the evening."

Captain Rogers ignored the last part of Heller's remarks. "I can assure you that your old sergeant major will see to it that you'll get opportunities to see everybody at Special Forces. You know, I was fascinated with your conversation this afternoon. These guys worship the ground you walk on," she thought, then apologized. "I'm sorry. You know what I mean. It will be some time before you get your feet on the ground."

"What do you think of my progress, Captain Rogers?"

"As you know our Army medical department is very thorough," she replied. "We have no miraculous cure for Vietnam casualties, who may be hounded by the horrors and afflictions still unknown in our field. Actually," she went on, "Dr. Markham and I are encouraged by your great progress and your attitude..."

"Captain Rogers," Heller said slowly and deliberately, "I'd like to have the privilege of taking you to the NCO club on my first pass. What do you think?"

Nurse Rogers hesitated before she answered. "I've never been there before. I'd love to go sometime," she said thoughtfully.

"But, there are Army regs. Tell you what, Sergeant Heller, let's think about it. Shall we?"

"Think? Think?" he repeated with boredom in his voice. "That's all I do, day and night."

"Would you care to tell me what you think about?" she persisted. "I'm really a good listener."

"That would take twenty-four hours."

"Try me!"

"All right, Captain Rogers," Heller finally agreed. "First, I'm thinking about getting the boot from the Army. I feel that this is the end of my days in the service."

"Wait 'til your cast comes off," she suggested positively again. "May I ask you a personal question?"

"Certainly."

"If you should get a medical discharge, what would you do?"

"That's the least of my worries," he told her. "You know my Dad is in commercial fishing. I'd most likely navigate one of our shrimp boats. I can do that from a sitting position. A handpicked crew of four or five will do the rest."

"I've often thought about trying for a big sail in the deep blue Gulf, off Key West, or Miami. Can I make reservations with you right now?" she laughed. "My problem is that I hate touching those worms."

Heller had to pinch himself to keep from laughing. He didn't want to good-naturedly tease her that fishing for sailfish takes larger bait than worms. Instead, he told her that sport fishing can be a lot of fun, but for those who make a living from it, it is dependent upon circumstances and can be trying.

"Dad and I spent many a day and night at sea. Luck has a lot to do with it, as well as the weather. For the fishermen, it's a constant battle. If not against the elements, it's against men and boats from foreign nations, as far away as Russia, who not only come in fleets of large ships, but even come with their factories..."

"You mean canneries?"

"That's right."

"That's interesting," she thought. "Aren't the Russians

restricted from coming too close to shore? I've heard we have a twelve mile limit."

"That's not good enough. We need a two hundred mile limit. Dad is an officer in the Florida Fisherman's Association which is now pursuing Congress to pass laws to curb wholesale slaughter of our fish by foreigners."

"Is Congress really doing something about that problem, or are they just giving lip service like they usually do?" she asked seriously, as if indeed she understood the dilemma.

"Let's say Congress is working in that direction. Most fishermen hope at least a hundred mile limit is not just a dream..."

"Well, sergeant, as you undoubtedly know, there are dreamers and workers in this beautiful world of ours. I assume you and I are not in that class of dreamers," she smiled broadly. "Don't you agree?"

"No! Sorry about that. Right now I wouldn't have very much of anything, if I didn't have my dreams."

"Really?"

"Last night I dreamed about the first Christmas I can recall," Heller grinned. "Dad and our neighbors had a ball with the toy trains, especially since no real trains run further down than Miami. We were all on our tummies, watching and waiting for Santa's train with the goodies. I was three, then."

"Since Christmas is just around the corner, so to speak," she wondered, "what would you like under your tree, sergeant?"

In a very long dissertation Heller told the Army nurse that, first of all, he hoped someone would bring a small tree.

"One with real branches. One I can smell. I wanna see a star on its top, a wreath on the door of my room and I hope to hear voices, singing or playing, *Silent Night* and *Tannenbaum* and all the rest of the joyous carols. I'd like to see the toy trains in our attic and my Dad on his tummy again in the living room..."

"Anything else, Sergeant Heller?"

"Certainly, Captain Rogers. Certainly," he said emphatically, looking into her baby blue eyes. "I'd like to see Dad walk through that door," he pointed, " and you near my tree with a big smile, wishing..." Heller stopped talking.

"Go on! Go on! Don't stop now," she urged him on. "Would you believe me if I told you I too anticipate Christmas with awe and wonder? For a brief time I can forget the sadness and the war in Vietnam!"

"I guess it will be a long time before I can forget the horrors I saw in my short time in our Army," Heller said with intensity. "But, as Dad says, life goes on and dreams are good for the soul."

"Would you be surprised to know that I too had a dream about my early childhood last night?"

"Was it pleasant? Please tell me about it? I've been doing all the talking."

"As it was, I dreamt about my mother, whom I never knew, except for what my Dad and my sisters told me about her."

Heller realized just how sentimental Captain Rogers was and quickly changed the subject back to his own dreams. "In many of my dreams I pretended I was one of Huckleberry Finn's buddies collecting lizards, frogs and seashells, throwing stones into the only fresh water pond in the Keys. Afterward, all of us took a long snooze under a shady tree. As I slept, a beautiful little girl would come up and kiss me. I woke up and who do you think was doing the kissing?" Heller laughed.

"Somebody's dog?" she said with laughter.

"Wrong," he smiled. "It was a small deer, like the one in the picture, The Yearling."

"Who in the world would have thought that?" she wondered cheerfully, trying to come up with something to add. Ultimately, she said, "I sure am glad you didn't collect snakes," shuddering and trembling with horror just at the thought of it.

Both laughed hilariously, but only for a moment. Heller's facial expression became solicitous again, full of anxiety and apprehension. "What bothers me, nurse, is that I have some terrible nightmares about Vietnam. If I could get past them."

Captain Rogers realized what was happening and quickly intervened, "Sergeant! That little ol' lake you mentioned, did it have a place to jump in, with lily pads and frogs?"

Heller turned toward her and let out one of his rare laughs. "Oh, yes," he replied. "While the boys caught frogs, the girls picked lily pads. I'm reminded of a little girl by the name of Susan, who thought she was really a boy. Most of the time she even dressed like one of us. That little ol' girl could splash and shout louder than all of us put together."

The Army nurse smiled at Heller with kindliness and compassion, before she said, "Sergeant Heller! When I was five, I wanted to be a boy. Most of my playmates were rascals, who ignored me. So, I did the next best thing. . . I used to hide behind windows and bushes and peek 'til something started crawling up one of my legs."

"What was it, Captain Rogers?"

"A black snake! I wasn't sure. . ."

"Did you yell for help?" Heller laughed.

"No! But I screamed so loud, the snake took off in one directin and I in the other," she told him, her eyes wide with astonishment, when she suddenly realized she was holding Heller's hand.

"Please, sergeant. Please," she said meaningfully and withdrew it gently, although she knew that indeed she was magnetically drawn to her special patient, Heller.

Heller was sleeping soundly on Christmas Eve. But the moment someone entered his dimly lit room, moving stealthily, obviously trying to avoid being heard or seen, he awakened. He was not certain whether he was dreaming. He rubbed his eyes, then he smelled the pine tree, which suddenly lit up with tiny lights, embellishing the beautiful ornaments, the evergreen and the star on its very top.

Heller pretended to be sleeping, until he recognized the big man with the beard, who had cautiously set the small Christmas tree on the bedside locker. At this time, Heller could no longer deny himself the joy and luxury of embracing his father.

"Dad! Dad!" he shouted with joy. "God! I'm glad to see you. How about one of those bear hugs of yours?"

Jim Heller roared. "I'm Santa's helper!" as he literally embraced and lifted his son from the bed, which started to roll.

Christmas came and went, and so did his father. There were

numerous cards from well wishers, from friends in Key West, from relatives and comrades, including one from Cartwright and another from his old buddy, Sergeant Zusette. In spite of all that moral encouragement, Heller was not entirely happy. He appreciated the lovely card from nurse Rogers, who mentioned that she would be in Charlston with her family and that she wanted to convey her warmest wishes to his father. Nurse Rogers had signed the card, "All good wishes, all the days of my life, Captain Pamela Rogers."

Captain Rogers returned from her two weeks leave the day after New Years. When she accompanied Dr. Markham at morning sick call, every patient was delighted to see her except Heller in room 600. When she told Heller that she had missed him, he avoided looking at her altogether and the medical officer could see it.

Later in the day the doctor told her that he was disappointed with her.

"You got to get Heller on his feet! He's been here almost three months now. His second cast should be coming off in the next few days, perhaps even in the morning. I'll give you the word. Meanwhile, I expect you to make some efforts to snap him out of the recurrent trauma. Unless you are engrossed with others of rank, why not reestablish a good relationship with Sergeant Heller this evening? You had him well on the road to total recovery..."

"Yes, sir, Dr. Markham."

"Well! I think this Vietnam hero deserves getting a little special attention. His life is really just beginning. Please bear in mind, Pamela, I'm not trying to get you two together. I'm a professional, as indeed you must be. Our chain of thoughts need to flow in the direction that here is a helluva soldier, who deserves more than the Veterans Administration will give him after we discharge him."

"I'll have Heller on his feet within ten hours after his cast is removed," she promised the doctor. "Why not get it off this morning?"

The following evening, nurse Pamela Rogers pulled out all stops.

"I guess you'll be going home soon, now that your cast is
f," nurse Rogers told him. "We'll miss you."

"I'm really in no hurry," he informed her much to her
rprise.

"I thought you'd be overjoyed and anxious to get out of the
spital," she told him, coining her words carefully and
liberately. "I'm beginning to believe you're actually afraid
go back to civilian life?"

"How dare you question my manhood?" he shot bluntly at
r. "Although nobody has actually said so, I know I'll be out
the Army. You know what that'll mean? I'll have to go back
Key West. I'm a person with a problem. I know the ad-
tments I'll have to make for civilian life," he told her clear-
reaching for a Psychology textbook by a Syracuse Univer-
y Professor.

"I'm not questioning your manhood, sergeant," the nurse
essed. "I simply care about you in a professional manner.
at's why I left that book for you to read."

'It might interest you to know, I've read the book up to and
luding page 211 'the technique of creative thinking.' Stop
ging me! I have no defense against your type of fire."

'I'm not judging you," she said in self-defense. "As I said
other day, life is just beginning for you. The world, the
s and the fish in the Keys are yours for the taking."

Heller controlled his anger. After a long moment of silence,
astonished the beautiful nurse by saying, "I guess life will
be the same without you, way down in the Keys."

Nurse Rogers stood near the bed wondering what to say.
expectedly, Heller caught her by the hand. But she freed
self from his grip and hastily walked to the window, where
turned and faced him. She almost said something, but
nged her mind and moved to close the door. Then she
urned to the foot of the bed and pretended to examine his
rt once more. With ridicule in her vibrant, regal and pro-
ional voice she blasted, "Heller! You better take a good
k at me, because this is my last visit. I loath patients who
their love for life. But, then again, so what? You have the
care," she mocked him, challenging him verbally, men-

213

tally and physically, now that she had taken the offensive. Bom
bastically, she demanded to know how long he intended to carr
on his defiance to at least try standing.

Heller was speechless. He sat up in bed. He knew she wa
right. There was simply nothing for him to say.

"Heller! Since this is the last time you'll see me, I dare yo
to get out of your bed and kiss me? Perhaps even love me?

Heller was stunned. The nurse amazed him. "What are yo
waiting for? Lock the door and come to me..."

"Not on your life! I wanna see you standing like a man! No
crawling like a worm," she berated him, moving toward th
door again. "I'll be back in ten minutes. If you have any gu
or manhood left, let me see it when I get back!"

"Damn that beautiful witch!" Heller said between his teet
"I'll show her a thing or two, if it's the last thing I do!"

With intense determination he turned his body in the be
sliding his legs out from under the sheet. He anchored his che
to the mattress. Slowly, he permitted the pressure of his weig
on his legs. The pain was excruciating, almost unbearable. Th
sweat poured from his brow. He drew back his lips. His tee
were rattling from pain. He finally tried to stand, first on o
foot, then the other. It was sheer torture. But Heller was dete
mined to show that he was a rare creature of God, that he w
far from being ineffective. Since he obviously knew, or b
lieved, he could not walk to the door, he decided to crawl. H
lowered himself slowly, then, like the creatures of the sea
the Florida beaches, he started dragging himself across t
room. After he had reached the door, he grasped the kno
and pulled himself upward, slowly, using the knob for levera
and finally accomplished standing up for the first time sin
the Battle of Loc Ninh.

Although he trembled feebly, he remained determined. "I
show that beautiful snot nose nurse I'm still all man,"
repeated several times, while he moved still closer to the w
behind the door. Cautiously, he tried a few small steps, th
some longer. When Heller heard the nurse's foot steps, he fr
against the wall. Suddenly the door opened. When nurse Rog
saw the empty bed, she almost screamed and flew into

214

bathroom. She almost fainted when he was not there either. In tears, she ran across the room to the open window. She literally ripped the thin curtains apart and noted the screen was gone.

"Good God! No! He wouldn't. He couldn't have jumped!" she reasoned loudly, remembering how she hammered him down to nothingness only minutes earlier. "He might have wheeled himself into the next room...but how could he? The wheelchair is here?"

Suddenly the door swung closed. A voluntary cough came from someone standing behind it. When she saw him, her eyes lit up. He was standing, astoundingly erect. Nurse Rogers was so mentally involved, she backed off and flopped wearily into the only chair near the hospital bed.

"Just like a woman!" he swaggered in an overbearing voice, boasting in exultation like a crowing rooster, who had just triumphantly succeeded protecting his flock. "Come to daddy and pay your due. I realize of course," he chided further, "your word of honor is not enforceable. But my little Florence Nightingale, may I collect that long overdue kiss for being a good patient?"

By the time he stopped bragging, Pamela had recovered. "You great big incredible idiot!" she cried, running toward him and into his open arms. "How...how...why?"

"Forget the hows and whys," Heller whispered softly, as he embraced her lovingly. "I'm waiting to get paid!"

"Darling," she cooed in his embrace, while nestling comfortably in his arms. "If you'll bend down just a little."

"Kiss me! Kiss me! Kiss me again and again," he urged her, "before I go completely mad and attempt rewriting the entire 'Code of Military Ethics' for officers and enlisted personnel."

After countless passionate kisses and loving embraces, the nurse looked momentarily perplexed, as Heller held her perspicaciously at arms length. Now that her shrewish nagging and scolding had been obviously replaced with love and affection, in which both were gloriously delighted, Heller looked into his beloved nurse's eyes as if he were trying to penetrate her soul and beyond.

215

"Darling," he whispered between kisses. "May I ask you two very important questions?"

"Silly. Ask them. Ask me anything you like..."

"Ever been in Paris? Paris, France?"

"What's the second question?" she teased, as Heller pulled her toward him and kissed her again.

"Please answer my first question," he insisted. "I have to have a yes or no to justify my next question..."

"Yes, darling, I've been in Paris. Why?"

"When were you there?"

"Why?...it was in June of 1964. A group of nurses from Walter Reed took a trip on a special hop to see the city, including the Palace of Versailles."

Heller again held her at arms length. He put his open hand over her mouth to shush her. "Now I remember...now I remember where we've met," he told her hugging her once more to his bare chest. "It was in the Palace..."

"Don't tell me you're the one who stood behind me and stared at my legs, while I was admiring the Venus de Milo?" she said with a feeling of surprise, recalling that one of the nurses told her that some frustrated Army Corporal was indulgingly gazing dreamy eyed at her legs. Suddenly her face lit up. "Why did you ask me for the time?"

"I wanted to prove something to my buddy."

"Really! What?"

"When I gave him the ol' elbow to take a look at your backside, he waved me off with his hand and told me he thought you were some rich debutante, who wouldn't give me the time of day," he told her grinning and whispering in her ear.

"And, you didn't believe him?" she wanted to know.

"Of course not. As a result of your pleasant reply, your remarkable smile and the gleam in your eyes, I dreamed and fantasized about you in Paris, even in Saigon, when I first arrived there. Then again at Bragg, and again and again and again while I was on a stretcher being carried into the operating room at this hospital."

"Oh! You poor darling," she cooed. "Surely you have a girl back home."

"No!" he told her honestly. "I never had the pleasure to be in love, physically, mentally, or morally. Somehow, I was hoping I would see you again someday," he confessed, shrugging his bare but massive shoulders, still cradling her like a father would a loving daughter.

"So? What are you gonna do with me, now that you have me in your arms?" she teased coquettishly, turning her beautiful face and lips closer to be kissed.

Heller hesitated to kiss her. Instead, he said, "Ah!" blinking one of his eye lashes and holding her at arms length. "Would you mind if I called you by your first name?"

Captain Pamela Rogers knew what Sergeant Raymond Heller was referring to. Before Raymond could continue with his verbal struggle to justify his longing, Pamela cuddled comfortably in his arms again. "Raymond! When we are alone, you may call me anything you like. Why?"

"It's very simple. You see I've been thinking about this moment for a long time..."

"Please tell me before I die," she begged with earnestness, using all of the feminine persuasive power within her. "Please!"

"A staff sergeant in the Army couldn't possibly propose to the girl of his dreams, an officer, without permission to call her by her first name," he joked to clarify his sense of humor.

"Are you proposing, Raymond?"

"Yes! Yes!" he declared positively and painfully knelt on one of his knees before her. "I love you, Pamela. Please marry me."

"Yes! Yes! I will," she answered, kneeling down before him. "Kiss me, Raymond. Kiss me..."

When the two young people embraced again, their hearts pounded. There was a passionate longing for each other. This was indisputable proof that love can heal what modern medicine might not, that Heller's perpetual pain and turmoil could be overcome.

Stunned and startled, their passionate embrace ended abruptly with a sharp knock on the door and the familiar voice of Dr. Markham echoing from the outside, "Is everything going well, Captain Rogers? Do you need any assistance?"

"Please don't bother, Dr. Markham," nurse Rogers studdered in spasms. "I've shut the door, because I'm giving the sergeant a sponge bath..."

"Very good, Captain!" Dr. Markham said officiously. "I'll see you in the morning?"

"Yes, sir," she replied, while Sergeant Heller shouted that he, too, wanted to discuss something pertaining to his discharge.

"Where you're concerned, your nurse has the last word," the doctor chuckled.

Before Dr. Markham could walk off, nurse Rogers stuck her beautiful head out of the door and said, "Heller and I will be in your office before you start morning sick call. By the time you get there, we will already have been down in the lobby to see Private Womack's picture and his Medal of Honor citation."

"That's good! That's very good, Captain Rogers. See both of you in the morning."

When the nurse turned, she flew right into the outstretched arms of her future husband. Her lovely head was still spinning from Heller's proposal. She had to be certain, since they were so incorrigibly inconvenienced by Dr. Markham's voice.

"Raymond! You were saying?" she asked, clinging to him and looking steadily into his eyes. "Would you mind very much repeating what you said, when we were interrupted a few minutes ago?"

"Oh!" Heller spoke vigorously and his brow showed concern. He tried to kneel again but the pain was overbearing. Words seemed to fail him.

"Raymond! Are you gonna ask me again, or are you gonna let me suffer?"

Heller finally found his voice. "Captain Rogers! I love you...Will you please marry me as soon as possible?"

"Yes! Yes! I will," she cooed like a hungry dove. "But, from now on, please call me Pamela, and," she added happily, "I don't give a damn if the Chief of Staff of the Army is listening."

Sleep simply would not come to Sergeant Heller that night. His thoughts were about his incredible nurse, Pamela Rogers, whom he had met two years earlier in Paris, France. "It's a dream come true," he mumbled to himself as he rushed into his first shower in months at five in the morning.

As usual, reveille was at 0600 hours. Customarily, the night nurse routinely stopped by Heller's room to give him his early medications. When she saw him standing on his own two feet, shaving himself in the bathroom, she was surprised.

At 0800 hours, when Dr. Markham and his staff made sick call, they found Heller on the floor in his room, doing pushups, sweating and grinning from ear to ear.

"As you can see, Dr. Markham," Heller boasted with a smile, somewhat out of breath. "I'm just about ready to return to my outfit in Nam..."

"Sergeant Heller!" Dr. Markham finally remarked. "If and when you find the time, may I know what motivated you to stand tall and proud again?"

"Well, sir! I've been in bed long enough..."

"That's true! It seems medical science is on a holiday," he stated to his assistants, who witnessed what Dr. Markham said was a scientific medical phenomenon..."

Somewhat later, after routine completion of sick call, Dr. Markham was unaware someone was at the entrance to his office. He spoke to his assistant, "It's entirely possible that our favorite nurse has much more than Florence Nightingale ever had. I believe Captain Rogers has a kind of feminine witchcraft called *l o v e,*" he said, spelling the word "love" good naturedly for his assistant. "What do you think, Jim?"

The two medical officers were so engrossed checking the night's new entries on the patients' charts, it took another minute before they became aware of their visitor.

"Frank!" said Dr. Markham. "This is a surprise. We've been so busy with these records, we haven't raised our eyes for a whole hour."

While Chaplain Cook and Dr. Markham shook hands, the latter remarked, "Chaplain I don't know if you have met my associate, Dr. Charles Evans? Charley, I'd like to have you meet Frank Cook of Special Forces..."

"Delighted to meet you, chaplain," Dr. Evans said, catechizing a question. "What brings you so early to us this morning?"

"Yes, Frank! Why so early?" Dr. Markham asked. "May we know your reason?"

"Certainly!" said the distinguished and enthusiastic chaplain in his lieutenant colonel's uniform with three rows of ribbons on his chest. "Last night, at 2300, I received an urgent call from Sergeant Heller in room 600. He was kinda restless and most anxious to have me visit him. So, here I am," the ruddy faced chaplain of Special Forces said with pride.

"Really, Frank? Actually we are impressed with Heller's remarkable progress," Dr. Markham said thoughtfully. "He's still bitter and grim. Angry, would be a better word, that the do-gooders and especially the media, who blatantly and vociferously want us out of Nam, are getting the upper hand in this country."

"With or without a clear cut victory," Dr. Evans added. "The domino theory, that all other little countries out there will fall systematically into the red river of no return, is not just an evolutinary phenomenon. Heller believes that."

"Gentlemen!" Chaplain Cook smiled, "May I visit with Sergeant Heller?"

"Frank, you don't need to ask," Dr. Markham said solicitously, showing apprehension. "Personally I think, purely specualtion of course, wedding bells may be ringing for our precious nurse Rogers and Heller..."

"She's a rare young lady," the chaplain emphasized. "For the past month, this utterly charming girl has been in our Special Forces chapel on her knees every day. I know she had a spiritual communion with her creator. I watched the silent movements of her lips and a sparkling light in her eyes, as she lifted her beautiful head toward the cross."

"Those two were meant for each other," Dr. Markham said with optimism, hopefully adding, "what about Army Regulations?"

The Special Forces Chaplain laughed. "Gentlemen! Love can get around the devil himself and that includes the Army!"

At exactly nine in the morning, nurse Pamela Rogers, rustled methodically through the long Womack hospital corridors. Her face and hair were radiant. Her perpetual smile and symmetry of motion was that of a positive bride. Her every move was feminine and like a quiet symphony. She was in love for the first time in her life, and she wanted everyone in the whole world "including the Army," she said, to know it.

When the Chaplain entered room 600, Pamela and Raymond were holding hands. "May I assume you have set the date for your wedding?" he asked them, shaking hands with Sergeant Heller and bowing his head and upper part of his body in respect and recognition of the Army nurse in uniform.

"Yes, sir!" they replied simutaneously. "Easter morning, Chaplain Cook."

The Chaplain smiled, "according to your equanimity and excitement, I see nothing but sunshine, and much happiness in the days to come. If it's possible, please see me in my rectory at noon this Sunday, if that's agreeable to you."

"It is!" Pamela and Raymond answered together. She, with her eyes twinkling and Raymond grinning with her endorsement.

After it became common knowledge to most staff personnel that wedding bells were on the horizon, nurse Rogers asked the Chief of Nursing Services for thirty days leave. At the same time she submitted her resignation to be effective on Easter morning. Heller on the other end got busy getting himself in shape. He continued to awaken at five, shower and shave. He ate two or three breakfasts and anything else he could get his hands on. Immediately thereafter, he appeared at physiotherapy in the basement of the hospital, without his crutches. The Army physiotherapist gave him a clean bill of health and the medical evaluation board approved his request for thirty days leave, starting Easter morning, after which time he would report to the Key West Naval Hospital for final disposition.

The hospital command sergeant major and the adjutant, who is the chief assistant to the commanding officer, worked feverishly and diligently, trying to persevere in spite of some difficulties.

With the help of many Army nurses, who willfully worked like soubrettes, ladies in waiting, Pamela Rogers acquired her fabulous wedding dress. The manager of the NCO club dictated working hours to get it ready for the biggest wedding reception Fort Bragg would ever see.

During these trying days and evenings, Pamela and Raymond were inseparable. Although Pamela was totally receptive to Raymond's wishes, the nearness of him and the tautness of his body, plunged them into intense emotional and physical need. Nevertheless, they agreed to wait until their wedding night, when they would share their love, all its earthly bliss, spiritual joy, rapture and ecstasy, according to the highest attainable level of ascending human value.

"Good heaven's to betsy!" Heller suddenly remembered in Pamela's presence. "I haven't told my Dad about us!"

"Let's get to the nearest telephone, darling," she cooed lovingly, almost dragging her 210 pound future husband, "There's one right down the passageway."

In a matter of minutes, Raymond had his father on the telephone. Even before Mr. Heller could open his mouth, Raymond shouted, "Dad! Dad! Are you listening?"

"Yes, son. I'm listening. What's on your mind?" he asked, trying to control the joy of hearing his voice again.

"Dad! I hope you still have my mother's precious rings?" Without waiting for him to answer, he added, "Please bring them!"

"Raymond! Raymond! Hold everything down," his father interjected suddenly. "Are you getting married, or something?"

"How did you guess that? I wanted to surprise you..."

"Oh! It's kinda' sudden, isn't it? The ward doctor told me you're doing exceptionable well. But, I would have never guessed you'll be carrying some lucky girl over the threshold. Are you strong enough? It takes guts and strength."

"She only weighs 107 pounds, Dad." he told him hurriedly. "Here she is, Dad! I want you to meet her. Dad, the next voice you'll hear will by my wife on Easter morning."

"Don't you think you ought to tell me her name, Raymond?"

"Oh! Pamela. It's Pamela Rogers, Dad. Here she is."

"I'm looking forward to see you again, Mr. Heller," she told him softly, waiting for a comment from him.

"Same here, Pamela. You said 'again'. . . . Have we met?"

"Yes, Mr. Heller. We've met. It was right after Raymond's return to his room. I told you his operation was remarkably successful, that we would put a special watch on him and that you were not to rouse him until he opened his eyes. . . Do you remember me now?"

"How could I forget? You looked like an angel without wings and you smelled so clean."

"As it turned out, Mr. Heller, we kinda' got Raymond on his feet, finally," she laughed and Raymond joined her.

"Pamela, I look forward to see you wearing Raymond's mother's rings," Mr. Heller said affectionately. "Now let me get back to my son for another moment. I'll see you in church," he emphasized.

Pamela handed the telephone back to Raymond. "What do you think, Dad? Isn't she something special?"

"I knew her before you even met her," he laughed. "Now settle down and tell your old Dad once more what you'd like him to do for you and when?"

"All right, Dad! Once more. Please drive up to Fort Bragg in my car, or anyway you can get here, as long as it is no later than eleven in the morning on this blessed Easter morning, and please bring my mother's precious rings!"

"I'll be there, son. Meanwhile, how's your cash. Need some?"

"No! Thanks. Thanks, Dad," he repeated. "I can cover everything, including our honeymoon."

"Good. Any idea of where you'll honeymoon, or is that a secret?"

"My little darling wants to go where it's warm. If everything goes well with me, we'll hop to the Bahamas and eventually end up in Key West."

"We'll see each other at the alter on Easter morning," Mr. Heller confirmed. "Give Pamela a great big kiss for me. . ."

After Raymond had replaced the telephone, he reached for

Pamela. "Come here, little angel. Dad wants me to kiss you for him."

"Here I am. You can kiss me if you can catch me," she teased him, attempting to get away rather leisurely only to get caught.

In the city of Key West, Jim Heller slowly and carefully removed from a drawer his wife's picture in the golden frame and kissed it.

"Darling," he implored, earnestly beseeching the Almighty, "I think the time has come for us to have new life in this old house. Be it your will that we may gain a daughter and not lose our son," he concluded, placing his wife's portrait upon a special shelf in the living room.

Meanwhile, at the Army hospital, his son Raymond was sitting on pins and needles, waiting with his beloved Pamela to see the Special Forces chaplain. For the occasion he donned his uniform with fourteen medals, including the Silver Star, the Soldier's Medal, the Bronze Star, the Joint Services Commendation Medal, the Military Order of the Purple Heart and the Good Conduct medal. For this special occasion, he replaced his crutches with a walking cane, which Pamela had given him as a present. Nurse Pamela Rogers was in civies. Since she had been at Tripler Army Hospital on Hawaii six months earlier, her wardrobe consisted only of bare necessities for the winter months. On this refreshing morning, she wore her full length dyed muskrat coat, over a pure virgin wool suit with a slim, split skirt. Being a typical outdoor girl, she wore creamy colored, quality stitched western boots.

"I'm delighted to see you both," Chaplain Frank Cook of Special Forces told them sincerely, as he shook hands with Heller, then gently embraced nurse Rogers, whom he had known from earlier years. The Chaplain took several steps to make himself comfortable behind his desk and motioned the betrothed to sit on the couch opposite him. After a searching look at each, he cleared his throat.

"Pamela and Raymond," he said with profound firmness in his voice. "Both of you have the most precious thing in life, which is youth. Today, many of our young people are confused, frustrated and alone. We live in the 20th Century Babylon, in which, if we believe the doom merchants, there's little to look forward to. Don't you believe them!'' he emphasized. ''If you face reality and consider fixed ideas, negativism, fantasy, withdrawal, rejection, hostility, think about developing your own personality in a way of life which makes numerous adjustments absolute. As you both know, there is a predominant myth in our times that sex is a simple phenomenon of nature. Never, never take that for granted. I am happy to know that you Raymond are chaste and you Pamela are pure, which makes your relationship as man and wife unique. So, learn to live and work together. Be considerate, sensitive, enthusiastic and communicate with each other, even when making love, where attitude and feeling are so important. Plan your family and how to best rear your children and go to church on Sundays. But the crucial point, most vital in a happy marriage is the level of communication. Let me read from Hepner's Psychology Book on *Adjustment in Dating, Courtship and Marriage:*

''The movies, novels, songs and comics proclaim romance as a power that overcomes all obstacles. In these fictions, marriage is pictured as a continuous state of ecstasy. Actually, marriage is like work and other important arenas of life.

''It is an arena where we have splendid opportunities to learn to enjoy emotionally satisfying experiences, such as companionship, and, to interpret life in new and exciting ways.''

''Pamela and Raymond,'' he continued, closing the book, ''After I pronounce you man and wife, I expect you to act worthy. Accept your responsibility and build a life for your children and theirs yet to come. If you live with faith, for better or worse, you may well have your feet in the door of the paradise yet to come. May the Divine Creator of us all and all earthly, human and heavenly elements, bless your forthcoming marriage and keep you well.''

Heller continued to have numerous visitors at all hours of the day. He was particulary happy to see his former commanding officer, Major Armstrong, who had been assigned to a teaching position at the John F. Kennedy School of Special Warfare.

"What's so pitiful, even contemptible," Major Armstrong stressed, looking straight at Sergeant Major Cartwright and three other NCO's, "is that our college and even university graduates come to us with degrees of reduced standards. Young graduates think and eat computers and really believe in push button warfare. They and their diplomas lack good old fashioned academic quality."

"Major!" Cartwright remarked, wanting to add his opinion, "High school seniors get diplomas and can't read the plan of the day, or standard operating procedures. Some of those youngsters our recruiters bring in are under the impression the Army is gonna educate them, and," the senior NCO continued, "higher education ought to help solve this critical national problem by teaching military science. After all, they teach everything else, like what Uncle Sam owes them, job placement, special counseling, how to make money in athletics, childcare, sex and family planning before and after the kids come into the world..."

"My wise mentor, teacher, guardian of Ulysses and me," Heller joked as others in the room laughed. "Now that I know I'm out of the Army, what do you suggest I ought to do, besides going back to Key West?"

Without the slightest hesitation Cartwright spoke. "First, you ought to discuss the future with your intended wife. She might have a few plans of her own. What do you think, Major Armstrong?"

"By all means. By all means."

"Bear in mind my Dad and I are in commercial fishing," Heller remarked truthfully. "It will not be a matter of income. After our honeymoon, we can move right into the old family house in Key West..."

"Hold it!" one of the NCO's remarked sitting on his haunches on the floor. "I'd go back to school, if I were you. Get some kind of a degree on the G.I. Bill. I understand you get paid while you're at school."

"And besides that, your retirement pension will be coming in every month, which should be considerable," Cartwright affirmed.

"We'll get down to the basics this evening," Heller assured his friends from Special Forces, then before they all left, he added, "Don't you let me stand up front on that altar all by myself! I'll need all of you, or I may chicken out!"

That evening, Pamela and Raymond rekindled their forth-coming marriage vows. "Ours is unique, like Chaplain Frank Cook told us the other day," Pamela smiled. "I doubt if anyone in the Army would believe that neither of us has been with a member of the opposite sex?"

"God! I love you," Heller told her. "Our wedding will be timeless."

At 11:00 on Easter morning, Sergeant Heller looked nervous-ly at the dozen frolicking and grinning combat veterans, stand-ing near him in total support. All of them knew that their com-rade could no longer be one of them. Most of them had seen Heller fight, bleed and suffer. He had led up front, where it counted. "But," they reasoned, "that was something he could handle." These veterans were not so sure, however, that Heller would survive this special ordeal today.

"What are you so nervous about?" Major Armstrong, who was Heller's alternate best man, asked in a whisper. "Tangl-ing with your Captain Rogers is gonna be a lot more pleasure than tangling with us, or the VC, don't you think?"

"I appreciate you trying to humor me, sir."

"Settle down! It'll be over in an hour..."

"Perhaps, major," Heller grumbled. "But, if Dad doesn't get here with the rings, my little Pamela might leave me stand-ing at the altar all by myself. What can I do, major?"

"Remember old Colonel Outlaw, who whipped the VC at Loc Ninh? Most people never knew that he had an answer for everything."

"How can I forget? I kinda helped him there, or have you forgotten already?"

"Of course, I haven't forgotten, Heller. I'm trying to keep you on course and I wanted to inform you that Colonel Outlaw had a theory about everything."

"I believe you're referring to the word 'necessitarianism'. The colonel used it so often in tight spots. That's the theory devised that every event is determined by absolute necessity, and that the action of the human will is never free, but is caused by previous experiences," Heller recalled. "So?"

"So, now is the time to practice what he preached!"

"This is not the time for jokes, major!"

"Let me spell it our for you, ol' buddy... If your Dad doesn't get here in time, I will still be your best man. Naturally, we'll have to improvise on the rings. When that time finally comes, I'll pass you my key ring, without the keys," he explained further. "Pamela might kill you right after the ceremony. But, she'll consider herself ringed!"

The laughter of the ushers and the major was so intensively loud, the choir was interruped singing the hymn of praise for a second and Chaplain Cook, trying to perform his religious functions, turned his head from his prepared text, wondering what was going on behind the altar.

Still desperate for the rings, Heller and his best man rummaged through their pockets for their keys, but in vain. "Now what?" Heller asked his practical comrade. "We don't even have a key!"

"One of you ushers have a key?" the major asked loud and clear, stepping in the direction of the groomsmen at the altar. "A key ring, perhaps?"

When no one volunteered, he became poetic. "It is written fury has seen no wrath as a woman's scorn! But wait, my friend," he added, walking briskly toward the side entrance of the anteroom, where he had just heard the screeching of car wheels. "I have a premonition the man of the hour has arrived."

Heller rushed to the window just in time to see his father fly from the taxi toward the anteroom and in his full naval commander's uniform, carrying his hat with the gold braided acorns and leaves under his arm.

The major swung the door open, and Mr. Heller ran into his son's arms. "It's an apparition! It's Davie Jones! It's my Dad! Dad! Where have you been? We'd given up on you!"

"Never throw in the towel, son," Mr. Heller said happily, with love and pride, embracing him, who still could not believe seeing his father. "By the way, I had to go on a crash diet to get into my old commander's uniform of which I am so proud."

Raymond cut him off. "Dad! We can wait with the entertainment. The rings! The rings! You got them?"

"Right here!" his father said softly, holding a small velvet jewelry box high above his head. "I'll keep them for you. Now, stop worrying and introduce me to your groomsmen and the major, and this is an order!"

There was considerable chatter and laughter during the introduction.

Meanwhile, a dozen bridesmaids and the matron of honor huddled excitedly around the beautiful bride, in the Special Forces anteroom. All were eagerly wishing the regular service would end, so that all gathered might see that dreams still come true for those who wait.

Pamela Rogers, radiant with happiness, was awaiting her finest hour, holding a bouquet of tiny violets, which had arrived earlier via an Air Force fighter pilot, who had been transferred from Homestead to Pope Air Force Base.

Her wedding gown was of ivory silk, peau de Soice, empire styled with portrait neckline. Her 21 foot chapel-train fell from a Dior bow. Ivory French Alencon lace applique accented the bodice of the skirt and sleeves. Her chapel-length mantilla of imported silk illusion was bordered with more Alencon lace. She was wearing her sister's white satin high heeled shoes and a gold necklace. One smooth, bluish-white pearl hugged her neck.

The matron of honor made a few last minute adjustments on the bridal train and remarked with admiration, "Pamela, I believe this will be the most lavish wedding dress ever seen in this chapel. You are the epitome of the most provocative and gorgeous bride in the whole world. I cannot believe a young woman can be so radiant, without lipstick, manicured fingernails, a dash of sexy perfume, long dark lashes and things like that."

"One compliment deserves another," she told the matron, with a smile revealing her perfect teeth. "And I've never seen you look lovelier and more abundantly happy. Take a look in that full length mirror behind you... why, you look like a bride yourself."

The matron turned and viewed herself in her Grecian burgandy satin gown, with a velvet sash, also styled on empire lines. Her headpiece was of matching satin tulle. Her bouquet of flowers were pink and white carnations. A simple gold necklace, a gift from the bride, was her only piece of jewelry. "The only difference between all of you and myself," she remarked, glancing at the bridesmaids, "is that I'm twice as old as most of you. I hate to admit it, girls, I believe I've missed the boat."

By high noon, the military ushers from Special Forces personnel had cleared the chapel, except for the wedding party. Late arrivals were quickly directed to their seats. There was the lighting of the altar candles. When the organist started "Ode to Joy" from Lidwig von Beethoven's Ninth Symphony, the bridesmaids and the matron of honor preceeded the flower-girl, who scattered her rose petals, moving toward the altar at a moderate pace.

At the first note of the traditional wedding march by Wagner, from the Opera Lohengrin, the bride in all her magnificence and grandeur entered the aisle with her father, Doctor William Rogers. While the bride moved deliberately, placing one foot firmly on the heavily carpeted floor, before lifting up the other, her father tried his best to keep in step with her.

After the veiled bride had reached the groom's side and her father answered "I do" to the Chaplain's question, "Who presents this woman to be married to this man?" he turned and took his assigned seat in the first pew.

"Dearly beloved," charged the Chaplain to the congregation. "We are gathered together in the sight of God and in the face of this company, to join together this man and this woman in holy matrimony, to be honorable among men. Therefore, it is entered discreetly and reverently and in the fear of God that these two willing persons present, will be joined into this Holy Estate."

The Chaplain paused for a long moment before he declared, "If any man or woman can show just cause why they may not lawfully be joined together, let him speak, or else hereafter and forever hold his peace?"

The military Chaplain addressed the couple. "I require and charge you both, as you stand in the presence of God, before whom all secrets are known, having duly considered the holy covenant you are about to make, you do now declare before this company your pledge of faith to each other?"

The Chaplain paused again, then in the declaration of intention the clergyman addressed Raymond first, saying, "Raymond, will thou have this woman to be thy wedded wife, to live together after God's Ordinance, in Holy Estate of Matrimony? Will thou love her, comfort her, honor and keep her, in sickness and in health, and, forsaking all others, keep thee only unto her, so long as ye both shall live?"

Raymond answered, "I will."

The clergyman now looked at the bride. "Pamela, will thou have this man to be thy wedded husband, to live together, after God's Ordinance, in the Holy Estate of Matrimony? Will thou love, honor and keep him in sickness and in health, forsaking all others, keep thee only unto him, so long as ye both shall live?"

Pamela answered, "I will."

Once more the Chaplain addressed Raymond first, then Pamela in their marriage vows, accepting the marriage contract.

"Please repeat after me," the Chaplain asked of Raymond, "I, Raymond, take thee Pamela, to be my wedded wife, to have and to hold from this day forward, for better or worse, for richer or poorer, in sickness and in health, to love and to cherish, till death us do part, according to God's Holy Ordinance and there to I pledge thee my troth."

Finally, lovely Pamela repeated her vow, barely above a whisper.

The clergyman then said, "For as much as Raymond and Pamela have consented together in holy wedlock and have witnessed the same before God and this company, and therefore have pledged their faith each to the other and have declared the same by joining hands and by giving of rings, I pronounce that they are husband and wife together, in the name of the Father, and the Son, and the Holy Spirit. Those whom God hath joined together, let no man put asunder."

The Chaplain smiled and promptly added, "Raymond, you may kiss the bride."

After the bride lifted her veil, the groom kissed her lips in an act of affection. Finally, the couple kneeled for the Chaplain's benediction:

"God the Father, the Son and the Holy Spirit bless, preserve and keep you; the Lord graciously with his favor look upon you and so fill you with all spiritual benediction and love that you may live together in this life, that in the world to come, you may have life everlasting."

The couple turned toward each other again in deep affection, then turned toward the aisle. The matron of honor and the best man followed, as did the twelve bridesmaids and their escorts. The happy bride and groom had every intention of stopping briefly at the entrance to the chaped to allow their friends and relatives to wish them well, even before they would meet them at the club. Both were in fact surprised that the chapel door was closed and not a soul appeared to wish them well, or to throw rice at them.

Suddeny the chapel doors opened from the outside. One hundred Special Forces combat NCO's were assembled in two rows, facing each other, their sabres gleaming in the chill, but bright, noonday sun. Sergeant Heller and his darling wife were speechless. While the couple momentarily stood flabbergasted, the commander of the Special Forces detail shouted, "Sabres, Salute!"

The highly disciplined Vietnam Veterans uplifted their sabres above their heads, forming an arch, while their happy comrade and his bride briskly walked the gauntlet of honor from the chapel to their waiting convertible totally encircled by military personnel and their families, showering the newlyweds with rice.

A short minute later, a military escort from the 82nd Airborne took them to the main ballroom of the NCO club for a festive reception.

The enormous table contained a ten tier wedding cake. A minature bride and groom was on its very top. When the time came for the newlyweds to cut the cake, several photographers snapped pictures of the occasion. While the several hundred officers and NCO's stuffed themselves with sausage balls, boiled shrimp, ham biscuits, chicken salad sandwiches, cheese rings, mints, nuts and pickles, others sipped the gentle wedding punch, which somehow, later, started to taste very much like scotch and soda. Finally, later in the afternoon, Pamela and Raymond danced the traditional "Straus Waltz." There was the traditional ancient custom of removing the bride's blue garter, which she had borrowed from her older married sister. Then, the lovely bride threw her bouquet of violets toward her matron of honor, who started crying after catching it.

When the proud groom announced his departure, the entire NCO Club emptied to see and watch a beautiful beginning.

"Dad! Chaplain Cook, ladies and gentlemen of the Special Forces. . .my wife Pamela and I are headed for a honeymoon resort in the warm Bahama Islands, where we'll celebrate our wedding with love and respect for each other. I've been told we'll have champagne breakfasts in bed, a heart shaped bathtub for two, candlelight dinners in a small cottage near the ocean with a dream bedroom and all those lacy pillows, ribbons and with clouds of color, of which I dreamed about in Vietnam."

"How are you gonna get to the Bahama Islands?" somebody shouted.

Raymond answered quickly. "As long as you realize you can't come along, I'll tell you that."

Raymond glanced at his lovely wife, who looked radiant, spiritually and graciously happy, before he answered, with a smile.

"Dad will drive us to the civilian airport, where a privately chartered Cessna 210 will fly us directly to Nassau..."

"Then what?" inquired an old buddy, grinning from ear to ear.

"Well! If you must know," Raymond answered, his face turning crimson. "After we get to our honeymoon cabin, I'll lock the doors and throw the keys into the Atlantic."

THE END

Silver Star

Soldiers Medal

Bronze Star Medal

Joint Services Commendation Medal

Army Commendation Medal

Purple Heart

Good Conduct Medal

National Defense Service Medal

Armed Forces Expeditionary Medal

Vietnam Service Medal

Vietnam Campaign Medal (RVN Award)

Presidential Unit Citation

Valorous Unit Award

Meritorious Unit Citation

SERGEANT RAYMOND J. HELLER'S AWARDS

THE BUTCHERY OF HICKHAM FIELD ON HAWAII

THE BUTCHERY OF HICKHAM FIELD ON HAWAII

A SPECIAL FORCES DETAIL OF PROFESSIONALS

CITATION
for
CONGRESSIONAL MEDAL OF HONOR

Private First Class Bryant H. Womack, Army Medical Service, United States Army, a member of Medical Company, 14th Infantry Regiment, 25th Infantry Division, distinguished himself by conspicuous gallantry above and beyond the call of duty in action against the enemy on 12 March 1952 near Sokso-Ri, Korea. PFC Womack was the only medical aidman attached to a night combat patrol when sudden contact with a numerically superior enemy produced numerous casualties. PFC Womack went immediately to their aid, although this necessitated exposing himself to a devastating hail of enemy fire, during which he was seriously wounded. Refusing medical aid for himself, he continued moving among his comrades to administer aid. While he was aiding one man, he was again struck by enemy mortar fire, this time suffering the loss of his right arm. Although he knew the consequences should immediate aid not be administered, he still refused aid and insisted that all efforts be made for the benefit of others that were wounded. Unable to perform the task himself, he remained on the scene and directed others in first aid. The last man to withdraw, he walked until he collapsed from loss of blood and died a few minutes later while being carried by his comrades. The extraordinary heroism, outstanding courage and unswerving devotion to duty displayed by PFC Womack reflect the utmost distinction on himself and uphold the esteemed traditions of the United States Army.

SGT. JOHN MORAN, 7th SPECIAL FORCES GROUP (Photo by SFC Ron Freeman, US Army)

A SPECIAL BREED OF MAN